T0153347

Keeping The Peace

Colette Maitland

Keeping the Peace

STORIES

A JOHN METCALF BOOK

BIBLIOASIS
WINDSOR, ONTARIO

FIRST EDITION

Library and Archives Canada Cataloguing in Publication

Maitland, Colette
    Keeping the peace / Colette Maitland.

Short stories.
Issued also in an electronic format.
ISBN 978-1-926845-92-0

    I. Title.

PS8626.A4178K44 2013   C813'.6   C2012-907642-2

Edited by John Metcalf
Copy-edited by Dan Wells
Typeset by Chris Andrechek
Cover Designed by Kate Hargreaves
Cover Photograph by T.W. Collins

Canada Council for the Arts   Conseil des Arts du Canada   ONTARIO ARTS COUNCIL CONSEIL DES ARTS DE L'ONTARIO

Canadian Heritage   Patrimoine canadien

Biblioasis acknowledges the ongoing financial support of the Government of Canada through the Canada Council for the Arts, Canadian Heritage, the Canada Book Fund; and the Government of Ontario through the Ontario Arts Council.

This book is a work of fiction. Any resemblance to real persons, living or dead, is purely coincidental and unintentional.

PRINTED AND BOUND IN CANADA

MIX
Paper from responsible sources
FSC® C107923

Contents

For Al

SHOOT THE DOG

"WE DON'T NEED the clinic's name on the cheque, Mona, we have a stamp."

Mona rewards the veterinarian assistant with a too-sweet smile as she signs her name. Eighty-five bucks to dip a sample of urine, prescribe a more effective arthritis medication and caution Mona when she broached the subject of putting Sadie out of her misery.

"Oh, it's not time for that yet, is it old girl?" Dr. Givins had asked the Golden Lab earlier in the examining room.

Easy for him to say, Mona thinks now, sliding her cheque across the counter towards his assistant's outstretched hand—he's not setting his alarm for 2AM, then lugging Sadie down off the porch steps to the darkened driveway so she can do her business. He isn't bathing her once a week to keep that old dog smell at bay or issuing cheques on an increasingly regular basis to maintain her questionable quality of life.

Mona bends at the knees, scoops the dog up and into her arms.

"Come on, Sadie."

"You're going to *carry* her?" the assistant asks.

Mona nods. "I'd like to get home today," she says, nudging the steel-framed glass door open with her mule-clad foot.

"You're killing me, you know that, right?" Mona whispers into Sadie's velvet ear as they cross the parking lot. Sadie's tail

9

thumps once, then twice, against Mona's hip. It almost makes up for everything.

Vinnie looks up from his paper, gets out of the truck and drops the tailgate.

"So, what's the verdict?"

"She will live to see another appointment, unfortunately," Mona replies, placing Sadie atop Trevor's forgotten velour bathrobe. *Go ahead*, she thinks, *piss at will.*

Vinnie gets behind the wheel, Mona climbs in and buckles herself next to him.

"Did you tell him about her peeing in the house?" he asks, shifting gears.

"Yes, but it's only happened three times—hardly a reason to have her put down, Givins said. Besides, everything would have been fine if I'd got to her in time."

Vinnie stops for a red light at the east end of town, tossing his calloused hands into the air.

"There you go again!"

"What?"

"Blaming yourself! A dog is responsible for its own bladder, Mona, just like a man is responsible for his own finances, *if* you get my drift." His heavy eyebrows arch dramatically, transforming him into Vinnie, rural secret agent.

"So what are you saying, Vinnie, that I'm trying to put down the wrong animal?"

Vinnie's mouth splits like a seam, his loud guffaw bounces off the windshield as he hits the accelerator, bringing them up to highway speed.

"Mona, you can be such a card sometimes! They say making jokes is good for what ails you."

She attempts to force the issue of gas money when they arrive back at the house, but Vinnie disowns her five-dollar bill.

"Put it away, Mona. What are friends for if you can't call on them when you need a hand?"

Out. Handout.

She's always been a giver—food-bank volunteer, blue-box committee chairperson, but now that the shoe is on the other foot, she's discovered it's pinching her toes. There's nothing more to say—Vinnie is as stubborn as a weed.

They lean side by side against the truck and watch Sadie's painful descent into a squatting position.

"How long do you plan on putting Sadie and yourself through this slow torture shit?" Vinnie's straight face asks.

"I don't know. Once I sell the house, if she hasn't improved … maybe then. It's not cheap—a hundred and forty, Givins said. Of course, that's the cadillac version where Sadie gets cremated and her ashes come to me in a tidy white box suitable for burial out back, next to the peonies."

"Why, that's highway robbery! My shotgun is always in the truck, Mona. Just say the word and I'll do her for you."

Will you blindfold her, offer her one last jerky treat before you nuzzle the barrel next to her ear?

"Thanks, Vinnie, but I can't bear the thought of you splattering her brains all over some field."

Vinnie shrugs.

"A shotgun to the head or a needle in the butt—dead is dead, Mona. It wouldn't be the first time that I've helped out a friend. Any bites on the house?"

"Not even a whiff of a sniff."

Her real estate agent had predicted no miracles.

"Isolated old farmhouses and single, older women have a lot in common," he'd said, peeking into her closets and poking around in her root cellar, "they both tend to stay on the market for a long time, no matter how many facelifts they've had."

Perhaps a new realtor was in order.

"Time to change agents," Vinnie confirms. "Shake things up. You don't owe Tucker anything. Besides, I hear he's a slimeball."

"Aren't they all?"

Sadie makes the agonizing shift to a standing position, wheeling about to smell her own shit before limping off to the garage where she will spend the remainder of the day lying on the old feather tick Mona dragged out for her after Trevor split with the Volvo.

"That's the biggest doghouse I've ever seen," Vinnie observes for the fourth time in three months. Mona doesn't even crack a smile.

"I'd best be on my way, I've got to be at St. Maria Goretti's for three to pick up my load of little darlings. You want me to swing by tomorrow for groceries?"

"Only if you let me fix you something to eat."

"It's a deal."

"How about after your pickup, say around five o'clock? We'll go to the store, you can run me home and I'll cook you dinner."

"Sounds great."

She watches Vinnie's silver truck turn to a puff of dust as it charges down her half-mile dirt road.

MONA LEAFS THROUGH one aged cookbook after another, trying to imagine what would appeal to a widowed, fifty-two-year-old bus driver. She hasn't prepared a proper meal since Trevor disappeared with half the town's life savings and their joint bank account, scribbling '*you can keep the house*' on the back of their last telephone bill. What the hell had he meant by that? She'd come to the marriage *with* the house, refusing as recently as seven months ago to sign it over for collateral when Trevor made mention of a minor cash flow problem.

What about a frittata and cold cucumber soup? No, too big city. Besides, Vinnie looks like the kind of man who might suck soup straight from the bowl without benefit of a spoon.

She first met Vinnie three years ago when they sat on the township recycling committee, otherwise she never would have known he existed, though he lived just one rural road over. Only three-quarter of a mile if you happen to be a turkey vulture, is how Vinnie had put it, as he pinched her fingers by way of introduction. Vinnie hadn't volunteered much at the committee meetings, preferring, he'd said, to sit back, smoke his pipe and let the womenfolk run the show.

What about liver and onions? He's too young to crave liver and onions, isn't he? She does have a six-month old chicken curled up like a frozen foetus in the freezer. She could stick it in a sink full of water for a quick thaw and make chicken and biscuits.

The reporters had come scratching and squawking just like poultry after Trevor's Canada-wide warrant was issued: his handsome business card face flashing on the local and national news, reprinted in the local and national papers. Had she known? Did she have any idea, inkling, or clue? Sugar-coated accusations politely plunged down her throat with each new revelation: Trevor's three American wives, his multiple aliases, and his less ambitious scams south of the border.

Media interest had died like a child's temper tantrum once the Volvo was discovered abandoned at the Ottawa airport. He'd fabricated another name, left for parts unknown, end of story.

Not for Mona. She still had to live here and watch folks in town walk through her as if she were a hologram. People she'd known her whole life.

She'd got THE WORD at the library two weeks after Trevor's vanishing act. Bob Butte, the town clerk, assured her it was nothing personal—though he himself had invested heavily in Trevor's Northern Ontario phantom diamond mine—blaming her dismissal on provincial downloading to the municipality.

No one was hiring in town. If her unemployment insurance ran out before the house sold she would have to apply for welfare, line up at the food bank, on the other side of the counter this time, with the less fortunate. These were the thoughts Vinnie had crashed into three months ago, as she dropped a last desperate resumé off at the Penny Parlour.

"Hey Mona, I heard somebody made off with your Volvo. D'ya need a lift home?"

She could have kissed both his ruddy cheeks right there and then on the King Street sidewalk.

Vinnie had refused gas money that day too, touching his hand to his baseball cap, digging the toe of his Kodiak work boot into the gravel of her driveway.

"I know how people can be when you're down and out," he'd said. "It happened to me and my Liza when she turned up with the breast cancer. The phone hardly rang while she was taking her treatments, feeling sicker than a dog, losing her beautiful red hair. She saw more of the V.O.N. than she did of her own women friends. Oh, they came out in droves for the two wakes and the funeral, dropped off a dumpster load of food once there was only me left to eat it...I know things are tight for you right now, Mona, so call me if you need a lift to town. Don't be wasting good money on taxis."

And so their alliance was formed.

"DO YOU MIND if we stop off at my place?" Vinnie asks as he loads Mona's groceries into the back of his pickup.

"No, of course not."

Vinnie fiddles with the radio the entire way back to his house, switching channels so often that Mona almost barks at him to stop. He parks the truck in front of his garage and reaches for a remote door opener on the dashboard.

"I want to show you something," he says.

The garage door slowly lifts to reveal an older model, navy blue, Honda Civic sedan.

"That there was the wife's." His voice splinters like a wooden spoon. He fumbles in the breast pocket of his overalls, dropping a set of keys into her lap. "You might have better luck finding a job in the city. Keep it for as long as you like."

SHE'S TALKING TOO MUCH. It could be the sparkling white wine—Vinnie's contribution to dinner—or the fact that she's been starved too long for a simple social conversation, or the feeling she has that she owes Vinnie some kind of an explanation for the sorry state of her life now that he's gone and lent her his dead wife's car.

"I married Stan straight out of high school. It lasted six months. He smacked me one time too many. Never with his fist, mind you, always with his open hand, as if he had nothing to hide. I decided I wasn't cut out for a husband or children after that experience. People around here fought me tooth and nail for years, inviting me for dinner to meet unattached relatives or old college buddies, insisting I hold every baby born within a hundred mile radius, telling me I was too pretty to stay single, as if marriage were an antidote. Thankfully, time marches on so that foolishness stopped when I reached my mid-thirties."

Vinnie chuckles as he fills his pipe bowl, but doesn't speak.

"Then I meet Trevor in the Caribbean and marry him without a second thought. I'd just buried my dad, my mom having passed away five years before him."

Vinnie nods in sympathy, striking match to tobacco.

"I don't know what got into me. Normally, I look at all the angles. I make informed decisions. Take my trip—I spent hours on the Internet, scouting out the best location, the cheapest airfare, a nice beachfront hotel. I had everything planned. But when Trevor sat down in the chaise longue next to me on that pool deck and started to talk—I lost all reason. Suddenly, being alone wasn't what I wanted after all. I see you're done there, Vinnie. Would you care for more?"

A loose fist goes to Vinnie's mouth smothering a soft belch. He shakes his head.

"No thanks, Mona."

"Are you sure, Vinnie? I'll only give it to Sadie later on, I don't eat big meals when I'm alone."

"I don't have the heart to take anything away from that poor gal. You've had her since she was a pup, I guess?"

"What makes you think that?"

"I just figured the way you put up with all her health problems she must have been with you a long time."

Mona picks up the wine bottle, empties the last of it into her glass and swallows it hard.

"Sadie was Trevor's idea. After we came home from the Caribbean he set about making local business contacts—he joined the gentlemen's hockey league, became a member of the

Rotary Club. I let him trade in my Chevette so he could buy the Volvo off of Jimmy Blodgett's lot. He paid cash for it too, which set a few tongues wagging. Then he comes up with this idea to sponsor a 'Pet of the Week' in the local paper for the Humane Society. Did you know Selma and Pat McGuire out on County Rd. 39?"

"I sure did. I used to clear their driveway every winter."

"Sadie was their dog. She was the sole survivor when their house caught fire. Apparently none of Selma and Pat's kids or grandkids were interested in a smelly old legacy like her, so she ended up in the pound. Next thing I know, Trevor shows up with her on a lead, saying how it would be good for business if it got around town about his compassionate nature."

Vinnie draws on his pipe and shakes his head, billowing smoke toward the ceiling.

"Talk about having all the angles covered." Mona hears grudging admiration in his voice.

"I'm curious, Vinnie. Why didn't you get caught up in the diamond fever?"

"I went to one of his meetings out there at the Journey's End Motel and listened to his pitch. I even pretended like the rest of them that I understood geology reports and flow charts, but when push comes to shove you have to trust the man, not the deal. Trevor was too flashy. Those *eye*-talian shoes. The pricey suit. That handshake. I went up to him afterwards with a few questions, but he wouldn't look a fellow in the eye. That's when I remembered what Liza once said about a time-share deal in Florida—if it looks too good to be true, then it probably is."

"I wish I'd had her with me in the Caribbean."

Vinnie is reaching across the table for her half-full plate, stacking it atop his own before she realizes where she has put her foot.

"God, Vinnie, I'm so sorry!"

"No harm done, Mona. She's been gone almost four years now. I'm at a point where I can let the little things slide." He pushes his chair away from the table, as if to stand.

"You know what bothers me most, Vin," Mona snaps his name in half, reaching to stay his forearm, "it's how I've been 'packaged' by this town, the whole country now, as a lonely, gullible, unattached librarian, who let herself get royally screwed."

"Come on, Mona, you're not any of those things."

"Am too."

"Well, you're not a librarian any more ... " he stops short. "Geez, now I'm the one who should apologize!"

Mona hears a bitter, unpleasant laugh. Did that just come from her? She releases Vinnie's arm and rises on legs that feel loosened from her hips, giving into the realization that she is about to fall flat on her linoleum floor.

Vinnie moves fast for a heavy-set man, catching her about the waist, easing her down onto her chair. For a second, she feels he might kiss her and she thinks she might kiss him right back but then, just as suddenly, he is moving off to a safe distance, his face newborn pink.

Vinnie grabs the plates from the table without looking at her and takes them to the counter, scraping leftovers into her frying pan. Keeping his back to Mona, he turns on the hot water tap and squirts too much Joy into her sink, watching it fill to the hot soapy brim before speaking to her again.

"I'll take the rest of this out to Sadie and stay with her until she's done. If you want, I can bring her back up for the night."

MONA RINSES THE PLATES and wipes the table. She runs to the bathroom to splash some sobering water on her face, returning to an empty kitchen to sweep the floor. She steals a look through the screen door; the truck remains parked out front, next to the Honda.

Looking toward the garage, she sees a stationary straw of light poking toward the rafters. Where did he get a flashlight? From his truck, maybe, while she was in the bathroom. What's he doing, spoon-feeding her? Afraid to walk back into the house and discover his naked, new best friend sprawled on the couch, eager to shake her tail at him? That thought makes *her* blush.

What if he's fallen, hit his head?

Mona slips her running shoes on and steps out onto the darkened porch. It is a moonless night, which means she will have to navigate the path to the garage in the dark, Vinnie's flashlight her only beacon. She stumbles immediately, once off the porch, giving her ankle a painful twist. Best to walk it off, she tells herself, whilst roundly cursing Sadie and all old, arthritic dogs who look like Sadie. And that is when she hears the single report of a shotgun.

Mona's feet stop moving, but her heart lurches forward. The echo of the blast lifts away from its epicentre, her garage, and pulses off into the darkness. She can't just stand here. She's got to choose—limp toward the garage and listen to what Vinnie has to say, or sneak back to the house, pretend she didn't hear a thing and wait for him to come to her. The perpendicular strip of light turns horizontal and begins to bob toward the door.

She meets up with him at the entrance to the garage. He's gripping the shotgun with one hand over the breech, its barrel angled toward the ground. The flashlight is in his other hand. He's looking at the ground, finding his way. He is not aware of her until she blurts out his name.

"Vinnie?"

"Mona? Ahh shit. Hey, don't go in there, alright?" Vinnie's voice sounds plugged, as if he's pinching his nostrils together.

"Why not?"

Limping past him and through the doorway, Mona's hand finds the light switch.

There are blood smears all over the feather tick. Tufts of gelatinous, golden fur are sticking to the snow blower, a couple of abandoned paint cans, the wheels of her mountain bike. It looks like someone has had a pillow fight with her dog.

"Where's Sadie?"

"She's over in the corner by the freezer, what's left of her. I covered her with Trevor's bathrobe, so you wouldn't have to see. Something got at her, Mona, must have been while we were eating dinner. I think it was a fisher."

"A fisher?" What about the gunshot? She backs up, just a little, and decides to play it his way. "What's a fisher?"

"They've been moving down here from up north. I've never seen one myself, but I've read about them in the paper. Imagine a fox crossed with a weasel and you've got yourself one vicious, sneaky little bastard. It probably snuck up on her while she was asleep there on the feather tick. She was over in the corner when I came in. I couldn't just let the poor old gal bleed out."

"So, you shot her?"

"I figured you wouldn't mind. Don't look, okay?"

Mona glances toward the corner, sees the bathrobe, considers the scenario, averts her eyes. Vinnie's right, she doesn't need to see.

"You're not mad are you, Mona?"

"No, Vinnie, you did the right thing." Poor, unsuspecting Sadie—Mona shivers, but cannot shed a tear.

Vinnie turns her toward the house, binding his words to her thoughts. "Say, I hear those fishers have got more powerful jaws than a fast-talking conman."

"Funny, Vinnie. Very funny."

They weave their way back to the house, Vinnie's flashlight illuminating the path.

"Shouldn't we bury her?" Mona asks, overcome by guilt, as they reach the porch. "There's a nice spot out back, next to the peonies."

"Nah," he says. "It's late. I'll come by tomorrow with a pickaxe and a shovel, get her done right. She's not going anywhere tonight, Mona."

"No, I guess not."

"Besides, you're in no shape to help dig a grave. What did you do to yourself?" he asks, spotlighting her running shoe with the flashlight.

"I twisted my ankle on the path. It's nothing serious." But Vinnie is having none of it.

"Sit," he says, motioning to the porch steps, "let's have a look."

Mona plunks herself down on the middle step and unlaces her sneaker; Vinnie takes a seat, too, his thigh grazing hers as he trains the flashlight on her ankle. Removing her shoe, she strips off the sock, to reveal an egg-shaped swelling just below her anklebone.

"Ouch," he says, wincing. "Now that's gotta hurt."

Which is when she realizes that it does hurt, quite a bit, actually.

"We need some ice," he says, handing her the flashlight. "Stay put, I'll be right back." Scrambling up her steps and into the house, he returns with a grocery bag poultice of ice cubes, two Advil and a glass of water.

"Take these." Handing her the pills and the glass, Vinnie goes down on bended knee to gently wrap the bag of ice around her swelling ankle. His other hand comes to rest on her knee. "We'll wait for it to get good and numb and then I'll help you into the house," he says.

Mona smiles. It's now or never. Tapping his shoulder with the head of the flashlight, she reaches forward to imprint his forehead with her lipstick.

"Sounds like a plan," she says.

Highway Salvation

SHE COULD KICK HERSELF for forgetting the watch. It was worth something, damn it! *A pretty penny*, Jared had said, when he gave it to her for her birthday. Just what had she been thinking, leaving it behind? She could have hocked it down the road. She could have used it now, too.

She hated not knowing what time it was. Hated it!

Chalk it up to the excitement of the moment, to the sound of Jared's high-pitched, niggling voice peddling forgiveness, in the name of *Jeeesus Chrrrist*! It made her want to grab him by his prim and proper, button-downed collar and heave him against the wall, or better yet the china cabinet. Breaking glass, Jared bloodied and bruised—might have been more fun than the rest of their time put together.

Goddamned rain. At least she'd had smarts enough to bring her umbrella and overcoat, though the coat did make her look fat. She cinched the belt a little tighter. The rain was pelting the umbrella's surface like a typewriter, reminding her of the weekend comics she used to read spread out on the floor of her parents' townhouse.

How Betty would stand out there suffering in the stick-pencil rain while Archie was inside putting the moves on that dominatrix, Veronica Lodge. What a dummy, she used to think. What did Betty see in Archie anyways? Pale face, too many friggin' freckles, head of carroty hair.

Men. God love'em, somebody should.

Hah! Her mother's expression—whenever Dad left the house for cards or the track—never to his face, though. She didn't have the guts.

She took it for as long as she had to and then split, leaving Tommy behind to fend for himself. Her one regret.

She remembered driving somewhere with them when she was thirteen, her mother pissed because they had to stop at the side of the road for her to vomit, Tommy taking shape inside of her. On their way to visit crazy Aunt Sue, her nerves so bad you could practically see them sprouting from her forehead, cracked like a pane of glass her mother was fond of announcing.

Two hours there, two hours back—her parents barely speaking, lighting cigarette after cigarette. She made her mind up right then that she would never, ever get hitched.

Of course it only got worse after Tommy—her mother hissing 'slut' over one shoulder as she mopped the afterbirth from the bathroom floor. Her father downstairs barricaded in his La-Z-Boy recliner, staring at the spot on the carpet where Tommy was conceived.

She left two months later in the middle of the night after nursing Tommy, changing his diaper and singing him one last, sweet lullaby. Sometimes she allowed herself to imagine her parents raising him as their own—changing his diapers, feeding him strained carrots, kissing his wounds, trips to the park. Did they ever wonder about her or where she'd flown off to? Not likely.

He'd be twenty-two now.

The cars were whizzing by, rain exploding from their windshields. No one had noticed her. Not true. The kids noticed—pressing their runny noses and damp fingertips up against the windows, mouths working overtime, trying to get mom, dad, somebody, to acknowledge the woman standing at the edge of the 401.

Maybe the umbrella conjured up images of Mary Poppins for them. Hah! Wouldn't Serge get a kick out of that one? Perhaps if she had to start dancing again she could work it into her act—an umbrella, overcoat, those cruel, black ankle boots with the tiny buttons? She could see the customers now—breathing a little heavy, grabbing their crotches under the Formica tabletops, stroking their little fellas through a layer of cloth while she did the bump and grind above them. And the tricks she could perform with that umbrella! It might even make up for those twenty extra pounds.

Serge had said he didn't give a tinker's damn about the extra weight when she'd run into him down at the Bear's Tooth Tavern after Jared's fifth attempt to steer her immortal soul toward safety. He'd come up from behind and bit her on the back of the neck.

"Don't give no shit about de weight, Missy. You're still de best, you know dat." Hot, leathery tongue poking in her ear. Sliding his beefy hand up her thigh. "Wanna go someplace? I got some extra cash."

She didn't go with him that time. Not that she minded taking money for it. After all it had paid the bills in the past. Especially when Serge's joint had come under attack from those holy rollers. Never lasted long though. Slick old Serge could be a pig with the girls, but he knew which palms needed the grease. Besides, getting paid for rolling a guy, it rang her chimes more often than not. Maybe that's what she needed from Jared—cash, sex, not some stupid watch that only served to remind her how much time she'd been wasting on him.

She yanked a pack of duMaurier's out of the side pocket of her trench coat. Two left. If he didn't show his milk-toast face soon she'd have to make a scene. Wave her hands above her head, strip naked, bleach-blonde hair blowing in the whistling wind. Now that'd be a sight! Guys liked it when a woman was afraid. Forget the diamonds, sometimes fear could be a girl's best friend.

And then there was Jared. The first time she'd seen him down at the Club Kahuna she couldn't believe it. Mr. Squeaky Clean! Mr. Born-Again! Mr. I-Have-All-the-Answers-Right-Here-in-the-Good-Book!

He came into the club armed with a Bible and a box of tissues—allergies—sat down and ordered a ginger ale, no ice and watched. And no matter which tricks she performed above him his hands stayed topside and his eyes never left her face. It drove her nuts and that's why she let him talk to her.

The cigarette tasted good and for the first time in four months she could take a puff, suck it deep down into her chest and exhale without Jared waving the newspaper in her face or worse, honking into a handkerchief and reading his snotty fortune. It felt good to be free. No more Jared, no more Jared's house, rules, questions.

He told her he'd started his own church—public works employee by day, redeemer of souls by night. Well, she just laughed and laughed straight into his calm, peckish, little face.

"Come live with me," he offered, the last time Serge got shut down. "I'll take care of you."

She figured sure, why not? She had nothing to lose. Besides it had been two months—every night at the Club Kahuna and his hands were still topside, his eyes still locked onto hers. So sincere, so *caring*. Maybe if she got inside his house she could get inside him, smash his beliefs into teeny-tiny pieces and save him from redemption!

He lived on a quiet, dead-end street with lots of trees and birds. *That* should have been her first clue. She knew as soon as they parked that she couldn't make herself fit whatever mold Jared had in mind.

He was too neat for one thing. He worked outside all day—un-plugging sewers, sweeping streets, fixing lamp posts, and then he'd come home at night and clean—tubs, toilets, windows. She never lifted a finger. Just sat in front of the television smoking one cigarette after another. He cooked, too, and he was pretty good at it. Didn't she have the twenty pounds to prove it?

On weekends he was up early baking—bread, muffins, sticky-buns. He'd bring it all into her room on a fancy tray with little silver pots of jam and marmalade and a big mug of decaf and then watch her devour it.

He cooked. She ate. He cleaned and she made messes for him. Sometimes she would spill milk or juice on the floor and wipe it up with a dish towel, leaving just enough behind to make the floor sticky for him, or sprinkle cereal all about, grinding it to a fine powder beneath her heel, then walk all over the dining room carpet. It kept her from climbing the walls, kept her from going over the wall too.

"You should get out more," he'd say. "Take a walk around the block and meet our neighbours."

Yeah, right. Like they'd want to make her acquaintance. She'd seen them congregating outside every evening after supper—their little brats riding up and down the street on spanking, new trikes, pointing at Jared's house, wondering why the woman who had gone in never came out. She did come out, late at night for cigarettes from the corner store.

The worst thing, besides the boredom, was her not knowing what Jared wanted. It wasn't sex. She'd tried a couple of times—three-inch spikes, G-string, redder-than-red lipstick and nail polish, then no makeup, soft, winding-white nightgown, lots of lace and pearl buttons, ordered from the Sears catalogue. Nothing. He'd just sit at the edge of his bed and shake his blushing head, look her straight in the eye and forgive her.

Made her want to nail him to a cross just like his mentor.

Then he started in on her past. Where did she grow up? How did her father make his living? Her mother? She knew what he was after, the same as those shrink-types at the drop-in center in the city after she'd left home—her *id*, her *dark side*, her *inner child*.

Finally, she let him have it but good, screaming it into his startled face, imagining her hot breath melting the skin right off of his hawk-like nose. She thought it would shut him up and get him off her back. But nooo! No way. Not him. Not Mr. 12-Step-Bible-Thumping-New-Wave-Preacher! Saint Jared, The Redeemer! Didn't she wonder about her son? Didn't she wonder about her parents? Well, maybe not her father, but certainly her mother? Were they still alive, did she think? What about forgiveness?

Forgiveness? Forget it! She spat it at him, just like that and more than once, too. He took it. He always took it, which only served to make her more angry.

Then, this afternoon while she was watching *Oprah*, smoking a cigarette and thinking about getting dressed, he crept into the living room and dropped two envelopes onto her lap—one apple-green, one long and white, both sliced open.

"What's this?" she'd said, her mind a fog.

"A letter from your mother."

That brought her out of it. She felt dizzy right off. Then she got angry, her head a torpedo that might just shoot off and hit Jared square in the stomach, spilling his guts out all over the crumbs on the carpet.

She couldn't remember her exact words, how they'd poured out...

He'd pointed to the long, white envelope. Her mother and father had given the child up a few weeks after she ran away. If she filled out the form in there she might be able to find out what had happened to him.

She shredded the envelope into tiny, little pieces, right before his God-fearing eyes. Then she called him every name in the book, the air blue around them. The boy was better off not knowing. Couldn't the numbskull see that?

"The truth will set you both free."

Well, that's all she needed, him bleating scripture. She yanked her suitcase out from under her bed and told him she'd had enough of him messing with her head. She demanded to be taken to the city so she could catch an express and get the hell away from him and his forgiving ways.

Jared did everything she asked. He didn't argue or try to change her mind. He even stopped with the scripture, watching her with those tractor-beam eyes as she stomped around the house gathering her belongings. He opened the car door for her and reminded her to buckle up.

She settled down some in the car. Her heartbeat slowed, her palms stopped bleeding sweat. After a couple of minutes he reached into his pocket, shuffling around and pulled out the green envelope.

"Here," he said. "You take this, in case you change your mind."

She glanced at the handwriting—sloppy lettering, wrenching to the right. Her mother would be fifty-four by now. Old? Frail? What a laugh! Hard. Mean. More like it. She snatched it from his hand, slid it into her pocket real casual-like.

"Does she say anything about my old man?" Blurting out the words before thinking.

"He left after the child was placed."

He glanced over at her.

"So you see, she's known loneliness too."

His eyes. The compassion, there.

She couldn't take it, didn't want it.

"Fuck you, Jared! Let me out of this goddamned car, RIGHT NOW!"

Smashing her fists against the dashboard, screeching obscenities. She scared him but good. He couldn't save her soul if he killed her in a fiery crash, could he? He pulled off the highway.

She grabbed the latch and swung the door hard, hinges rocking. Breathing heavily, she pulled the suitcase from the backseat.

"Get away from me, Jared. Go find someone who NEEDS you meddling in their life 'cause I sure as hell DON'T!" She slammed the door. He drove off.

Coward! Milk-toast! Whiner! She couldn't remember, did she yell those words inside or outside of her head? It didn't matter. The cigarette was burning her fingers now. She dropped it on the gravel, grinding it beneath the sole of her high-heeled shoe.

She needed a plan.

She couldn't stand here much longer.

It was time to pull a rabbit out of her hat. Sit her arse down on top of her suitcase, put her head in her lap, start shaking and sobbing. Surely the deadbeats would notice then, wouldn't they?

The taxi passed her just as she was planting her bum on the ridge of her wobbling suitcase. It was the one from town, she recognized the driver's hill of flesh. Stuck her hand up and waved just like she might if she were sitting out on Jared's front porch.

The driver flashed her four-ways, went off to the shoulder and backed up slowly, her tires eating, then spitting gravel. She stopped a foot shy of the suitcase and heaved herself out of the car, clomping around to the passenger side while hitching her man-sized jeans up over the crack in her bum.

"You the one what's been staying with Jared?" Glasses sliding down her nose.

"What if I am?"

"He told me to take you wherever you want to go. Bus station, train depot, his place. Whatever."

"Let's shove off, then." She stood up, grabbing her suitcase and umbrella and opened the back door to toss them in.

The smell of fresh bread.

"Here," the driver said and pushed an aluminum tray across the seat, five out of six buns still accounted for. "Jared said to give you these. Hope you don't mind me taking one, they smelled so blessed good I couldn't help myself."

"Don't sweat it."

"This is for you, too." Handing over an envelope, then waiting, curious to see the contents, before she pulled out onto the highway.

Five twenty-dollar bills.

The watch.

A note: *Come back when you're ready.* Jared's phone number at the bottom.

"So where'm I takin' you, honey?"

"The city. Bus depot."

She stuffed the note in her coat pocket beside the green envelope, put the money in her wallet and the watch on her wrist, then yanked out her last cigarette, lighting up with shaking fingers.

Money in her wallet, watch on her wrist.

No time to lose.

MISCONCEPTIONS

BERNICE'S CRUSADE BEGAN with a haunting discovery, one bitter November morning in 1973, as she heaved her matronly bones up the steps of St. Maria Goretti's rectory—a sturdy, rectangular liquor box, wedged between the metal screen door and its massive oak counterpart.

"Anyone could have found it," Bernice confessed to Constable Osborne, when he dropped by that evening to record her official statement. "Just anyone." *Now why do you suppose God chose me?* Bernice's unspoken, anxious concern, as the distressed fingers of her right hand sought solace from the tiny silver crucifix that graced her neck.

On a milder Eastern Ontario evening in September, or even October, situating a cardboard box between two doors might have afforded some protection against the elements, but on that clear, crisp November night the temperature took a predictable tumble.

Bernice recalled setting a brisk pace on the morning in question. Nestling her twin chins deep within the collar of her woolen jacket, she walked the two blocks to St. Maria Goretti's in record time for a woman of her considerable girth. Even so, Bernice found upon arrival that she had lost all feeling in her gloved fingertips. All she could focus on was getting inside to thaw her hands over the range element while setting a pot to boil for Father Simon's bowl of Red River Cereal.

It was not that unusual for parishioners to place offerings at the doorstep for Father—baked goods, scrap wool scarves and mittens, the odd bottle of spirits. No one bothered to knock or ring the bell after eight PM because everyone knew he turned his hearing aids off.

Confronted by the liquor box, Bernice thought nothing of bending forward to scoop it up, as she had so many times with gifts in the past. She was caught off guard, however, when the object inside lurched to the left, almost causing her to lose her grip. Much too heavy to be cookies or muffins or knitted goods, Bernice remembered thinking of it as dead weight. Later, in the comfort of her own kitchen, with Howard and their three children, Maggie, Madonna and Owen, bearing witness, Bernice would employ the phrase several times over as she spoke to a sympathetic and patient Constable Osborne.

Since the box was not addressed to Father Simon and since there was no card, Bernice allowed her natural curiosity to get the better of her, pulling back the cardboard flaps to view the contents.

She called the police station straight off.

Constable Osborne and his partner arrived before Father Simon could fumble into his black clothes. They took charge of the tiny body and cardboard coffin as he was biting down on his false teeth and jacking the volume on both hearing aids.

"I wish now I'd rushed the poor thing straight to Father before calling you," Bernice reproached Constable Osborne that evening. "The sooner last rites are performed the better," she added, assuming the Anglican constable's ignorance on the subject of Catholic sacraments.

"Did you touch the infant before we arrived?"

Bernice blinked, fighting with her conscience.

"I know that earlier I said I didn't, but I was not being entirely truthful. I did roll the baby over to see her little face, praying to Mother Mary that it would turn out to be a child's doll, a prank. But when I saw her, well, it was obvious."

"And there was no sign of life?"

"No, sir, she was as blue as your shirt."

"I meant, you didn't notice anyone hanging around outside before or after you entered the rectory?"

"Why no, I never saw a soul."

The Toronto Coroner took his time releasing a report, which, when it came out, told Bernice little that she didn't already know. The baby was female, seventeen and a half inches in length. She weighed a scant 5 lbs., 3 oz., suggesting a premature birth. She was just hours old when swaddled in a threadbare flannel blanket and placed inside the cardboard box. Cause of death: hypothermia as a result of exposure to the elements.

No one wanted to believe that the mother could be home-grown.

Over the next several months all women known to be pregnant, and all teenage girls suspected of being pregnant, were informally tallied by the local population, each of their offspring accounted for over steaming mugs of sweetened coffee, half-drunk beers and stubbed-out cigarettes.

Public concern strained at the seams throughout the winter, shrinking several sizes by early spring. No one came forward with any leads. The case remained a mystery. Most everyone within the parish community and beyond came to accept the tragedy for what it appeared to be—a pregnant teenage runaway, passing through town, frightened and alone, going into premature labour, leaving the baby on the rectory doorstep in the middle of the night, thinking she was doing what was best for her bastard child. And though God would most certainly hold the teenage mother to account for a plethora of mortal sins, even he would find her blameless in this one respect—not knowing about Father Simon's hearing aids.

Sad, yes, the whole sorry business, but over now, the child's soul consigned to Purgatory, her earthly remains laid to rest God knows where, since no one came forward to claim the body; time to let it be and move on, while thanking one's lucky stars and the Lord above that the baby's mother wasn't your daughter or the daughter of anyone you knew or happened to like or respect.

But Bernice could not let it go. No. God had placed that sweet child directly in Bernice's path, if not to save her, then why? The question refused to be banished from her thoughts, swirling about inside her head alongside an almost continuous replay of her discovery at the rectory door. A dead infant, what God meant for Bernice to do—she poured all of it into Father Simon's ear through the confessional grate the following Saturday, and for several consecutive Saturdays after that, and although he did his best to comfort her, absolving her of any perceived responsibility she might have felt for not finding the child in time, he could provide her with no answers as to why God might have chosen her to find the child's body.

Have you prayed about it to our Holy Father? he asked, feeling a bit of a failure, both for not having heard the baby's cry on his doorstep and for being unable to furnish Bernice with a clear-cut response to an earnest question. Of course she had prayed, she replied, the question had kept her up at nights praying—*all* night on more than one occasion. He might have noticed her stifling a yawn or two as she went about her household tasks at the rectory, and for that she apologized. Down on her knees by the bedside while Howard snored away in blissful ignorance—nothing could wake that man once he was asleep—praying, praying to God, Jesus, Mary and Joseph, to Saint Maria Goretti, Patron Saint of Youth, and all the other saints she could name. And though she listened very hard, and with what she sincerely believed to be an open heart, she heard nothing.

Nothing.

His ways are mysterious, her confessor reminded Bernice, *perhaps more patience is needed on your part.*

Father Simon, who had many years before shepherded Bernice through her conversion to Catholicism so that the bleats about excommunication from Howard's mother could be silenced, was counseling patience. What other choice did she have? She would obey; she would plant the seeds of patience and allow them an opportunity to germinate. And while she waited, praying nightly, shedding sleep, she also managed to lose her appetite and with it went ten pounds, then twenty, then thirty-five. One of her chins completely disappeared. Behind her back, Bernice's women friends agreed that she had never looked better. To her face they cautioned, *Don't lose any more, Bernice, or you'll start to look sick.*

HOWARD FINALLY TOOK notice of his wife's weight loss late one Sunday evening when, by chance, he glimpsed Bernice's naked body through their opened bathroom door as she was toweling off after a sudsy soak—a leg, bent at the knee, raised navel high, the instep of her foot pressed against the edge of the bathroom counter. He had a fine view of her diminished backside, a partial view of one jiggling breast—also reduced in size. Sitting at the end of the bed, not saying a word, almost without breathing, he watched as his wife carefully and thoroughly dried every nook, crease and fold. Bernice had always been modest—he could count on ten fingers and six toes the number of times she had removed all of her clothing in front of him during their married life, and since relations, which happened less frequently than he would have liked now that the children stomped about until all hours, were silently negotiated between Bernice and himself with the lights off, well, he had simply failed to realize or appreciate the drastic changes in his wife's physique. But now that he had, he first grew excited, then slightly ashamed at his excitement, then accepting of his lawful and natural appetites, then alarmed by the sight of his wife. Bernice was too thin. He would have to fatten her up.

He began by bringing Dairy Queen treats home after his day at St. Maria Goretti's elementary school was done—Buster Bars, Blizzards, Banana Splits. *Oh, I couldn't, Howard,* she'd say with a wan and distracted smile, a rosary always within easy reach, *why don't you give it to one of the children?* He made outlandish Sunday dinner requests: spareribs, fried chicken, roast beef and gravy, twice-baked potatoes with sour cream and crumbled bits of real bacon, chocolate cake. Bernice cooked all of it for him without complaint, but now that he was paying attention he began to notice how little actual food she arranged on her own plate. The praying, the weight loss and sleepless nights, the abandoned baby—they were all con-nected. Bernice, he yearned to say, do you really believe a lov-ing God would want you to leave three children motherless, and me a widower because of an illegitimate child abandoned on the rectory steps?

But he knew not to come between Bernice and her God. Over the years, she had become the better Catholic—a true believer, a living saint, more willing to follow the Church's laws and precepts than he would ever be. Case in point: his vasectomy. Arranged and executed within the sanctity of his family doctor's office not long after Owen's birth, without a word to his wife. Bernice would have been happy to keep on having a baby every eighteen months until she was too old to conceive and they were financially ruined, but Howard, the eldest of nine raucous siblings, valued peace and quiet, a comfortable house and a fifty-dollar bill in his wallet at all times more than he did the idea of a large family or the Church's position on birth control. But his wife took all of the Church's teachings as Gospel. So now, instead of suggesting she might want to cut back on the prayers, which he knew she would never do, he decided to join her at the side of the bed, two heads being better than one. Their communion went on for several weeks. To Howard's surprise and delight, it brought them closer—not because of the prayers, but because they retired much later, long after the children were asleep, which resulted in something of a sensual revival. Unfortunately, all that praying, combined with more time in the missionary position began to take a toll on Howard's middle-aged knees—first they creaked, then they swelled and then they began to ache. Late one Friday evening near summer's end, as Howard was beginning to accept that he might have to sacrifice prayer and, by extension, sexual relations, because of his knees and arrange an appointment to see young Dr. Mills, there came a loud and prolonged knocking at the front door.

IT WAS CONSTABLE OSBORNE and his partner. Bernice had not spoken to either officer since that dreadful day back in November. She regretted seeing them now even more than she had then because between them they were supporting the full weight of her and Howard's fifteen-year-old daughter, Maggie.

Where had she got that halter top?

Those hip-hugger cut-offs?

Lipstick, fine, but blush, eyeshadow, mascara? No one had agreed to any of that.

"There was a party," Constable Osborne explained to Bernice, overtop of her daughter's drooping head, "60 Pine Crescent. Do you know the address?"

Bernice nodded. "The Petersons," she said. Presbyterians, she was certain of it. They had a son, two years older than Maggie. He attended the public high school in town. By all accounts a hooligan. He'd already made one young girl pregnant, mercifully no one that Bernice knew. He and his ilk were one of the reasons why she and Howard had made the decision to send Maggie to high school at Regiopolis Notre Dame in Kingston.

"No parents present," Officer Osborne was saying now, "out on an island at the family cottage, the son said. We're seeing it more and more—the parents go away and leave the kids to play. We cleared everybody out; found your daughter, alone, in an upstairs bedroom. She was in no shape to make her own way home."

"Yes, I can see that." Bernice moved closer to Maggie to get a whiff of her breath—gin, a hint of sour vomit. Jesus, Mary and Joseph. Taking hold of her daughter's chin between her thumb and forefinger, Bernice lifted her face, sternly proclaiming her daughter's name: "Maggie!"

Was she faking unconsciousness, like she sometimes faked sleep on Sunday mornings when Bernice rapped at her bedroom door to rouse her for Mass?

To test this theory, Bernice slapped her daughter across the cheek, just once and not nearly as hard as she would have liked because of the police presence.

"Maggie, for heaven's sake. Wake up!"

She stirred, then, her eyes opening almost halfway, the corners of her mouth pulling down in a vague acknowledgment of the slap.

"Maggie?" Howard said, so hopefully it crushed Bernice's heart. Then their daughter's eyes rolled to somewhere near the back of her head, and her eyelashes fluttered down.

Lights out.

For a moment, no one spoke.

"We'd be happy to assist you in getting her up over the stairs," Constable Osborne offered.

Bernice sighed. "No, no, that won't be necessary." Motioning toward Howard to grab their daughter under one arm, Bernice took hold of her by the other.

Howard cleared his throat.

"Will there be any charges, Constable?"

Good Lord, Bernice hadn't even considered charges, she'd been too shocked, too embarrassed, too angry to think about charges.

"No, sir. It's her first brush with the law, obviously she's from a good family, and like I said, it's becoming *really* common."

"Not in this household it isn't," Bernice said. "Thank you, Constable. Thank you both, and God bless."

TOGETHER, BERNICE AND HOWARD managed to drag and guide Maggie up and into the room she shared with her younger sister. Creaking stairs and floor boards, grunts, whispered directions from Bernice to Howard, from Howard back to her, the *fummph* of Maggie's body as it hit the mattress—through it all, twelve-year old Madonna, Bernice's little angel, serenely unaffected by teenage hormones, not yet swayed by teenage peer pressure, a Good News Bible lying open on her bedside table, slumbered on. Thank God for small mercies. Madonna worshipped Maggie—her sinful, drunken, slatternly big sister.

Bernice felt Howard's arm come around her shoulder, gathering her in close, his palm sliding up and down the outer part of her upper arm. She never quite knew how to react to this type of gesture, felt paralyzed by it, in fact. Was he offering her comfort or asking for it? She wasn't sure. Up, down, up down, causing her arm to feel irritated, making it difficult for Bernice to concentrate. She stepped away from him, closer to the bed, closer to their drunken daughter, Howard following, hands now limp at his sides.

"Even if we could wake her," he said, "she'd be in no shape to discuss the consequences of tonight's behaviour. It's late. We should go to bed. Tomorrow'll come soon enough."

"You go. I'll be there in a minute." Waiting for Howard to leave the bedroom, Bernice fished the rosary from a pocket in her robe.

Friday—the Sorrowful Mysteries—Jesus in the Garden of Gethsemani, brought low by thoughts of imminent betrayal; Jesus whipped by the soldiers, crowned with thorns, forced to carry the cross. Crucified. Bernice pressed the crucifix to her lips, tried to pray for her daughter—Our Father, Hail Mary, Glory Be, but her mind refused to settle into the predictable and comforting rhythm, her thoughts straying to the mortal sins her daughter may or may not have committed while in that boy's home. While lying to Bernice and Howard about her plans for the evening—a sleepover at Sherry Calhoun's house—was certainly a grave sin, it may have been the least of her transgressions. Drinking underage, lewd dress, lustful thoughts, letting some boy touch her where no boy should ever, *ever* touch her until she was properly wed—the gravity of her daughter's situation drove the rosary back into the pocket of Bernice's robe. In her current state of mortal sin, if Maggie were to stop breathing right now, if she were to, say, succumb to alcohol poisoning at this very instant, like that boy from Queen's did last fall on Homecoming weekend, God would have no choice but to send her straight to hell. The first order of business, tomorrow, once they had given her a chance to relate her version of events, to apologize for her behaviour, and after they grounded her for a suitable period of time, was to get her over to the church and Father Simon so that she could confess her sins and be absolved.

Snoring lightly, now, her breathing relaxed, without a care in the world, stretched out atop the quilt that Bernice had presented to her for her last birthday. They'd gone to the fabric store together, she'd allowed Maggie to pick out all of the material. Maggie had even assisted Bernice in cutting some of the fabric, appearing to take a real interest.

That was then.

Now? Drunk and not slightly so. No. Falling down drunk, like Bernice's father used to get, every Friday and Saturday night of Bernice's truncated childhood. How many times had she put her father to bed like this? He'd died years ago, long after her mother. Funny, while she could replay every significant moment of her mother's illness, she could never remember the exact year of her father's demise, but the children were small—Maggie in grade one, Madonna at nursery school, Owen not yet weaned—a fall down a steep set of stairs that led up to his bedsit, his neck broken. Drunk, of course. A profound relief to Bernice—no more phone calls in the middle of the night, him asking for money which she and Howard could ill afford to supply, him calling her a liar and a bitch. His death had marked the end of all of that—or so she had thought.

This little snip had no idea how lucky she was—two healthy, loving parents who took their responsibilities seriously, who only wanted to guide her along a sober and righteous path.

Halter top. Cut-offs. Eyelids weighed down by all that glop.

Bernice's gaze drifted to her daughter's belly button, displayed for all to see above the waistband of her cut-offs—rounded and taut, as yet un-stretched by successive pregnancies.

What if she were to become pregnant?

What if sperm and egg were meeting up inside her virgin womb at this very moment, like the child-mother of that other ill-fated little one?

It was happening all the time—an epidemic of sorts, according to the medical community, the media. Recently, young Dr. Mills had displayed a poster in his office—a high-school girls' basketball team—row upon row of healthy, pony-tailed athletes. *One in five girls will become pregnant before they graduate*, it said. *Speak to your doctor about preventing teenage pregnancy.*

Two girls from Maggie's grade *eight* graduating class had already been caught. Fourteen. One had given hers up at the hospital without ever setting eyes on it. The other? Living at home with her parents, brazen as could be, passing the child off as if it were a baby sister, when everyone in the parish, in the town, knew better.

The shame it would bring to the family—to Howard, Vice Principal at St. Maria Goretti's Elementary, where Madonna would soon be a grade seven student, and Owen in grade five; to Bernice, who cleaned and cooked for Father Simon. It would kill Howard's mother, while at the same time confirming every misgiving she had ever voiced or felt about Bernice as a suitable wife for her son and mother for his children—at least she would die vindicated.

And Maggie? She would have to be sent away—there would be no other choice—Howard had a cousin out west.

Bernice's little family would never be the same.

Bernice now had a focus for her prayers. Withdrawing the mass of beads from her pocket, she bunched them to her lips.

Please God, no.

DONNA WAS NOT ASLEEP when the police officers arrived at her family's front door. Awake for hours since her 10PM bedtime, she'd been entertaining a flurry of impure thoughts about Robert Redford, inspired by a photograph she'd seen of him in the city newspaper—bare-chested and golden—running through the ocean surf. Sure he was older—thirty-seven, the paper said—so, not quite as old as her dad, but he was so handsome, so s-e-x-y, and not stupid at all like every single boy in her dumb school. Thinking about him—his blue eyes, the perfect blond hair, his square jaw and oh-so-white teeth and smile it all made that tiny spot *down there* beg for the attention of her fingertips, and so she had spent the better part of the past hour agonizing over whether or not she should give in to this pressing urge.

Her mother at home, her teacher at school, Father Simon during the special 'facts of life' retreat for the Grade Six girls that took place in the last week of Lent—they all spoke with one voice—masturbation was a serious sin, and not just masturbation—anything at all having to do with 'it', with S-E-X.

God is always watching us, even when we believe ourselves to be alone.

Was God watching her right now? Was he hovering somewhere in her room, maybe over there by her closet, or over there by the window, waiting to see if she would endanger their special friendship by breaking one of his sacred laws? According to her sister, Maggie—uh, no. God has *way* more important sinners to keep tabs on—thieves, murderers, warmongers. Think about it, if God were to spend his spare time monitoring all the people in the world getting themselves off, all of the people in the world doing *it*, wouldn't that make him, like, a total creep? Who'd want to believe in a god like that? Not me, little sister.

Maybe she was right. But then there was Father Simon.

A girl must have conviction if she is to be a witness to Christ. She must make up her mind that no matter what happens she will avoid sins against purity.

Most of the time, Donna felt as if she possessed the kind of conviction Father Simon had spoken about during the retreat. She didn't swear, ever, not like a certain older sister she knew. And though she hadn't completely made up her mind, yet, how far she might let a boy go if she really, really liked him and he really, really liked her, one thing she knew for sure—she would be a virgin on the day that she married. But touching herself, *down there*, that was proving much harder to control.

Why even *try* to control it, Maggie had said. It's perfectly natural. People do it all the time. Every girl I know does it. I bet even your dried up old teacher, Mrs. Marshall, has done it. Mom and Dad, too.

Well, maybe not Mom.

That was when Donna covered her ears and begged Maggie to stop.

During the retreat, Father Simon had told them the story of St. Maria Goretti, Patron Saint of Youth and namesake to their very own church—how when Maria was twelve-years-old, the same age that they all were now, her life was taken from her by a twenty-year-old brute named Alessandro Serenelli, who wanted her to commit impurities with him. Except Maria was blest with conviction and true devotion to our Lord; she knew that what the young man wanted her to do with him was a sin, so she told Alessandro no, but he would not take no for an answer. Maria struggled with all of her might, she screamed but no one heard her. She warned the young man that he would go to hell for what he was about to do, at which point he pulled out a knife and stabbed Maria fourteen times.

Little Maria forgave Alessandro on her deathbed—telling her confessor that she hoped to see her killer in Paradise—too good to be true, some might say, but the Holy Father and his Cardinals knew that she was simply too good to live. She is a saint today, Father Simon said, because she chose death over sin.

Let this be a lesson to you all.

Not only must a girl keep the salvation of her soul in the forefront of her thoughts, Father Simon continued, she must also guard against becoming occasions of sin for others. A person should not become less of a friend of Christ because he is a friend of yours. How to keep that from happening? Begin with these three simple precepts:

Dress moderately.

Don't dance too close.

Keep your tongue in your own mouth.

Ewww.

Sometimes Donna would French kiss her pillow, the back of her hand. Were these sins? Did they count?

And what about times like right now, when she couldn't keep her impure thoughts about Robert Redford from invading her mind, her hand as if by its own accord snaking its way down to that surprisingly damp and warm place? Was it a sin if she couldn't help it?

Mom, Mrs. Marshall and Father Simon all said yes.

Maggie said no.

Was Maggie turning into a bad influence? During the retreat, Father Simon had warned the girls away from friends who made fun of God's laws, who had foul mouths. But what if the bad influence was your own flesh and blood?

Maggie said f-u-c-k all the time. And s-h-i-t. She took the Lord's name in vain, too.

She didn't appear to be concerned at all, anymore, about her immortal soul, or about being a witness to Christ. That all seemed to stop when she turned fourteen and went to high school.

What happened?

Boy crazy, she'd overheard her mother saying to her father, and he'd said *we have to trust her, Bernice, until she gives us a reason not to.*

What they didn't know: that recently, late into the evening after everyone was in bed, Maggie had been lifting up their bedroom window and climbing out—the hockey jock, Will Peterson, standing below and ready to break her fall. They didn't know about the secret stash of makeup in the closet, the cigarettes, or the slim pack of pills she had obtained from Dr. Mills. Donna wanted to tell her parents, not only because she was worried that Maggie was heading down the wrong path, but because not telling her parents was a serious sin of omission—but Maggie said being a loyal sister came before being a snitch to one's parents. Besides, Maggie knew there'd come a time, and not too long from now, when Donna would want to be alone with a boy, and if Maggie was still living at home she promised she would do the same for her.

Right now, all Donna wanted was to spend a few minutes with Robert Redford. But just in case Maggie's logic proved faulty, and before Donna allowed her fingers to reach their destination, she vowed to God that if he could turn away for a few minutes and stop watching, that she would go to confession tomorrow afternoon and admit her impure thoughts to Father Simon. It would be a hard and embarrassing thing to confess, but she knew Father Simon would forgive her, he always did, and she would leave the confessional with a purified soul, her conscience unburdened.

Moments later, a loud banging at the front door put a halt both to Donna's fingers and her imagination. Guiltily sitting up in bed, she listened to her parents' panicked rush down the stairs and the slide of the deadbolt. Her mother's greeting to Officer Osborne catapulted Donna to the foot of her bed, the better to hear, except maddeningly, as if on cue, all of the voices in the hallway quieted. A murmuring of subdued voices before her mother's final, "Thank you both, and God Bless." Donna repositioned herself beneath her covers and listened as her mother and father dragged Maggie's butt up the stairs. Closing her eyes, slowing her breathing, she took in all of what happened next: the whispered discussion of consequences, her father leaving the room, her mother's rosary beads.

Please God, no.

No, what?

A deep sigh, and then,

In nomine Patris, et Filii, et Spiritus Sancti. Amen …

And then,

Veram paenitentiam meae culpae cupio …

(I Desire True Repentance for My Sins ...)
I Desire a Spirit of Mortification ...
I Desire Moral Courage ...
I Desire the Virtue of Patience ...
I Desire the Grace of Final Perseverance ...
And then the creak of the wood floor as her mother struggled to her feet, coming to stand over Donna's bed. And then the feel of her mother's hand as it smoothed a lock of hair away from her cheek, accompanied by a choking sob.

SPARK

"**THE BEETLE IS ONE** of our top sellers, Mr. and Mrs. Reed. Dependable, fuel efficient, not to mention incredibly cool."

Cool?

The salesman—Derrick is his name—is a kid. Twenty-one, twenty-two years old at best. Suit and tie, hair on the crown of his head sculpted into short frosted spikes, a smudge of dark blond beard beneath the curve of his lower lip. Hockey-jock shoulders. Reminds Foster a little too much of Cody. He wonders if Lynette has noticed.

Cody.

A boy's name, not a man's. Cute enough while he's a kid, Foster had said when Lynette first proposed it after his birth, but what about when he becomes a man?

Moot point, now.

Derrick places a proprietary hand on the car's rounded roof, the colour of a ripened tomato.

"So, would you and your wife be interested in taking it out for a test drive, sir?"

Foster looks to Lynette, who signals her agreement with a flutter of eyelash and a shrug of her purse-strapped shoulder. Irritation creeps up the back of Foster's neck. First time in their married life that they are about to buy new, not to mention the exact make of car that Lynette used to talk of owning once the kids were grown up and gone. Would it kill her to show a little more interest?

"Mr. Reed?"

"Yes, that would be fine," Foster says.

"Great!" Derrick removes his hand, leaving a slick imprint of fingers on the roof. "I'll go get the keys and the temporary license plate from inside."

Silently, Lynette steps away from Foster and around to the passenger side of the vehicle. Shaking her head, her mouth forms what has become over the past eleven months an all-too-familiar frown.

"I'm sick of red, Foster."

"It's only a test drive, Lynette. If we like it, you can pick any colour that you want."

"So long as it isn't red," she says.

BUYING A CAR USED to be a blast. Driving out to Blodgett's Family Dealership on the edge of town, shooting the shit with Jimmy Blodgett—Mr. Family, himself—letting him point a pudgy index finger toward one model, then another, taking one or two vehicles out for a spin, then getting down to the nitty-gritty: gas mileage, rust proofing, transferable warranties, taxes, hidden charges. Foster never bothered with the hired help, always went straight to Jimmy, because when it came to hammering out a deal it was Jimmy who had the final say. And, since they each ran their own business, Foster liked to believe that Jimmy was cutting the margin as close as possible, just as Foster would do for Jimmy if he needed some electrical work done at the dealership or at his riverfront estate out on the Golf Club Road. (Lynette would snort whenever Foster talked this way. She and Jimmy had dated, briefly, in high school—she had his number. Don't kid yourself, she'd say, we're getting the same deal as anybody else, which is no deal at all.)

The best time Foster had buying a car was the very first one that he and Lynette ever owned. A second-hand Colt hatchback, purchased from a younger, slimmer, unmarried Jimmy, when Lynette was pregnant with the girls. When the shock over the ultrasound results wore off, "I'm going to need a car of my own," was the first thing out of Lynette's mouth (after "Holy shit, Foster, what did you do to me?"). "Otherwise, I'll never get out. And I'll need to get out, Foster, or I'll go crazy." Even back then, Foster had a truck, but that was strictly for the business. So, off they went to the bank to secure a car loan, his ball cap in hand, her swollen belly requiring no explanation.

They made the Colt last until Marjie and Melanie were no longer in car seats. By then, Cody was on the way. His arrival ushered in the minivan phase of their married life—three over the course of the years, all bought second-hand from Jimmy— one beige, one blue, the last one, red—each of them, at any given point of the day, crammed full of kids or teenagers, gro- ceries or hockey equipment. More room in the front seat than the Colt had had both front and back. Still, if he allowed him- self to, Foster could get pretty damned sentimental about that little hatchback. It had to do with his girls—strapping them into those car seats whenever he was around to do so, kissing their warm, sweet smelling foreheads, grabbing hold of their velveteen feet to make them giggle.

Foster wishes they could have dealt with Jimmy Blodgett this time around, as well, but he knew it would be asking too much. Eleven months since the accident, and Jimmy's daugh- ter, Kelly, was still not out of the woods. Alive, unlike Cody and Mark and Allie, but facing months of rehab. Who knew a person could suffer so many broken bones and survive? Immediately after the accident, when the story got out about what those kids had been up to, and with Kelly's prognosis still uncertain, Jimmy wouldn't even make eye contact with

Foster if they happened to pass each other on the street. Now, at least, he would acknowledge Foster's existence with a slight nod of his head. But, going to Jimmy's place of business, trying to replace the vehicle that had caused him and his family so much grief—even if they were to deal with one of the other salespeople—at best, it would be rubbing salt into a festering wound. It could still make Foster very angry, thinking about all of the relationships that Cody's stupidity had ruptured. Life had been so much easier when the kids were little.

"Remember the Colt, Lynette," Foster says now, as he pulls away from the Volkswagen dealership and out onto a city street, leaving Derrick to cool his heels in the lot until their return. "It didn't have much room, but it sure was a good little car."

Lynette doesn't respond, just stares out the window, her eyelashes fluttering. A nervous condition which first presented itself after the birth of the twins. At the time, Lynette blamed it on sleep deprivation—you try nursing two infants round the clock, Foster, see if it doesn't make your eyes go a little twitchy—and it did disappear once the girls were weaned, just as the thievery had done, only to resurface at other times of extreme stress—Cody's birth, her mother's long and terminal illness, the aftermath of the accident.

"I need to pee," Lynette says, now. "Take me to the mall."

"Chapters is closer."

"I don't like their washroom."

She doesn't like the camera in the alcove outside the washroom doors. A book is harder to hide than, say, a Bart Simpson Pez dispenser, or a rectal thermometer, or a men's left-handed golfing glove.

She's never been caught by anyone other than him, but there's always a first time and Foster would like it very much if this were not to be the day.

54

"I want to go out on the 401 to see how she handles, then we'll head straight back to the dealership. Ten minutes. You can wait that long, can't you?"

Lynette glares at him, crosses one cream-coloured pant leg over the other.

"If I have to."

Foster merges smoothly into traffic, behind a transport truck and in front of a shiny black SUV After a lifetime of driving a pickup, he finds being this close to the ground a little disconcerting. He wonders if Lynette will feel the same way after driving a van for the past fifteen years.

"You really should get behind the wheel, Lynette. It's not the same as the van. You're not so high up."

"Maybe I will, once you allow me to relieve myself."

By God, she's prickly today. If this is about Cody—and she makes everything about Cody—well, she's not the only one who lost a son is she? But he won't get into it with her now, not with a transport truck a car's length in front of him and that SUV breathing down his neck. The last time he tried to make a little room for his grief, he and Lynette had the biggest fight of their married life. The things she accused him of regarding Cody, the things he said back to her, well, they were awful, terrible things. He slept in the girls' vacant bedroom for two months afterwards—alternating between Marjie's frilly four-poster bed and Melanie's no-nonsense futon—unwilling to risk an escalation in hostilities by setting foot inside the shrine that their son's bedroom had become. He moved back into the master bedroom one day before the girls came home from college for their Christmas break. The first Christmas without Cody would be hard on everyone. The girls didn't need to know that he and Lynette were pushing through a rough patch.

"Wasn't that the turn-off, Foster?" Lynette asks, now.

"Shit! Yes, it was. Sorry. We'll have to take the next one."

"Which will bring us to the mall where I can take a pee."

"Fine. But just a pee."

"Oh, and what's that supposed to mean?"

"It means that I'll wait for you in the car."

FOSTER STARES OUT at the chrome and glass doors of the Sears entrance from his parking spot. It's been fifteen minutes since Lynette walked away from him and the car. The washroom facilities are at the other end of the store. Taking into account the time she would need to make her way through the store, then do her business, then walk all the way back again, Foster figures she should have been pushing through those glass doors five minutes ago.

Unless she stopped to 'browse'.

He should have gone with her. He could have acted as a deterrent. Of course, if that were true, Lynette wouldn't have stolen anything over the past eleven months, since without the van she had become dependent on him to drive her pretty much everywhere she needed to go once his workday was finished.

He discovered Lynette's latest stash quite by accident, in the cedar-lined cupboard down in the basement rec room four months after Cody's death. They had had their blow-up only a few days before. Lynette wasn't home. She'd taken the bus to her sister's place in Ottawa to get away from everybody—him, the nosy neighbours and well-meaning friends, and the parents of the other kids who had been traveling in the van with Cody.

Melanie and Marjie had returned a week earlier than was necessary to their respective campuses—relieved, he was sure, to be away from their mother's unrelenting grief. Foster was alone in the house for the first time in his life and realized within five minutes that he didn't much care for it. Lynette—who spent hours of each day leafing through photograph albums, fast-forwarding through family videotapes, or simply lying on Cody's bed staring up at his ceiling—had let the place go since the funeral. Nothing mattered, she would say, now that she no longer had her son, so Foster decided to spend his time alone cleaning out the basement. Perhaps when she came home from her sister's and saw what he had done for her, perhaps it would make a difference.

She hadn't tried very hard to hide it. A blue plastic bin half-full of disparate items: a tool belt, four key chains, a box of dominoes, water wings, a can of Klik, two garden gnomes, several hundred feet of dental floss, a putty knife, a disposable camera. And of course, the Pez dispenser, the thermometer, the golfing glove.

She didn't deny it when he confronted her with the container—not like the first time when the girls were still infants—neither did she express remorse over what she had stolen.

"A can of Klik will not be missed," she'd said.

And when he pressed her on why, she short-circuited: "I can't explain it! I can't control it! And I'm not about to change my spots now!"

Were there any other items hidden in the house?

No. Generally, she kept the stuff for a short while, and then gave it away to the church, or to the Goodwill or to the food bank. I always make sure it goes to a good cause, she said.

Why not let Foster make an appointment for her with Dr. Mills? He'd even sit in on it if she wanted him to. He was sure that Dr. Mills would know of someone who could help her with this problem.

"I don't have a problem," she said. "It will only be a problem if I get caught."

Here she comes.

Pushing through the metal doors, she pauses on the lip of the curb to stare down cars in both directions before stepping out into the crosswalk. Foster scans her cream-coloured dress pants and sleeveless silk blouse for bulges that weren't in evidence when she left the car—all the while thinking to himself how she is still one fine looking woman. Nothing. And she isn't being trailed by a security guard—another good sign. Of course, that bag of hers could hide a filing cabinet, but far be it from him to violate the sanctity of a woman's purse. He's not that foolish.

Grateful for the opportunity to stretch his legs and intent on switching places with his wife, Foster climbs out of the driver's seat.

"What are you doing," she asks as she reaches the car. She sounds angry.

"I thought you wanted to get behind the wheel."

"No, that's what *you* wanted."

Without another word, she opens the passenger door and slips inside, stowing her purse at her feet. Foster drops back into the driver's seat.

"Why not put your bag in the back, Lynette, it'll give you more leg room."

"My legs are fine," she says.

Her eyes have stopped twitching, but the rest of her is a mess. She didn't want to come car shopping today, but he insisted. They'd been putting it off for months, ever since the insurance claim had been settled. She needed a car. He needed her to have a car.

What to do? He could stretch his hand across the space between them and massage the knot that is always present between her left shoulder blade and the base of her neck, and then he could ask her what is wrong. But he already knows what that is, and there is nothing that either of them can do to make it right. So, he turns the ignition key, instead. The engine comes to life with barely a rumble.

Derrick was right—this is a cool car.

Wouldn't Cody have loved to get his hands on this one? And, knowing how Lynette could deny him nothing, it wouldn't have been long before he was zipping all over town, ignoring stop signs, speeding through yellow lights, parking in no parking zones, not wearing his seat belt, like every other teenage boy with his G2 license and access to a vehicle.

An accident waiting to happen.

PROM NIGHT. Cody, Kelly, Mark and Allie. Lynette offers to cook them a romantic dinner, complete with candles and cloth napkins and her best china. It will save the boys a bundle of money, and besides, she wants to do it for Cody. Since Marjorie and Melanie are not interested in catering to their younger brother or his peers, Lynette will act as both chef and server. Foster will be expected to take pictures and then get out of the way before he can do or say something that might embarrass their son in front of his friends.

Foster snaps the requisite photographs when they arrive— the girls in their strapless, shimmering gowns, hair piled high, and the boys in their tuxedos—then he disappears with a cold beer and a bag of microwave popcorn into the basement rec room. (Foster still carries one of these photos in his wallet. Cody, Kelly, Mark and Allie, arms across each other's shoulders. Girls and boys. Forever.)

They are good kids—athletes, all. They get decent grades, they come from stable homes, at least as far as Foster can tell. What possesses them to do what they do that night? The sole survivor, Kelly Blodgett, says that she can't remember anything about the evening once they leave Foster and Lynette's. Convenient, Lynette likes to say, whenever she and Foster find themselves circling the events of that night, but Foster tends to believe Kelly. She wasn't the driver, after all, she has no reason to lie. And if she was on what the blood analysis tests later show that Cody was on, it is no wonder that she can't remember much.

Alcohol. Ecstasy.

There are two parties after the formal—one in town, the other out in the boonies. The police report that the kids go to the one in town first, and that they are on their way home from the second party, somewhere between two and three AM, when the accident occurs—a single vehicle crash involving a telephone pole.

Cody is ejected from the vehicle on impact. The other three are trapped inside the van until the fire department can arrive with the Jaws of Life. Cody is pronounced dead at the scene. Mark and Allie die before the ambulances can reach the Kingston General Hospital.

Just before dawn, the sound of tires biting down on gravel causes Foster to open his eyes. The walls of the master bedroom are awash in a pale, pulsating red light. *Aliens*, his first confused thought. *Cody*, his second, more lucid one.

THIS WILL BE DERRICK'S first sale. He can't thank the Reeds enough. Would they object to his taking a photo of them with his cell phone? No? Because his mom isn't going to believe him when he calls her, she's going to want to see the Reeds for herself. Foster and Lynette have spent the past half-hour with Derrick filling out the paper work in a glass cubicle inside the showroom. Lynette has made her colour selection: pale yellow, like lemon chiffon pudding, she says. Not Foster's first choice, by any stretch of the imagination, and they will have to wait up to six weeks for delivery, but at least she's engaged enough to care. The only thing left for Derrick to do, after taking their photograph and saying goodbye to his mother, is to go upstairs to his dad's office to have the paperwork approved.

"How long will *that* take?" Lynette asks, picking at a speck of lint on her thigh, then brushing it away.

"Ten minutes. Five," Derrick adds quickly, when he sees a frown beginning to form on Lynette's face.

Lynette stands. The photograph and the telephone call to Derrick's mother have taken their toll, Foster sees. Lynette's eyelids have begun to twitch. The tips of five fingernails touch down on his shoulder.

"I need some fresh air," she says, and then she is gone.

She has upset Derrick.

"Is she okay?" he asks.

"She'll be fine," Foster says. "You remind her of our son, Cody. We lost him last May in a car accident."

"Oh." A long pause as all of the meanings sink in. "How old was he?"

"Eighteen."

The boy clears his throat.

"I'm twenty-two," he says.

Bingo, Foster thinks.

Derrick looks down at the desk, he toys with the smudge of beard beneath his bottom lip with the tips of two fingers. Being young, he is unschooled in the etiquette of death. He doesn't know what to say to get them past this moment. Foster helps him out.

"She'll be fine," he repeats. "She just needs a couple of minutes to collect herself."

"Shall I take the paperwork upstairs, then, sir?"

"Sure thing."

Scooping up the papers, Derrick swivels out of his seat. He hesitates in the doorway, "And Mr. Reed?"

Foster knows what is coming. He closes his eyes.

"I'm *really* sorry for your loss, sir."

"Thank you, son."

Now Foster needs some fresh air, too. Leaving the cubicle, he strolls through the showroom with its potted plants and pristine vehicles and granite floors, out onto the car lot to look for his wife—the thief. Sure enough, there she is, crouched at the rear of the red Volkswagen Beetle. Is that a brand new Phillips screwdriver in her hand? Why yes, he believes it is. She must have picked that up at the Sears store. And is she unscrewing the temporary license plate from the back bumper? She certainly seems to be doing just that, yes. Well.

He doesn't know whether to laugh or to cry.

In a bid for heavenly guidance, Foster looks up toward the sky only to discover Derrick looking down at Lynette from the second storey window of his father's office, a baffled look on his face. His confusion changes to grim understanding as Lynette removes the license plate from the back bumper of the car and unzips her purse. Lynette is too preoccupied to notice either her husband or Derrick, which means that Foster still has time to fix this.

Soundlessly, Foster waves his arms above his head in a bid for Derrick's attention. It works. Foster puts a shushing finger to his lips, works his bushy eyebrows up and down, then points to the interior of the dealership. Foster's wallet is out and flipped open by the time he meets the boy at the foot of the stairs.

"Did you say anything to your father?"

"Uh, uh. Not yet."

"Good. I'd like to keep it that way. My wife has a problem, Derrick. She's getting help," he lies, "and she was doing quite well until this thing with our son."

"I see. Okay. Well, just get the plate back from her and we'll call it square."

"I can't do that." Foster pulls five twenties from his wallet, shoves them toward the boy. "Will this cover it?"

"No."

"How much, then?"

"You don't understand, Mr. Reed, I need to have the license plate back."

Foster glances towards the car lot. Lynette has taken up a position just outside the showroom doors. Her back is to them, her head is down, and her shoulders appear to be quaking.

Sweet Jesus.

"No, son," he says, turning back to Derrick. "You don't understand. It's taken me months to get her to look at a new vehicle. If you make a big deal out of this, I can pretty much guarantee that you *will* lose this sale."

Derrick's shoulders sag. Suddenly, he's looking years older.

"I'm perfectly happy to pay for it," Foster presses on, "just tell me how much."

"You don't get it, sir," Derrick says, gesturing up towards the closed door of his father's office. "My dad is really anal about stuff. He'll want to know what happened to the plate."

"Tell him you messed up, that you didn't tighten the screws enough, that it must have fallen off during the test drive."

Derrick doesn't look convinced.

"Look, son. You just made your first sale, he's going to cut you some slack—I'm a father, I know. Especially if you accept responsibility and offer to pay for the plate." Foster pulls the last three twenties from his wallet. "Come on, Derrick. What do you say?"

"I SAW WHAT you did back there," Lynette says to Foster, ten minutes into their drive home. The accusatory words cause his heart to race, but her tone is light. He glances over at her. There's a smirk haunting her face. She's perched forward a bit in her seat, sitting on her hands, the way she used to do before the accident, like a child who can't wait to see what is around the next bend in the road. He decides that it is safe to play dumb.

"Lynette, I have no idea what you're talking about."

"Oh, come on, Foster!"

And then she does something he hasn't seen her do in nearly a year—she starts into a fit of laughter.

"What?" he asks.

"You, waving at that kid up there in the window, the look on your face—I can't get it out of my head!" A snort escapes through her nose, causing her to laugh even harder.

"You *saw* me do that?"

Lynette can no longer speak, so she nods her assent instead. Suddenly, her quaking shoulders back at the dealership take on a whole different meaning for Foster, and for a second time today he is unsure whether to laugh or to cry.

Lynette is doing both. Tears are welling up in her eyes. She needs a tissue. Unzipping her purse, she fishes out the stolen license plate, dropping it to the floor by her feet, which triggers another round of laughter, this time from the both of them. God, it feels good. Finally, Lynette locates a bit of rumpled tissue. She wipes her eyes, blows her nose, goes quiet. Foster goes quiet, too. Lynette's hands come to rest in her lap.

"Oh Foster," she finally says, after a kilometre or two of silence, "I really do have a problem, don't I?"

Keeping the Peace

SYBIL AND GWEN DRIVE EAST along the main street of
their adoptive hometown in Sybil's used, but reliable subcom-
pact. ("Like New," Sybil was assured by the salesman when she
purchased it in the spring.) All four of the windows are wide
open. Still, Sybil can feel sweat pooling in the usual crevices.
Now that August has arrived with its reputation intact, she
is wishing she'd picked a vehicle with air. If Martin had been
with her in the car lot, he would have insisted on it. He would
have looked at a bigger car, too, one that could accommodate
his daddy-long-legs.

Six years, this past February.

Gripping the steering wheel a little more tightly, Sybil
shifts her attention to their fourteen-year-old daughter and
her impending job interview.

"Are you nervous?"

Gwen snorts through studded and un-studded nostrils.

"Because it's not unusual to feel a bit nervous, especially
the first time."

"I'm fine."

"Well, good. Good for you." She looks over at her daughter, who continues to stare straight ahead. "I threw up before
my first job interview. Twice. I was that nervous."

"Red light, Mom. RED LIGHT!"

The male driver of the beige minivan that Sybil has nearly
hit raises a middle finger. He mouths obscenities at her

through his closed window—obviously he has air condition-ing—and speeds off. Sybil makes it through the intersection and pulls up to the curb next to the single-storey, brick post office.

"Mom, what are you doing? I'll be late. You're going to make me late!"

Sybil's heart has relocated—it is in her ears, in her throat. She must guide it back to where it belongs. "I just need a second. You won't be late. I promise." She closes her eyes, puts a hand to her chest—come here little heart. Why couldn't it have been a woman in the other car? A woman would have rolled her window down, wouldn't she? A woman would have given Sybil an opportunity to apologize. But maybe not.

"Mo-om! LET'S GO!"

"Yes. Okay. All right." Sybil clicks her left signal light on, checks her side-view mirror, looks over her shoulder to elimi-nate any possibility of a blind spot. All clear. She pulls into the right hand lane. They roll along in sweating silence to the next red light. A thought occurs to Sybil.

"Aren't people in small towns supposed to be friendly?"

"Maybe they draw the line at manslaughter. Green light, Mom!" Gwen's fingers fly to her temples, her voice drops to a scathing whisper. "God, you're *so* stupid!"

Sybil forgives the barely audible comment. Gwen is ner-vous even if she won't admit it. A lecture on respect will only make things worse.

"Did you bring your resumé?"

"No. Stephanie told her boss everything she needs to know about me."

"And you trust Stephanie to speak for you?"

"Of course! She's my friend. Why wouldn't I trust her? She got me the job interview, didn't she?"

"True enough. It's just that Stephanie seems so ... " 'Slutty' percolates to the surface, but no, she'd better not say that! "So, 'mature' for her age."

Gwen expels one of her trademark dramatic sighs. "She's the only girl who's given me the time of day since *you* decided *we* had to move here."

HIGH SCHOOL IN THE CITY had not proceeded smoothly for Sybil's daughter. Gwen had gravitated toward the wrong crowd. Classes were skipped. Grades slipped. Two months into the first term, Sybil was invited to the high school for an 'intervention meeting' with Gwen's guidance coun-selor—a warm, intelligent, well-dressed woman who laid pamphlets out in front of Sybil as if they were tarot cards. They chatted about leaders and followers, boundaries and choices, personal responsibility and the special chal-lenges faced by single parents. Sybil left the school feeling refreshed and purposeful. She read each of the pamphlets over and tried to discuss them with Gwen. Things calmed down until February, when Sybil received another call from the school, this time from the vice-principal. The story was that Gwen and another female student had fought over a male student, although neither girl would talk when they all met in the vice principal's office to discuss the two-week suspensions.

Gwen's suspension worked wonders on Sybil. It brought clarity. There really was nothing holding her in Kingston. The cursory friendships she had established with some of the other military wives had not survived Martin's death and Sybil's move off base and into the city. Martin was in an urn on her dresser, which made both him and his memory portable. She was a waitress. She could work anywhere.

Clarity led to opportunity a couple of weeks later, when Sybil came across a promising advertisement in the Whig Standard—an employment fair for a charity casino being built at the edge of the 401 between Kingston and Brockville, outside a small tourist town with an unpronounceable name. The casino was on track to open its doors to the gambling public by June. Hundreds of jobs were up for grabs, including a call for experienced waitresses to staff an upscale restaurant located inside the facility.

Sybil went shopping and culled a new skirt and blouse from the sales racks at the Bay. She dyed her hair to cover her premature grey, then asked her hairdresser to cut it short. She drove to the town on the appointed day, bringing her resumé and an extra dose of panic medication with her. She stood in line for hours first outside, then inside a tiny movie theatre where the interviews were to take place. She answered with verve all questions put to her by a tribunal of impossibly young, impeccably dressed people, then was told she would be notified by telephone within two weeks. She was offered a position ten days later and given twenty-four hours to accept. Now came the hard part.

Sybil re-read the high-school guidance counselor's pamphlet on family meetings before sitting Gwen down to present her case. The casino would be open round the clock. Sybil would be working some pretty crazy hours. The thought of driving the 401 in all kinds of weather, her small car a hyphen between transport trucks, was enough to bring on a mild panic attack. Things would be easier if they lived where Sybil worked. The little town had a high school. Gwen could start fresh, meet some nice, wholesome, small-town kids. Sybil's mind was made up.

Gwen put on an impressive show—sullen silence rapidly escalating into threats of moving out to live on the streets, followed by tears over her ruined adolescence, followed by an oath *never* to forgive her mother, followed by more silence.

They moved when the school year ended.

Gwen made Stephanie's acquaintance at summer school, both girls having failed to obtain their grade-nine math credit.

SYBIL SPOTS STEPHANIE as she is executing a cautious left turn off the main street and into the motel parking lot. Stephanie has plunked herself down between the furry hind legs of the nine-foot grizzly bear that stands guard outside the entrance to the motel. She is smoking a cigarette.

"I hope you aren't smoking," Sybil says, as she steers toward an end parking spot. "You know how I would feel about that."

"I know."

Stephanie has dropped her habit to the asphalt by the time she reaches Gwen's side of the vehicle.

"Hi Stephanie," Sybil says, and plunges right in. "You lose five minutes of your life every time you light up. Did you know that, sweetie?"

"Yes, Mrs. Paquette."

"They used to say it was one minute, then three minutes. Now it's five. And it won't keep you thin," she adds, scanning Stephanie's enviably perfect adolescent figure. "I know that's what you girls think nowadays."

Gwen turns her face from Stephanie towards her mother and stares at her, hard.

"Fine," Sybil says, "I'll stop now. Do you want me to hang around?"

"Why?"

"In case you don't get it."

"Gee, thanks, Mom."

"Gwen's the only one that Theresa called, Mrs. Paquette."

"Oh. Well, that's a good sign, isn't it? Wait a minute, what about that thing?" Her index finger flutters in the general vicinity of Gwen's silver nose stud.

Gwen kills her with another look and climbs out of the car.

"Well, it doesn't look very professional. That's all I meant."

"Yeah, like a chambermaid needs to look professional." Gwen tosses this tiny grenade over her shoulder and walks away fast.

Sybil watches Gwen and Stephanie cross the parking lot, arm linking arm, the best of buddies. She was Gwen's best buddy, once, before their life got blown to bits. Memory plays a trick—Gwen shrinks to age eight as she reaches the motel entrance. Suddenly, she's walking through another door—all ponytail and plastic barrettes—while holding the hand of a grief counselor paid for by the military. The woman has given eight-year old Gwen a choice: shall Mommy come in or stay out? Angry, sad Gwen has chosen the 'stay out' option. Gwen, who refuses to speak of her father to Sybil, opens up to this complete stranger, while Sybil is left to cool her heels outside the door. The counselor's assessment? The bed wetting, the temper tantrums, the trouble at school are punishment, whether conscious or subconscious, for promises made but not kept: Six months will go by in a heartbeat, sweetie. Don't worry—your Daddy won't get hurt. Not your Daddy.

—How long could she expect this to go on?

—It was hard to know.

*

"God, she drives me nuts," Gwen says, as she and Stephanie step past the nine-foot, glass-eyed sentry and into the front lobby.

"At least she's your real mom."

Reality's shifting nature became an issue for Gwen's friend last March Break, when Stephanie's mother and father had defined 'surrogate mother', then told her about their decision to divorce. Stephanie's mother, an accountant, got the house and the Neon. Her father, a computer software designer, got the sailboat and the BMW. All monies, securities, stocks and bonds were split right down the middle. A carefully worded custody agreement would allow each of them to retain a piece of Stephanie until she reached the age of maturity, whenever that might be. "Hi everybody," Gwen remembers her saying, that first day of summer school, when asked to stand and tell the class a little bit about herself. "I'm Stephanie. I was conceived in a test tube, implanted into my real mother's womb and raised by two complete strangers!"

Gwen had liked her straight off.

Gwen follows Stephanie through the front lobby. They pass by a gift shop full of shot glasses, T-shirts, key chains and coffee mugs. They push through a swinging door and into a loon-papered hallway, walk past the entrance to the indoor pool and hot tub, down another hallway with numbered doors painted forest green.

"So, Gwen, are you ready to meet 'Thereeesa'?"

"Sure," Gwen says, ignoring Stephanie's creeped out voice.

Why should she care if Theresa is a lesbian? The woman has a steady girlfriend, according to Stephanie: fat Marsha, the taxi driver. Besides, Gwen is into boys—one boy, at least. Unlike Stephanie, who says she has made it with three guys since the start of summer holidays, right here in the motel's hot tub. If her mother knew what Gwen knows, she would totally not be here with Stephanie right now applying for this job.

They come to the end of the hallway. Stephanie knocks on an unnumbered door.

"Come on in."

Theresa is exactly as Stephanie described her last night, while she and Gwen were sharing a joint down at the berm— short, big boobs, thick waist, compact legs. She's sitting at a card table. The bare light bulb that is screwed into the ceiling above her bleached, commando-styled hair causes her white uniform to glow at the edges. It also highlights the chain-smoker shadows beneath her slate-grey eyes. There are no windows, but there are plenty of pails, mops and spray bottles to complement a diminished fleet of linen trolleys. Gwen's first job interview is about to take place inside a large broom closet.

"Theresa, this is Gwen, the girl I was telling you about."

Theresa motions to the folding chair across from her. "Take a seat. Stephanie, you can get started on your rooms. We'll handle things from here, right Gwen?" Theresa smiles, revealing nicotine-stained teeth. Gwen smiles back—lips only.

There is an awkward period of silence as Stephanie turns away to load her trolley with chambermaid essentials: towels, sheets, all-purpose cleaner, glass cleaner, tiny bars of soap, dwarf-sized bottles of shampoo and conditioner. Theresa folds her arms and stows them high on the shelf of her chest. She stares daggers into Stephanie's back, but Stephanie appears not to feel them.

"You're supposed to restock the trolley before you go home in the afternoon, Stephanie. How many times am I going to have to remind you?"

"I did. Mine isn't here. One of the other girls must have taken it."

"Look, come back if you run out of something. I haven't got all day."

72

"Yes, ma'am."

"I'll get right to the point," Theresa says, once Stephanie is out of earshot. "I don't care for teenagers that much. Most of them are spoiled rotten. I go through lots of girls in the summer. They always start off gung-ho, thinking about how much money they're gonna make. But once they realize I'm actually expecting them to work they up and quit. Are you gonna do that to me, Gwen, if I decide to hire you?"

It is word for word what Stephanie mimicked last night down at the berm as she flicked the end of their communal joint into the St. Lawrence. Gwen is prepared.

"I won't quit," she says, adding 'ma'am', like Stephanie does, for brownie points. "I'm not afraid to work."

"Good. That's exactly what I wanted to hear." Her arms slide from their shelf and drop into her lap. "Now, Stephanie has told me a little bit about you and your mom. She got hired on at the casino, is that right?"

"Yes. She's a waitress in the restaurant."

"Well, bully for her. Some of us, who've lived here our whole lives, weren't so lucky." She stops to let the meaning sink in. "But that's not your mom's fault, now is it?"

"No, ma'am."

"Stephanie told me about your dad, too. She said he was a soldier, that he died overseas when you were eight or nine?"

"Yes."

Gwen looks down at her neatly folded hands. When pressed about her father, she offers the same two pieces of information—my father was a peacekeeper, my father died. Most people step back and draw their own conclusions. They make it easy. Not Theresa. She leans forward in her chair. Closer. Her breasts come to rest on the edge of the table.

"What part of the world was he in, dear?"

"Bosnia."

Gwen looks up. Both sets of high beams are trained on her. She might as well give this bitch what she wants and get it over with. Gwen's fingers weave themselves into a tight red ball, which bounces lightly against the tarmac of her thigh.

"It was a landmine."

"Goodness," Theresa says, her rough voice softening. "That must have been real tough for you. Real tough on your mom, too."

"It was." She counts to five. Slowly. "So, am I hired?"

Theresa pushes back in her chair, all business now that she has satisfied her curiosity. "Sure. What you're wearing will do for today, but I'd like to see a uniform by tomorrow. White, nothing fancy, and it comes out of your pocket. The boss doesn't pay for uniforms."

"I'll see what I can do."

"I'll take you through the first unit, show you how it's done. After that, you are on your own. You'll be assigned the same eight rooms every morning. The boss allows half an hour for each one. If you get done early, good for you. If you take too long, we'll be having a different sort of chat. Are we clear?"

"Yes, ma'am."

"Okay. Grab a linen cart and follow me."

*

Grocery bags hang like ballast from Sybil's wrists, as she treads across the five patio stones that lead from the curb to the front door of her cheaply built, hastily rented townhouse. It took Sybil less than twenty-four hours to regret her signature on the twelve month lease—the length of time it took for her to discover that there was no soundproofing between the units.

A young couple with a baby, Lisa and Taylor, live in the unit to her right. They argue all the time. Lisa spends too much goddamn money, Taylor doesn't make enough. He pays no attention, whatsoever, to his own son, she spoils the kid rotten. Why did she have to go and get herself knocked up in the first place? How stupid do you have to be in this day and age to let something like that happen? Stupid is as stupid does. What the fuck is that supposed to mean? Go to hell, Taylor. Go straight to hell! So far Sybil has not seen or heard anything that would require her to place an anonymous call to the police—no black eyes or bruises, no furniture smashed against the common walls of their housing unit. And the baby is beautiful.

She gives them six months.

The plastic handles of the grocery bags are digging trenches into her wrists by the time she hoists them onto the kitchen counter. Normally, she would have made two trips to the car, but it is almost eleven o'clock and she doesn't want to miss the start of the televised memorial service. Armed with a brand new box of tissues, Sybil slips into the living room.

"Gwen?" she calls.

No answer. She must have got the job. Good.

Sybil locates the remote beneath a pile of newspapers. She pushes a red button and tunes in to collective grief.

A new century, a different mission, another country, and still the same old story. Two Canadian soldiers this time: a private and a corporal—with two wives, one ex-wife and five children back at home—killed in their sleep by a rocket propelled grenade which punctured the tin can wall of their temporary barrack—their 'little home away from home', as Martin used to call it—before blowing them to bits.

The families sit in the first few rows: spouses, children and grandparents, brothers, sisters and in-laws, aunts, uncles and cousins. The politicians take up the row directly behind—a sandbar in a sea of sadness, they separate family from friends.

"It's really sick that you watch these things, you know," Gwen would say if she were here right now. "Wasn't living through it once enough for you? God!" Then off she would go, stomping upstairs to her room or out to the local piercing salon to have another hole put in her face.

Martin's death was singular and pre-911, before grief became everybody's business. No one asked to televise it. No politicians came forward at the end of service to hug Sybil or to touch a hand to the top of Gwen's French-braided hair. The truth is that Sybil can remember very little about Martin's funeral service, other than holding tight to Gwen and feeling an over-whelming thirst. Sedatives have a way of doing that to a person.

She doesn't know why she watches.

*

Gwen is rinsing out her last bathtub when a hand grabs onto her shoulder from behind. She doesn't flinch or scream, unlike the first day. She knows who it is. Stephanie's back-pack is slung over one tanned, bare shoulder. She has already changed into her bright pink, postage-stamp bikini.

"Hurry up," Stephanie says, sliding her own hand along the length of her slim hip. "There's nobody in the hot tub or the pool. We'll have the whole place to ourselves."

"I'll be done in a few minutes."

Theresa's rule—if the rooms are done early they can use the hot tub and pool, provided they stay out of the customers' way and do not engage in any monkey business.

Gwen transfers sweat from her forehead to the shortened sleeve of her uniform. Christ it's hot in here! That's because each morning at checkout time, their cheap-assed boss turns the air off to all the units so he can save a few cents on his hydro bill. "Take care of the pennies, young lady, and the dollars will take care of themselves," being the only thing that he has actually said to her. She doubts that he even knows her name.

Gwen moves as fast as she can. Still, by the time she is done restocking her trolley twenty minutes have passed. She hurries to the change room and strips off her uniform to reveal last summer's swimsuit—a modest, navy two-piece with a tank top. Sybil, who was quite willing to pay for Gwen's uniform, drew the line at bankrolling a new swimsuit—"I've had a lot of expenses with this move. You'll have your own money soon enough. Then you can buy whatever you want."

Gwen's jiggling reflection meets up with her in the full-length mirror attached to the back of the door that leads to the pool. Despite her mother's comments to the contrary—"You're not fat, Gwen, you're ample"—and despite her own last ditch attempt to count calories, there is no denying it—she has grown. The tank-top portion of the suit, which last year crested just above her belly button, is now riding high on her rib cage. Her 'ample' butt cheeks are overflowing from the bottom half.

She should have brought a T-shirt—too late now. Besides, it's only Stephanie. She pulls the door open.

Stephanie is in the hot tub. She's not alone. A boy with short spiked black hair and a farmer's tan sits next to her. Gwen has seen him before, getting a lecture from one of the town cops for skateboarding on the steps outside the post office. In the past, Stephanie has used words like 'stoner' and 'dirt bag' to describe him. And now? Stephanie is laughing loudly over something he has just said.

Stay or go? Gwen takes too long to decide. Stephanie has seen her.

"Finally!" Stephanie says.

The boy twists halfway around to have a look at Gwen. His eyes briefly connect with her face, before traveling south to size up her breasts and crotch. He completes the circuit with a smirk. Emotions collide like molecules. Gwen feels offended, embarrassed, but also somewhat flattered. She doesn't know where to look.

Stephanie provides a focus. She stands in the hot tub. Frothy hot tub foam traces a rabid path down portions of her reddened body. The boy's hand reaches out to scoop a mass of bubbles from her outer thigh, which he then transfers to his chin. Stephanie acts like she doesn't notice, urging Gwen forward with a wave of her arm. Gwen crosses her arms over her bare midriff and speed walks across the pool deck toward the raised hot tub. She comes to an abrupt stop when she spots a pair of sodden swim trunks laying on the second step.

"See, Kurt," Stephanie says in her new breathy voice, as Gwen takes note of the shrink-wrapped condom positioned on the edge of the hot tub, "she is real! Gwen, I need you to do Kurt and me a little favour, okay? Go stand outside the door and don't let anybody in."

*

Sybil is dreaming. In the dream, it is a Sunday morning. She and Martin are in bed. They are both naked. She is lying on her back, arms behind her pillowed head, legs together and bent at the knee. Martin is on his side, facing her—his torso propped up by his elbow, the Canadian flag tattoo waving on his biceps. He is tracing a circle around her belly button with the index finger of his free hand. It doesn't tickle, which is how she knows she is dreaming. Sun streams through their open bedroom window. She can smell lilacs. She can hear birds. Crisp white sheets, pale yellow walls, Martin's untroubled brown eyes taking all of her in, making her feel warm, safe, desirable.

He's telling the story again—it is an intricate tale with many twists and turns and several teaser punchlines that will lead, eventually, to the ultimate comedic prize. The whole madcap adventure is made more complicated by the fact that he is speaking in a foreign tongue. Sybil doesn't understand a word, but that hasn't stopped her from laughing, has it? Her sides are aching, threatening to split like a milk pod. Not because of the story, but because she is so happy, so relieved to see him in one piece and back where he belongs.

There is a soft knock at her bedroom door.

The room grows dark. Martin fades away.

"Mom?"

Sybil's door opens, letting in a strip of daylight.

"Mom? Are you awake?"

Gwen pads into the room. She takes Martin's place in the bed. It makes Sybil want to cry, to grab Gwen, hug her to her chest and tell her all about the dream. But she doesn't. She won't. Sybil opens one eye.

"What time is it?"

"Just past two."

Sybil closes the eye and groans.

"I don't need to be in until four. I could have slept for another hour."

"I know. But I have to tell you something."

Sybil hears Gwen breathe in, but she does not hear her breathe out. Sybil opens both of her eyes and looks at her daughter.

"You're not going to like it," Gwen says. "Don't freak out, okay?"

And as Gwen begins to explain about how she is no longer employed, and about how Stephanie is no longer her friend, Sybil's gaze is drawn up and over Gwen's shoulder, to the urn that sits atop her dresser—Martin's 'remains'. And not for the first time, she imagines a miniature Martin trapped inside there like a genie, waiting for the right set of hands, the perfect string of words to set him free.

UNTIL DEATH DO US PART

MARTHA SURRENDERS over toast and coffee. She agrees to meet Keith at twelve thirty sharp, next to the chip wagon in the town park. Their son, Mick, will be in school. Martha can leave Ellie with her boss at the municipal daycare. Fiona won't mind. She and Fiona do this sort of thing for each other all the time.

She and Keith will have some fries and a hot dog, and then head across the park to the open house. Keith only wants to look. He's curious—like everyone else in town. What's so bad about that? Curiosity killed the cat, Martha warns, right before giving in.

Her capitulation makes Keith's day. The crusts of toast at the edge of Mick's plate, the splash of fruit punch on his vinyl placemat, go unpunished. And Keith kisses her goodbye—a graze of lips, which startles Martha's cheek into submission as she is spooning oatmeal into Ellie's mouth. Keith whistles in the mud room as he laces up his steel-toed work boots.

They all hear it.

"Daddy happy," Ellie sings from her high chair.

They all listen, too, to the sound of his half-ton truck as it backs down the driveway: beep, beep, beep.

Mick's arm becomes a crane. Beep, he says, as thumb and forefinger sweep down to pinch a crust of toast from his plate. Swinging the crane upwards, Mick drops the crust into his empty glass. Beeeep.

Ellie laughs, claps her hands for the best show in town. "Again!"

It is on the tip of Martha's tongue to tell Mick to stop. Keith hates it when Mick plays with his food. But Keith isn't here.

"Again!" Ellie shrieks.

"ARE WE GONNA MOVE into that house, Mom?"

"No."

"Swear."

MARTHA LUCKS IN, nabbing the most coveted parking spot, right next to the chip wagon, at twelve thirty on the dot. Sunny, cool spring day, greasy french fries—an irresistible combination. She thought it would be busier, but the park is virtually empty except for a couple of goths who are splitting a large fry and a Pepsi at one of the picnic tables. Black hair, raccoon eyes, piercings everywhere. Is this what she can expect from Ellie in ten or twelve years—sweet little Ellie, her ray of sunshine?

There is no sign of Keith.

Should she go ahead and order? She hasn't eaten since last evening—a jumbo bag of salt and vinegar chips, all by herself in front of the television, once the kids were in bed and Keith had left for the rink. The inside of her mouth still feels raw.

A hot dog and large fries for Keith, then, and a hot dog for herself.

What if she orders and he is delayed by some problem at the work site? He won't be happy if his lunch is cold. Better to wait. What are a few more minutes if it means avoiding a scene?

A silver sedan glides into the parking spot next to Martha. A woman gets out—fifty-ish, tall, slim, wearing a tailored suit, earrings the size of conch shells. She walks around to the back of her vehicle and opens her trunk—an Open House sign and a string of multi-coloured balloons. Closing the trunk, she takes aim at the car with her set of keys. Bleeeep, you're dead. Crossing the road in high heels, she centers the sign on the sidewalk out front of the house.

"Boo!"

Keith.

Jesus!

"Jesus, Keith!"

His pupils shrink to periods. The smile vaporizes. She has made him mad.

Hands in pockets, he walks to the other side of the chip truck where B.J. Ford, a buddy of theirs since kindergarten, steams hot dogs and shovels fries into cardboard containers for a living. Martha catches up, falling in behind him, as Keith places his order.

"Large fry, hot dog, and a Pepsi, my man."

"And the wife?"

"No fries for me, B.J., just a hot dog and a bottled water."

"You're not on another one of those crazy diets are you, Martha?"

"No, B.J., I believe I've learned my lesson."

As did everyone else, after reading about it in *The Oracle*: *Police and Emergency Services responded to a call at an area grocery store, Thursday, February 14th at 12:15PM, after a female patron, aged 32, collapsed in the produce aisle.*

The grapefruit diet.

Keith changes the subject—not because he wishes to save his wife from embarrassment, Martha knows, but because he is sick of hearing about the incident from every Tom, Dick and Harriet in town.

"Good game last night, eh?"

"Sure," B.J. says, handing Keith his fries. "If you happened to be on the winning team, that is."

Hockey.

Martha shifts her attention to the house across the street—peaked roof, white wooden siding, black trim, and a red door. Side yard cleared of twigs and rotted leaves, flower beds churned up, primed for annuals. A wrought iron bench, wooden slats bowing under the weight of past snowfalls. Normal. Inviting, even, but for the knowledge of what went on in there a couple of months ago.

"He's always played dirty, ever since he was a kid," Keith is saying. "I'll give you that."

The police tape has been removed. When did that happen?

"And he is a puck hog. No doubt about it." Keith bloodies his fries and hot dog with ketchup.

No sign of the real estate agent now. She must be inside, flipping light switches, fanning copies of the listing out on the kitchen counter.

"But you have to admit, B.J., the guy can skate circles around anybody out there."

Martha's hot dog is up—a squirt of yellow mustard, a spoonful of sweet green relish. She passes on the ketchup.

*

The story was all over town within hours. Martha was one of the last to learn of it. If she had not passed out in the grocery store over her lunch hour, if she had not been transported to hospital via ambulance, if she had returned to the daycare after her break, like every other day, she would have been one of the first to hear, because the daycare was where the police went next after learning from the neighbours about the existence of two preschoolers.

Not his. Hers.

The deaths warranted only the briefest of mentions in the Police Beat section of *The Oracle*, right below the account of Martha's fainting spell: *Police were alerted by neighbours to an Oak St. residence, early Thursday afternoon. A woman, aged 34, and a male, aged 27, were discovered dead at the scene. Names are being withheld pending notification of kin. Police continue to investigate.*

The article in the city paper was longer, carrying opinions and speculation from two experts in the field of domestic abuse, but it, too, was short on details.

He killed her and then he killed himself. That much was known. And they weren't from town. (Martha's mother, who, like Martha, had been born and raised in Kanawasaguay, took great comfort from this fact, as if it explained everything.)

Keith heard from a reliable source that the guy had used a gun.

Fiona claimed the same thing about a knife.

Martha didn't want to think about it.

Fiona was also hearing rumours of a coroner's inquest. If that happened, there was a good chance that both she and Martha would be called as witnesses. If they call an inquest, Fiona said, you and I would need to make sure that we are singing from the same hymn book.

What could Martha possibly tell an inquest about the children? They'd only been at the centre for two months. Adrianna liked to pick at her chapped lips during story time. Sometimes, not often, she would cause them to bleed. Timmy, her younger brother, had been so enamoured of a new pair of red rubber boots that he liked to point them out to Martha each morning upon his arrival.

See, Marta, see? Look what I got!

*

Martha's hot dog is getting cold. How long can two grown men go on about one lousy hockey game? She nudges Keith with her elbow.

"What?" he says, as if she has poked him with a sharp object. B.J. gets busy, wiping down his counters.

"I've got to be back at the centre in thirty-five minutes."

"So?"

"So, we need to eat now. Otherwise, we won't have time to view the house."

B.J. lays down his cloth.

"You're not thinking about buying that place are you, Keith?"

"I'm considering it. It'll go cheap after what happened. I could fix it up, flip it, and make myself a tidy little profit."

"Sure, if you can find someone who doesn't mind living with a couple of ghosts."

"We're only looking," Martha interrupts. "We're not buying."

"Right," B.J. says.

"Sure," Keith adds. "Go grab us a table. I'll be over in a minute."

Martha is finished eating by the time her husband sits down across from her.

"So much for having lunch together," she says.

"I didn't think you'd mind. You weren't too happy to see me when I got here, remember?"

"You scared me. What did you expect?"

"Oh, I don't know, maybe a wife with a sense of humour?"

"Look, I'm sorry."

Not good enough. Keith glances around her as if she is a dead bug on his windshield. He finishes the hot dog in silence. He is three-quarters of the way through his fries when she decides *fuck this* and stands.

"Sit down!" His gunshot voice turns the heads of the goths at the next table, and it embarrasses her enough to do what he has ordered.

He extends the carton of french fries across the silence that follows.

"No thanks."

"Whatever," her refusal a further example of what he has to put up with. Tipping his baseball-capped head back, he shakes the congealed mass into his mouth—chewing, swallowing, and belching.

Lovely, Martha thinks.

He stands. She stands.

"Let's go."

THE HOUSE HAS BEEN emptied of personal effects. No furniture, curtains or laundry, no red rubber boots in the front hall closet, no toothpaste mollusks in the main floor bathroom sink— nothing to suggest that anyone ever thrived here, or perished here. Why, then, does Martha feel as if she is trespassing?

"God, no, they weren't married." The real estate agent sets Keith straight on that score. "Not even close. The husband, the father of those two beautiful children, described it as a 'trial separation'. Apparently, she won a bit of money on a lottery ticket a year or so ago,... let it go to her head. That's what the husband says. Hers was the only name on the deed.

Since they were still legally man and wife, the house became his property after her death. He wants nothing to do with it, of course. He's taken the kids back to Orillia. It's a wonderful opportunity, really, for the right buyers."

Are you the right buyers? her eyes ask. Martha looks away.

The front door opens. Another couple—Foster Reed, the electrician, and his wife, Lynette. Keith doesn't look happy.

"Foster," he says, with a quick nod of his head.

"Keith."

"I'll let the two of you take a look around," the realtor says to Keith. "The master bedroom is at the top of the stairs, to your left. The carpet has been removed and the wood floor sandblasted, then refinished. The room has been freshly painted, as well. It looks lovely. You'd never know."

Martha follows Keith up the stairs. Taking a right, Keith moves through the two small bedrooms and the bathroom, pointing to a crack in the plaster here, evidence of a roof leak there. He talks himself into new windows, drywall and carpeting, and then considers the cost of blown in insulation. He saves the master bedroom for last. Refusing to step through the door with him, Martha stands in the hallway. Keith paces the entire perimeter, then comes to a full stop in the centre of the room.

"You know what, Martha?" Martha hears the excitement in his voice. All is forgiven, for now. "That agent is right. You would never know what happened in here. I bet I could get it for a song."

For the first time since they walked into the house he looks directly at her. She recognizes the tentative expression that used to flip her heart before she came to understand it as an opening salvo to an argument he was determined to win.

She goes through the motions anyway, sickened by his opportunism, but never directly addressing that issue because it might hurt his pride. Sure, he might get it cheap, if Foster Reed's wife decides that they aren't interested. But even then, even if he replaces every wall, floor, carpet and window, there's a good chance that this house will stay on the market for years. If that happens, Keith should know that there is absolutely no way that she will ever let him sell their present home to cover his costs, or move in here with the kids. She promised Mick this morning. A stack of bibles and a pinky swear. That's what it took for Mick to agree to get out of the car and join his buddies on the schoolyard.

"Do you hear me, Keith?"

He stopped listening to Martha when he heard the word 'but'.

And now he is on the move again, edging past her down the hallway. Martha reaches out, touches Keith's arm just above the elbow, but it does nothing to slow him down.

"Where are you going?"

"Basement. I want to check the electrical panel."

He is gone before she can say another word.

Footsteps. Lynette and Foster are coming up. Martha meets them on the stairs. Lynette passes by her as if Martha is ethereal, but Foster sees her.

"Excuse us," he says.

Downstairs the real estate agent is greeting a trio of women in the front hall.

"Yes, it certainly is a lovely day. Feel free to look about. The owner is anxious to sell, as you can well imagine."

Martha has to be back at work in five minutes, but Keith is still in the basement. She'll have to go without him. The realtor, who continues to speak with the other three women, seems unaware that Martha is standing right behind her: "A terrible tragedy, especially for the children. Imagine growing up without your mother, knowing how she died. It's bound to leave scars."

"Excuse me," Martha says.

"Oh!" A hand flies to the agent's throat, she turns to glare at Martha. "Oh my goodness. You scared me half to death!"

"I'm really sorry, but I have to leave. My husband is down in the basement. Would you please explain when he comes up that I've left him? That I couldn't stay another minute?"

THE PLAN

A MAN'S FREEDOM and dignity are worth a few casualties.

He got her attention. Isn't that what Judith had encouraged Walter Bogart and the others to aim for during their initial get-together in the nursing home's gathering room?

Take risks, she'd said. Let your mind explore the 'impossible possibilities'.

Walter shot an open leer Judith's way that first day, his one good hand jerking suggestively beneath a thermal blanketed lap. None of the others saw it, his wheelchair positioned behind them and closer to the door. Disgusting old fart. Judith kept her eye on him through the next session, while she walked her geriatric students through descriptive language. She needn't have worried. Walter just sat and scribbled, hunched over in his wheelchair, seemingly oblivious to her and to her lecture.

This week, he'd presented her with a ballpoint-pen blitzkrieg. Three pages, single-spaced, plastered against Judith's hip with an inarticulate grunt as the orderly rolled him into the gathering room. It must have taken him days.

"Your submission should be double-spaced and as clear of grammatical errors and spelling mistakes as you can make it." To the best of their ability, the others had complied, but not Walter. He hadn't stuck to the past, either.

Judith sought out the charge nurse after the workshop, Walter's wilted pages at her side.

"What's the story on Walter Bogart?"

"Why, what did he do?" *Now,* lingering in the air, the nurse's take-charge eyes narrowed in anticipation.

"He didn't follow instructions. I'm wondering, has the stroke left him with any mental impairments to, uh, complement the physical ones?"

"He's mental all right, but not because of the stroke. He's a Second World War vet. Decorated for bravery. Used to getting his way at home, from what the wife tells me. His way or the highway, I'm sure you've met the type. Sometimes these vets can go a little squirrelly locked up in here."

"That explains a lot."

The nurse's eyes narrowed once more.

"Why, what's he got to say? Anything about me?"

"Not you, exactly. This place. Welcome to 'Nursing Home Armageddon'. He's just blowing off steam. I don't think it's anything to worry about. Really."

The charge nurse's gaze leveled Judith.

"We had an orderly stabbed in the leg with a letter opener a few months ago by a sweet old lady who would never hurt a fly." Her efficient hand reached out. "I'd better take a look. Can't be too careful these days."

GUILT BROUGHT JUDITH to the nursing home.

The weekly calls from her mother documenting her father's crumbling health finally ate through her resolve to keep her life the same. *The doctor says he's depressed, but who wouldn't be? He's got nothing to look forward to. The food is terrible—everything is pureed. I'd bring him home if I could, but the doctor says I wouldn't be able to manage it, not all by myself.*

A leave of absence had been possible.

Judith cleared the idea with her principal last spring after her father's stroke, when her emotions were in a muddle and it became clear that his body would not surrender, but she never filled out the paperwork. She flew to Edmonton over the long weekend that May, to hug her worried mother and to view her father's wasted body in the hospital bed. She made small talk about movies with her two brothers, ate dinner in their comfortable homes, caught up with their wives and children on the latest triumph or disaster—the lead in a school play, a flooded basement, the missed promotion, a new pet lizard.

Judith slipped 'nursing home' into the conversation like a bookmark as her much younger sister-in-law, a stay-at-home mom with the most to lose, drove her to the Edmonton airport.

"Thank God!" her sister-in-law had said, squeezing Judith's forearm at a stoplight. "I thought I was the only one."

Judith returned to Edmonton one week into her summer break to walk the florescent halls of prospective long-term care facilities with her mother and brothers. Her mother became tearful: the rooms were too small, the beds too close together, the noise level too high, the lack of privacy an outrage. In the end, they chose. Judith flew back east and learned to dread the sound of the telephone. Teaching creative writing at the local nursing home became her atonement.

JUDITH USED TO PRACTICE in the bathroom mirror when still a teenager, still under his roof, under his militaristic thumb: "Dad, did anyone ever tell you what an asshole you are?" Dreaming of the day when she would be financially independent, emotionally secure and ready to bring Drill Sergeant Drummond down a peg or two. She never did say it and now, she supposes, she is happier not to have done so. Not because it wasn't true, but because with enough time and distance she had come to realize how she would have been diminished.

A surprising number of people with whom she became friendly in her adopted province claimed to have accepted their parent's idiosyncrasies and absorbed their old fashioned traditional values, framing the entire buzzing ball of wax within a modern, more caring context, of course. They would insist over wine and cheese, strawberries and chocolate, that Judith was being too hard on her father.

"Look what they went through—a depression, a world war. It was a different time, a different era. Besides, all teenagers hate their parents."

When Judith attempted to clarify, they would take vague sips from their wine glasses and refuse to meet her gaze, smiling grimly through her evidential anecdotes: the golf club brought down across her flinching, slipper-less toes, toys destroyed in a fit of rage because he couldn't repair them, her bicycle locked away for an entire summer when she was ten because she left it lying down in the garage, doors secured one second after curfew. *My house, my rules, Miss. If you don't like it, there's always the street.* With these friends she learned not to even graze the surface of his alcoholism.

Over the years there were others—strangers that Judith would encounter at school-board seminars or weekend retreats sponsored by her church. There was also a hairdresser who moved away and a married man with whom she conducted a guilt-embroidered affair. A shyness in all their eyes that pulled Judith to them and said: "Tell me your secrets and I'll tell you mine." The childhood trauma would spill like loose change with the intensity and passion of a one-night stand. Yet, once the bloodletting was done, Judith found there was no lasting intimacy, but rather a kind of embarrassed distancing.

When she was twenty-nine, Judith married a teaching colleague in a civil ceremony at city hall. She called her parents with the news and her mother cried. They separated after a year when it became clear to them both that he was gay.

Judith entered her thirties unattached, throwing all her pent-up maternal energy into motivating high-school kids who didn't want to take English seriously because they already knew how to read and write. At thirty-five, she won a provincial teaching award, but she did not inform her parents until after its presentation. Her mother cried then, too.

"HELLO, MISS DRUMMOND. Are you there? Hello? This is Walter Bogart's wife and I think you should know you got him in a whole lot of trouble. They're going to ship him out to the hospital's psychiatric unit for an assessment, all because of that story he wrote for you. They're worried he might hurt somebody. Please, Miss Drummond, if you get this message, would you go down to the home and explain how it was only a story? I don't know what I'll do if they transfer him to the hospital. I don't drive. I'd never get to see him..."

Judith charges the charge nurse.

"You've got to be kidding. Walter isn't dangerous! He can't walk—he can barely feed himself! How can he be considered a threat to the other patients?"

"He expressed a desire to burn this facility to the ground with everyone in it. Where there's a will, there's a way."

"But it's fiction. It's not real! He's a sick old man with nothing to look forward to."

"Exactly. He's got nothing to lose."

"That's not what I meant. What about freedom of expression? He has rights."

"As do all the other patients in this facility. Have you asked yourself what would happen if he hurt one of them? I'll tell you what would happen—a great big lawsuit, naming all of us, yourself included, Little Miss Creativity, for not taking him seriously. And don't tell me he's harmless. Look what they did in the States with box cutters. He's got to go. End of story."

THE RESTAURANT is pseudo-Italian. Papier mâché tomatoes, heads of garlic, and red and green bell peppers dangle from the ceiling. The lighting is low, the music loud. Judith has to practically shout to be heard by her companion, who sits across from her at a table with barely enough space for dinner plates, bread plates and wine glasses.

His name is David. They met at the nursing home—his eighty-year-old mother one of Judith's students. He sat in on one of Judith's lectures—selecting the right point of view. With the occasional nod of his head, he took copious notes, a somewhat self-satisfied smile sneaking across a set of lips that supported a well-trimmed white moustache. And then he asked her out.

This is their third date. He seems nice enough. A retired OPP officer, but with only half his pension—his ex-wife saw to that—he teaches part-time at the college in the city. A little older than Judith, to be sure—he admitted as much on their second date, after chewing his way through a bit of gristly steak—but still fit, still with it. Until yesterday, Judith had half-considered inviting him home for a drink after dinner, but not now. Walter Bogart has got her rattled. He is all she can think about or talk about.

"I feel so bad, you know? His wife, she's so upset, though God knows why—from what the nurses say, he's miserable with her when she comes to visit. She's left three messages on my machine. I get nowhere with the charge nurse, nowhere with the guy who owns the facility. I feel like there's something else I should be doing."

"Like what?" David asks.

"Oh, I don't know, go over their heads, I suppose."

Earlier in the week, Judith had considered alerting the local paper and television news outlet, letting them explore the 'impossible possiblities' of Walter's story by working the whole human rights angle into a rabid, frothy media event, but she could not bring herself to pick up the telephone. She does not suggest it now to David and she has skimmed through enough self-help books to know why—because he might say "What a great idea. Do it!" And deep down, Judith is not so sure that this old man, who reminds her so much of another old man, is deserving of such an unequivocal show of support.

David reaches for the bottle of Merlot—the one he insisted she would adore when he ordered it with his appetizer.

"Do you want my opinion, Judith?" A splash for her, two splashes for him, followed by a swirl of his glass, and a longish swallow as he awaits her go-ahead-and-tell-me nod. "Rules are rules, Miss Drummond. And your man, Walter, being ex-mili-tary, should have known better. He's made his own shitty little bed, so let him marinate in it. Why, just look at the state you're in! He's nearly ruined a perfectly good evening. Let it go, I say."

"Oh," she says. She wasn't expecting a tirade.

He drives her home after dessert and decaf. There is a clasping of hands, a brushing of lips at the door. She decides she is not a fan of the somewhat abrasive moustache.

"Can we do this again?" he asks, not letting go of her hand. No.

"Well, I don't know," she says. "Why don't you give me a call?"

IT IS THE ONE childhood memory that Judith has never shared with anyone. Not the hairdresser, her married ex-lover, her gay ex-husband, not any of her friends or acquaintances, and for sure not her brothers or their wives. Some memories have the power to change everything.

She is twelve, budding into a training bra. Acne. Mood swings. Armpit hair, the other kind, too—*pubes*, her older brother has sneeringly referred to them, *short and curlies*, but only when their parents are out of earshot.

No period. Not yet, but her mother and gym teacher have warned her. It's coming. You just wait.

Saturday night. Her mother, who has a job for the first time since before the kids were born, is delighted to be called in for an extra shift at the bar. She will make great tips, which will help with the upcoming Christmas bills. Judith's younger brother is at a sleepover, her older brother decides to hitchhike into town for the evening. Her dad sits in his chair in the living room, watching TV, studying the newspaper, smoking cigarette after cigarette, downing yet another beer.

Judith is equal parts bored and envious. Everyone has something to do but her. She decides to take a bath. She does not lock the door. Why would she?

She likes it when the water is very hot. She enjoys the initial slide into the tub, the squeak of her wet and warming skin against the shocking cool of the porcelain. She likes to soak a facecloth, then lay it sopping wet across her chest. It takes her breath away.

He doesn't knock, or anything. Just pushes open the door, cigarette dangling at the corner of his mouth, the weekend paper spread wide and clutched between his two hands, a chuckle caught in his throat. Here, you've got to see this, kneeling awkwardly next to the tub.

Facecloth plastered across her chest, shoulders rounded and hunched, one hand covering her pubes, she tries to focus on the comic strip at hand—Andy Capp, drunk again, his wife, the rolling pin—and now her dad is not looking at the paper. She can smell the beer on his breath, the smoke from his nearly spent cigarette, he is that close. And the newspaper, initially held high and spread wide for her benefit, begins to droop and wilt in his hands as his eyes slip from her face, to her neck, to the washcloth and down.

Act like this is normal.

Act like this is normal.

Heh heh, that's real funny, Dad. But I need to get out of the tub, now, so.

And that is all it takes for him to snap out of it. Swear to God.

Are there other memories she may have repressed? *Where's there's smoke*, the self-help books and talk-show hosts will tell you.

Everyone's an expert.

DAVID'S CAR PULLS away from the curb and Judith enters her quiet house. Going to the kitchen, she uncorks a half-full bottle of Cabernet Sauvignon—the good stuff—and pours herself a generous glass. The light on her message machine is blinking. She presses the button. It's her again, Walter's wife. Sipping from her glass, Judith listens to it all the way through before pressing delete.

RESURRECTION

DAD PASSED AWAY on Good Friday of this year—his body sprawled at the base of the cellar steps.

The coroner ruled the death suspicious and ordered an autopsy, which in our town pretty much guaranteed standing room only at the funeral home and the church.

Turned out he'd swallowed too many blood-pressure pills. Combine that with a couple of ales to mark the Good Lord's crucifixion and you have yourself one tipsy handyman. The coroner said he likely got dizzy and took a tumble, but his ruling didn't become public until weeks after Dad's Easter Monday funeral.

So, me and Beth and Jill had to contend with three hundred sets of eyes gnawing into our backs as we mourned the old man into his next life. Of course, Jill had no worries, being in Vancouver at the time of his death, and finding out the way she did—by email.

I met Jill's plane at the Ottawa airport. Her first words as she handed me her carry-on?

"I would have preferred a phone call."

"Don't blame me," I said. "Beth handled notification of kin. I dealt with the funeral home. Speak to her."

Jill didn't bring Karl or the kids, and she decided to bunk with Beth and Arnie, which came as no surprise to me—sisters stick together, no matter how much milk is spilt between them, and believe-you-me, Officer, Beth and Jill used to argue about everything—closet space, chores, the telephone, the bathroom, boys. I used to think the reason Mom split was because she got sick of listening to the two of them.

Not that either was anything to look at in those days. Beth still isn't. The way she's let herself go—it's a mystery to me why Arnie hasn't started tapping another tree. But Jill? You should have seen her at the funeral—all decked out in a black suit and fancy hat—afterwards at the Legion a couple of my buddies came trolling for her phone number. I think she's had some work done. Of course, it could just be the hair and makeup. Whatever it is, I sure wish Beth would tear a page from Jill's program before it's too late for her and Arnie. She won't listen to me. Anytime I bring up the subject of her weight, Beth sticks her fingers into my gut like she's about to knead me and tells me to mind my own beeswax. Maybe when I get out of here I'll go on a diet.

What's that, Officer? Well, that's a whole other story, but if you've got the time, I don't mind telling my side.

Arnie was all set to take Jill back to the airport the day after the funeral when he got called in for a shift at the plant, so that's how it came to me. Not that I cared. I've always loved to drive, and with Dad gone I figured I'd grab up the keys to the Lincoln and Jill and I would travel to the airport in style.

The old man's car had it all—leather interior, heated seats, GPS, tinted glass, a compact disc player. I brought along a few of my favourite CDs—Johnny, Garth and Shania. Jill hadn't been too talkative when I picked her up in Ottawa, but wouldn't you know it, now that I was prepared for silence, all she wanted to do was yak.

She told me about her cardiologist husband, Karl, her three kids, Ashley, June and Charlie, and her interest in community theatre, but I got the feeling from the way she was going on, all fast and fidgety, that she was warming me up for the main event.

I was right.

We'd just come through Smith Falls and stopped at that little market. You know the one I mean—it's at the curve in the road just before you get to the hospital. Jill bought us a couple of Empire apples—so crisp and juicy you'd think they'd just been picked. Off we went, me chewing on my apple and her biting her fingernails. Nothing from her for five minutes, and then she iced the puck.

"I want to make you aware of something I've done," she says. "I already spoke to Beth about it and we agreed that you should know, too."

Here we go, I thought, they're going to contest the will.

"Is it about the house," I asked, "because you know I've practically paid off the mortgage myself over the last ten years with what he's been charging me for room and board."

No, she said. As far as she and Beth were concerned the house was mine, considering what I'd had to put up with while they were off making lives of their own. And that's when my back went up.

"It wasn't so bad. Dad and I got along all right."

"So long as you jumped through his hoops."

I didn't have a comeback for that one, but I could feel my neck tightening up like a tap outfitted with a new washer. Then she says:

"I hired a private investigator a year ago, to look for Mom."

"Mom?" I said.

It got real quiet, so I reached over and put Johnny on—not too loud, but enough to fill the spaces.

"My life with Karl was perfect," Jill said, "until I had Charlie, and then it all went to hell. Panic attacks, depression, booze. It took me a while to see the pattern—two girls and a boy." And she looked out her window as if she were watching an instant replay. "Finally, Karl took the kids to a hotel. He threatened to leave me for good if I didn't get help. Everything's okay now, but we had it pretty rough for awhile."

What did she want me to say? We'd never been thick, Jill and I. She was always at the library studying, or at work, or out on the town with her friends when I was little. She never looked out for me the way Beth did when it came to the old man.

"Has your detective had any luck?"

"No," she said. "Last time we spoke he asked me if I'd considered foul play."

"You mean he thinks somebody hurt her after she left us?" I asked.

"Maybe. Or, that something happened closer to home." And she looked me over like my high-school math teacher, Mrs. Pike, used to—as if I should know what she was talking about. Well, I didn't.

"Jill, what the hell are you getting at?"

"Remember when Dad shoved Mom into the kitchen cabinets and broke her nose?"

"No."

"What about when he knocked her down the stairs and cracked two of her ribs?"

"Nope. Don't recall that either."

"Do you remember her leaving?"

"No."

"Neither do I. All we had was Dad's word for it, the next morning. Remember?"

"Sure, I guess." There were beer bottles lined up on the kitchen counter. Dad's head cradled between his hands. Between you and me and the bedpan? It was the only time he ever put his arms around me.

Anyway, then Jill says: "I never believed that bullshit about her leaving because of us. It was him she could do without. Let's face it, Mack, he was one, mean son-of-a-bitch."

Everything stops for me right there. I know I got Jill to the airport because she's back in Vancouver with her family.

They keep a nice bar out at the Ottawa airport. I'm thinking that's where I got my start. Your fellow officers snapped up twelve empties at the scene, so I must have stopped off somewhere before I slammed into the market at Smith Falls. They really ought to straighten out that road before someone gets killed. What's that, sir?

Broken leg and pelvis, two cracked vertebrae, but I can wiggle all of my toes, so I'll walk again, eventually.

Pardon me?

Right! That's why you came by in the first place, and here I've been talking your ear off. I'm as bad as Jill! Did I mention she phones me every day? She wants me to come out to Vancouver after I get the wind back in my sails—even offered to spring for my fare. I haven't decided if I'll take her up on it. I've had a lot of time to think in here between the sponge baths, the bedpans and the morphine shots—I'm not a big reader and I can only stomach so much of the tube. The thing I keep coming back to, the thing I've found hardest to shake, is this detective's idea that the old man did harm to our mom, see?

Our dad had an awful temper. Handcuff that to the drinking and, well, I don't need to tell you what it's like. I bet you deal with plenty a mean drunk in your line of work.

Once I allowed that he could have done something to her, a few ideas cropped up—things I took for granted because he was my old man and I didn't know any different. Like this business of him crossing himself whenever he went down to the cellar. He never did that upstairs, or on the escalator at the mall, or anywhere else.

So last week, I'm lying here wondering why he'd do such a thing, and it came to me: what if, twenty-some years ago, he pushed Mom down those steps? What if this time, Mom broke her neck instead of a couple of ribs? What if she lay there dying and he got scared for his own self and for us and decided to cover it up? What if every time he went down those steps he worried he might see a ghost?

Thing is, once I allowed for the possibility of him pushing her down the cellar steps, it opened my mind to something else. Each spring, on the anniversary of Mom's disappearance, the old man would get good and hammered, see, and then he'd bugger off. The girls and I figured he was out at some bar or other.

The year I learned to drive, he took me with him. He handed over the keys to the truck, said he didn't want to risk losing his license. First, we went to the grocery store where he bought some flowers. Then, he directed me out onto the highway. Fifteen minutes later, he told me to pull off and we turned down a gravel road. I parked the truck near a grassy knoll overlooking the river and there we sat in the high grass, him drinking beer and reminiscing about their courtship. Turns out, he'd asked Mom to marry him at that exact spot. We stared out at the river for a while, then he stumbled back to the truck to grab the flowers from the front seat and he set them down between us.

The township has turned that whole area into a beach now, eh? They brought in truckloads of sand, slapped down a few swings, and installed his and her washrooms. Thing is, once the township took it over, the old man didn't want to go back. I remember feeling cut loose, you know, because other than the day Mom left, it was the only time I felt like he and I were on the same path.

What's that? Jeez, but you're quick!

Dad was strong as an ox back then, and our mother was not a big woman. He could have picked Mom's body up, down there in the cellar and carried her to the truck, no sweat. He could have buried her out by the river and been back in time to serve up his cover story with our breakfast cereal.

The son-of-a-bitch.

SHOES

FERN REFUSES EYE CONTACT with the others as she takes a seat in the waiting area. She stows her purse and the plastic bag containing her street clothes between the chair's cold chrome legs, then studies her clean-shaven, middle-aged counterparts.

"We all look like members of a cult. Kool-Aid, anyone?" a woman in slingbacks trills. The green-gowned adults shun her, but the blue-eyed boy who swings his feet across from Fern whispers to his mother: "Will *I* get Kool-Aid after this?"

A young man in cross-trainers emerges from a change room. His head is threaded through one of three armholes. Fern is treated to a partial view of his sprinting backside. The baffled look he displays as he takes the seat beside Fern under the fluorescent lights reminds her of Kyle. The mother hen is aroused.

"All three are arm holes," she instructs. "One of them overlaps."

"Ohhh," he nods. "Now I get it!"

He jerks to a stand. Yanking the gown tight to his hip, he sprints back to the change room. Minutes later, when he emerges, he sits as far from Fern as is possible.

"Mr. Smythe?" The tiny, blonde technician calls. No answer. "Mr. Smythe?"

"He's in there," Fern volunteers, pointing to another door. "Perhaps he's having trouble with the gown?"

Goldilocks raps at the door.

"Is everything all right, Mr. Smythe?"

"Yes, fine, goddamn it!" His muffled reply.

The door swings wide. A grizzled Mr. Smythe—all three of his armholes properly positioned—lurches out in plaid bedroom slippers. Droplets of sweat cling to Mr. Smythe's forehead and fragile comb-over. He focuses on the technician through the lenses of his drug-store reading glasses.

"Where do you want me now?" he growls.

"Follow me, sir, they are all ready for you."

"And for that I suppose I should be grateful?" he snaps, over her petite shoulder.

Fern forms a teepee with her hands, covering mouth and nose as he limps past, safeguarding against his unwashed, old man odour. There's no excuse for it, she'll tell Buck when she gets back to town. *If ever I reach the point where I refuse to bathe, get rid of me!*

Buck offered to accompany her this morning, but she turned him down. He feels about hospitals the way she feels about nursing homes, and the last thing she needs during this procedure is Buck complaining about palpitations.

Fern glances at the clock's round, institutional face: 8:45AM Buck is opening the store right now. Pulling the blinds, making room in the display windows for the new fall stock that arrived last evening. Sitting back behind the cash to sip his Double-Double and to watch friends and neighbours flock like pigeons to the Penny Parlour across the street.

Fern's abdomen issues a massive rumble of protest.

Absolutely no food or drink after midnight.

Fern turns, ready to offer an apology to the heavyset woman in Birkenstock's who is reading *Hannibal*, but she appears not to have noticed.

Can I brush my teeth?

Of course, but don't swallow any water. Your stomach must be empty for the X-ray to tell us anything.

Buck refused a poached egg on toast this morning in a show of solidarity. He's not fooling her—he's eating a blueberry fritter right now, make that two, and watching a teenage mom flick her cigarette into the gutter before pushing her little consequence through the entrance. Or maybe it's one of those old widows on a fixed income trailing a lightweight shopping cart.

They cater to hostages like these.

It wasn't always so, not back when Buck's father ran O'Brien's. When the oil crisis made Kingston seem distant and fuzzy, like Toronto, and people were content to take quality over quantity. If she has to endure one more customer leaning across the counter to tell her how they are doing her a favour because they could get shoelaces cheaper in the city she may expose her backside and tell them to pucker up!

Buck winces whenever she talks that way. It's not the customer's fault, he'll say, it's the politicians—local, provincial and federal. Buck may only have his high-school diploma, but he stays current, reading between the lines of *The National Post* at the breakfast table, flapping newsprint like the clipped wings of some endangered, exotic bird. He'll talk a person's ear off, if given half a chance, about free trade and welfare for the rich, holding the line on municipal taxes and this town's failure to attract new industry. He plans to spoil his ballot come the next election. In the end, nothing he has to say will halt their slow slide into bankruptcy.

Buck won't see it, won't hear of it.

Are you under any personal stress, Mrs. O'Brien?

No.

When Keeley phoned last month to whine about how far her apartment was from campus, didn't Buck run straight out to Blodgett's and buy her a Tracker! Second-hand, but still.

I had a car when I was nineteen, his lame defense.

What if she quits like Derreck did last year on Babe?

She won't quit. She's not a quitter.

Hel-lo! Remember piano lessons, guitar lessons, art classes, tae kwon do?

Fern had had to bite her combative tongue. Keeley could do no wrong in Buck's eyes. Babe would have understood. She wished Babe would come back.

Friends since kindergarten, married to their high-school sweethearts, they'd even acted as each other's labour coach, leaving the men out of it. She'd been Babe's shoulder when Harley decided to go find himself and never did. Babe provided the voice of reason last winter when Fern found Kyle's stash of downloaded porn in his sock drawer.

An embolism.

Fern removing the garden shears from Babe's lifeless hand, closing her startled brown eyes, covering her with the blue gingham tablecloth from the picnic table. Fern sitting cross-legged on the grass in the still spring sunshine with Derreck for twenty-three minutes, waiting for the ambulance to make its way back from the Brockville General.

Have you suffered any recent losses?

Well, I did lose a close friend, this past year.

Four months of heartburn and stomach aches before Doc Mills managed to yank the right string and get her in to see a specialist who, during a fifteen-minute consultation, pronounced a probable ulcer and ordered a barium X-ray for confirmation.

It's the little boy's turn.

"Remember," his mother admonishes as she hands him off to a smiling, male technician, "you *have* to drink it."

"Ya, ya, I know."

What if it's cancer?

Fern didn't have the guts to ask the specialist.

Her town so often hushed these days by the solemn, paralytic scent of cancer. In the grocery store, or milling about down at centennial park during the craft fair, or serving up casseroles at the community potluck supper. Did you hear about so-and-so, went in for surgery and damned if they didn't find a tumour. Malignant, radiation, chemo, nothing else they can do, sad-so-sad, you just never know do you? Mashed or scalloped potatoes?

There must be twenty people down here in this windowless cavern. Everyone booked for 8:30, no one expecting good news. A cold clutch of panic takes hold of her stomach and clamours onto her chest.

Buck should have come, after all. They could have gone out for lunch to one of those fragrant, dark places on Brock Street. She could have made a few Christmas purchases, though God knows her list is shrinking each and every year. Both of Buck's parents dead. Her father gone. Her mother insisting she no longer has need of material things while shakily affixing her grandchildren's names to all her worldly goods with masking tape and ballpoint pen.

And now Babe.

Fern had loved to open gifts from Babe. Unlike her presents from Buck, which Fern paid for, then wrapped, she never knew what to expect from Babe. It might be a book Fern had mentioned months earlier and then totally forgot about, a Santa figurine for her collection, a homemade ornament for her tree. Always thoughtful and measured, well-planned and executed. Not like her death at all.

The boy busts out of the radiation room, shadowed by his male technician.

"Your son did great."

"It didn't taste like nothing," the boy reports in a rush, "but it jumped around in my mouth like it had feet and when I was done? I had the second biggest burp of my whole life!"

The gowned ones chuckle. Even the woman in Birkenstocks permits a quiet snicker to escape while turning a page in her book.

"Mrs. O'Brien?"

Her turn. Goldilocks stands at the X-ray room entrance, a bright smile fixed to her lips. Fern returns the smile and steps through the door.

FAITH AND JOY

"DID YOU TAKE IT?" Billy asks, his words homing in on Faith from somewhere above her head.

They are in the kitchen—she is seated at the table, he is standing guard behind her back. On the counter, the baby monitor, alive with breath sounds and the occasional sigh, but no cries—not yet.

Faith smoothes blue terry cloth along the length of one arm, her fingers teasing out tufts of white lint—the result of one of Billy's laundering faux pas. She rolls the lint ball between thumb and forefinger and adds it to the tiny cloth mountain that she is producing in her lap.

Her husband asks a second time—he will not be ignored.

"Yes," she says, without looking up.

"When?"

Why won't he shut up? Can't he see that she's into a rhythm, here? Smooth. Pluck. Roll. Deploy.

"I don't know, a while ago."

He leans down, speaks softly into her ear, aiming for cute.

"When I was in the shower?" he asks.

Smooth. Pluck.

"Before that."

"Oh."

Roll. Deploy.

Billy unfolds, taking his warm breath with him. She doesn't need to look at him to see that he doesn't believe her.

"My glass is in the sink. You can lift my prints if you feel the need." What is wrong with her voice? That was meant to sound pissed off, but her words came out flat, devoid of intonation, like her students when she calls upon them to read poetry aloud.

He gets the point.

"Look, I didn't mean to ... "

"Suggest that I was lying?" Still not looking up at him, because she is afraid to see how he is looking down at her, remembering a time, not so long ago, when finishing Billy's sentences seemed proof of their unshakeable domesticity.

"Yes, I mean, no. Christ, Faith, I'm worried about you. This should be the happiest time of your life!"

Our lives. He means 'our lives', but he won't say it that way—too much pressure.

He squeezes her shoulder instead—gently, as if she were bruised fruit from the farmer's market. Juicy tears well up, bypass her cheeks, drop into her lap, singly, in pairs—the first cry of the day. Fuzz Mountain is overwhelmed. Faith imagines tiny lint people rushing for cover. She cannot stop.

"I'm sorry."

"Don't." He comes around and crouches at her feet, grabbing her hands with his. "You didn't cause this."

He is trying so hard. Why then does she feel this urge to slap him, pull his nose, box his ears, him Curly to her Moe?

She looks at him, drills him with a stare.

"How long?"

"How long what?"

"Until I feel normal?"

"Dr. Kline said you might notice some improvement within a couple of weeks of starting the meds."

She sweeps the drowned lint from her lap and onto the floor.

"They aren't working!"

"It's only been three weeks, Faith, you've come a long way."

"Yeah, right." Her voice betrays her, once again, turning what was meant to be sarcasm into a whisper.

"You are improving," Billy says. "You're sleeping better, you're able to nurse, the baby's healthy."

I can't seem to find my way out of your bathrobe, the laundry is spilling from every doorway, the fridge is emitting a nasty odour.

"The house is a disaster."

"No more than any other household with a newborn. We'll hire a housekeeper."

"Uh-uh."

"Just until you get you bearings."

"No!"

"Why not?"

"It's a small town, Billy. People talk." Must she really explain it?

"So let them." Spoken like a true city transplant.

"No."

He drops her hands, changes tack.

"How about some tea?"

Herbal tea. No caffeine because she is breastfeeding, which means no guts, but her dry mouth craves liquid.

"I guess."

"Let's see," he says, going to the cupboard. "We've got decaffeinated green tea, berry blast or," moving boxes like chess pieces, " apple-cinnamon. You pick."

"I can't."

"What do you mean?"

"I mean stop asking me things! You decide. I don't want to talk!"

Billy chooses berry blast and scalds tea for two in silence. He pops two slices of wholewheat bread into the toaster, and forages for several seconds inside the refrigerator before coming up with an almost empty jar of marmalade. He sits across from her—chewing, sipping, waiting.

More baby sounds crackle to life over the monitor on the counter, causing Billy to smile.

"Somebody's awake," he says.

"She'll be squawking like a chicken any second."

"I'll get her, drink your tea."

Alone, Faith brings the cup closer and submerges a forefinger—one, two, three, four, five, six. She pulls it out, red, raw, steaming, and blows on it like a gunslinger. This is what crazy people do, she thinks.

Billy's voice floats out over the airwaves. "Hello, sweetheart! Look at you!" There is a pause as Billy scoops the infant up. "Come on, let's go see Mommy."

Mommy—that's her—still so hard to grasp. The others had passed from her body barely formed—bits of tissue and blood—while Billy stood guard outside the bathroom door. Four miscarriages in seven years and now this one, born alive, without benefit of a medical explanation, on the cusp of Faith's thirty-eighth birthday. A miracle. She should be happy. Why isn't she happy? What the fuck is wrong with her?

Billy comes into the kitchen, their daughter's head cupped in his hand, her infant body balanced on a tightrope of forearm between his wrist and crooked elbow—as if he's been carrying infants around for years. Faith hides her finger beneath the table.

"There's your Mommy," Billy says, bringing the child alongside Faith. "Isn't she the most beautiful Mommy in the whole wide world? Yes she is, she sure is!"

"Liar. You still have one slice of toast left."

"You eat it. I'm not that hungry."

Sneaky Billy, making sure she eats, drinks, takes her crazy pills, all the while cooing for two into their daughter's wide-awake eyes.

"Any plans for today?"

"No."

"Dr. Kline suggested you set a goal every morning, no matter how small, remember?"

How about this? Today I will brush my teeth. Today I will remember to flush the toilet after I pee. Today I will strangle my happy husband.

She takes a breath.

"Today, if *she* allows it, I will grab a shower and get dressed and then I will attempt to get a handle on the laundry."

"Great! Did you hear that, baby girl, Mommy's got a plan!" Billy nuzzles his daughter's cheek. Faith wonders if he's got his own drug supply stashed somewhere in the house.

"God, Faith, her skin is so soft, it's softer than anything I've ever felt." Billy chatters on to his captive audience of one, while Faith chews his toast. He parachutes kisses onto his daughter's cheek, touching her because he wants to, not because he must. Faith feels jealous and not for the first time, either. She imagines wrestling Billy to the linoleum floor, terry cloth robe swirling, and sucking all the love he has for this child right out of him.

He shifts the baby into his lap, propping her up against his button-downed belly. Her head flops to the left. Her eyes focus hard on the chrome edge of the table, a tiny fret line appears between her eyebrows, as if to say, "Now what the *fuck* is that?"

The blue melamine table with its cuff of polished chrome was a flea market discovery, snatched from a bar-cum-warehouse outside of Ottawa a year ago, after they closed the deal on this house. She'd had big plans for this table and her new kitchen, naively announced to two of her colleagues in the teacher's staffroom while sipping fruit juice from a drink-box balanced on her bucking belly. Blue and white gingham curtains made from a pattern she'd come across while flipping through an ancient magazine at her gynecologist's office. Sanding the kitchen cupboards, then painting them white before replacing the brass handles with chrome knobs, and new countertops to match the table. Maybe a new floor, too. She'd have loads of time to do it, she remembered saying, while cooped up at home on maternity leave ... Billy's voice pulls her back to reality.

"Joy called last night after you went to bed." His voice has shifted to neutral. "She asked if we had a name yet and I told her no." Faith rolls her eyes. "And then she said that she'd like to come over today after lunch to see her granddaughter because she hasn't seen her in weeks. You're to call if you *don't* want her to come."

"Typical."

"I can phone her, tell her to wait a bit longer."

"No." Faith lets him off the hook, knowing his views on third party negotiations. "Let her come."

"Alright, then. Are you ready to take her? I've got to head out."

"Sure." Not so sure. "Give her over." Faith's arms extend.

"What happened here?" His finger grazes hers. She should have known it would not go unnoticed. Billy's radar is on high alert these days.

"Nothing. I'm fine." Minimizing, unwilling to provide another nail for her psychological coffin.

"Well, I'm late. Gotta go." He drop-kisses both their heads, steps into the hall for a moment to retrieve his coat from the closet.

"I'll get the groceries after work," he announces, pulling on his parka. "Is there anything in particular you'd like for dinner?"

"You decide."

Faith's lips make contact with the baby's forehead for Billy, so he can go to the X-ray clinic without conjuring images of her at home looking wild-eyed into the bassinet, pillow in hand. Staring at the child staring back at her, she sends a telepathic message of good will: I will love you. Soon. You'll wait, won't you?

Billy pulls his hood down over his forehead and ears until it makes contact with the frames of his glasses.

"You look like the Unabomber."

"I know. I'll call you later." He opens the kitchen door. Frigid air assaults Faith's bare toes. Untying her robe, she slips the child close. The baby feels her mother's body, smells her heat and turns her head, rooting.

JOY SITS AT FAITH'S blue melamine kitchen table, her hands laced and white-knuckled. She has not bothered to remove her plum-coloured parka or her knitted tam, although her black leather slip-on boots stand together on the mat at the kitchen door. She's been talking non-stop for ten minutes—her brick and mortar words filling the empty spaces left by Faith because of her 'condition'.

Had Faith heard about Sam Weston falling face first onto his shovel while clearing his front walk dead before the shovel could break his nose and him with a heart condition he should have known better an educated man like that but then I guess when it's your time it's your time he could have died just the same climbing the stairs to his bedroom he and Ida should have closed the deal on that bungalow over on Elm Street when they had the chance before prices went through the roof less lawn to cut and hardly any walk to speak of with the added benefit of having no stairs to climb.

The baby is snoozing in her lounging seat on top of the table between her mother and grandmother. She is surrounded by stacks of folded laundry—Billy's jockey shorts, dress pants and work shirts, Faith's nursing bras and sweatpants, spit cloths, towels, sleepers, a scrap wool sweater made by Billy's mother while sitting poolside with Billy's father at their condo in Florida.

(They haven't seen the baby in the flesh yet, and won't until they fly back with the geese in April. Faith hopes she'll have her shit together by then. Billy hasn't told them how things really are.)

Faith rushed to get the laundry washed, dried and folded before Joy's 1:00PM arrival, then left it all out on the kitchen table as undeniable proof of her mental stability. So far, her mother has not seen fit to comment—although her critical eye did manage to linger on the dishes piled high in the sink, the splattered stovetop and the unwashed floor, as she made her way from the door to the table.

How about that Linda Litcomb leaving them in the lurch at the salon to open up her own shop had her house renovated to do it now that must have cost a pretty penny and wasn't it a big risk to take the way things were she sure hoped Linda knew what she was doing in a small town like this where there were more hairdressers than you could shake a stick at and just what was she supposed to do now she certainly didn't want to hurt anyone's feelings she'd been going to the same salon for years to have her hair set but Linda's prices sure were more reasonable and her only getting the one pension since Dad passed away.

Faith is beginning to wonder when her mother will get around to the real reason for this visit—Joy hasn't looked twice at the baby since she walked in the door, so the point is clearly not to see her grandchild no matter what she might have told Billy on the telephone yesterday—when her mother abruptly stops speaking and reaches a hand down inside the black organizer purse that sits by her side.

"Here, I brought this for you and that husband of yours." She hands her daughter a slim paperback.

Name Your Baby. Faith catches a whiff of must. The book is dog-eared, the pages rippled, as if it may have languished at the bottom of a cardboard box in someone's moist basement. Nine diapered toddlers frolic over the block letters of the cover, ecstatic, Faith assumes, because they have names.

"I picked this up at the used bookstore. Now it seems to me there ought to be one name in there that will suit you and Billy." Joy's head bobs up and down in agreement with herself. Her trifocals slip over the bridge of her nose.

Faith dutifully thumbs through the pages. Names slip past like street signs on a subway line—Agnes, Candace, Henka, Marjorie. Next stop—Barbaras, Ignatius, Timothy. She places the book beside the baby's lounging seat.

"Thanks."

"A child should have a name, Faith."

"We know that, Mother."

"Most parents pick a name before the child is even born."

"Yes."

"Sometimes before a child is even conceived."

"We're taking our time. We want a name that will grow with her and give her room to breathe." Not like 'Faith', coiled and ready to spring at her as she slid into the world.

"What nonsense! It's been six weeks. Everywhere I go people stop me—friends, acquaintances, people who went to school with you—and they ask me all about my granddaughter. Who does she look like, how much does she weigh, what is her name? And I have no name to give them. How do you think that makes me look?"

Old? Confused? Uncaring?

"I've been a little preoccupied," Faith says, instead.

"Yes, well *that*. But you're better now, anyone can see that." Joy pushes her glasses over the bridge of her nose.

"No, I'm not."

"Of course you are. Why look at you," Joy waves a hand over her like a televangelist. "You're dressed, you've got colour, the child is healthy."

"I'm not better." Faith serves the words to her petulant mother as if they were diced bits of liver on a rubber-tipped spoon.

121

"Well, you're certainly better off than a lot of new mothers. You've got this healthy baby, a husband with a good job, a nice little house…" Her eyes stray from Faith to the dishes, the stovetop, the floor, then back to her daughter. "Why I was reading just the other day about a young girl out there in Vancouver. Sixteen, native, on welfare—arrested for trying to sell her six-month old to an undercover police officer. She said she couldn't afford to keep him. Can you imagine! Now, why she didn't just give him up, I don't know… My point is, you read things like that and it makes you realize how lucky you are."

Catholic Guilt Speech #1: Always Be Thankful for Who Thou Art Not. A young native girl, big city, helpless infant, black market… how can a measly post-partum depression possibly compete? Get over it, already! Joy must have combed the newspaper for days looking for just the right piece.

"Yes, but does the child have a name?"

Joy hesitates, wondering too, but then her lips pinch like a clothes peg. "That was not my point and you know it."

Faith surrenders in silence. It is useless to argue. Her mother simply washes over what displeases her, drowning dissent.

"Have you got her on any kind of a schedule?"

Here it comes.

"More or less."

"Every four hours?"

"Whenever she wants."

"That's no schedule, it's a recipe for disaster," Joy announces.

"She's not a souffle, Mom, she's an infant. Every book I've read about breastfeeding stresses feeding on demand."

"She'll get fat and spoiled to boot if you keep picking her up every time she cries. And you can take *that* to the bank!"

Faith makes a mental deposit.

"Breastfed babies are less likely than formula-fed babies to become obese." Faith rattles off the fact in a monotone. Her mother ignores the comment and with the bit in her mouth jumps the next hurdle.

"Is she sleeping through the night?"

"No."

"There you are," her hand displays the evidence, palm up. "It's no wonder you're so run down! Why don't you try her on a bit of cereal? It worked for my Glen," speaking of Faith's brother in the past tense as if merely dead rather than gay. "Knocked him right out and he wasn't any older than she is now."

"The books say no solids until six months."

Her mother snorts.

"Hogwash! You were both on cereal before then."

"The pediatrician says the same thing."

"What about common sense?"

"My common sense tells me to listen to my doctor and to follow what I read."

Joy sits back in her chair as if slapped.

"Suit yourself."

Translation—*Don't come crying to me when your daughter grows up sticking needles into her arm in a dark alley somewhere all because you were too stubborn to listen!*

"Would you like to hold her?"

Joy looks at the child for the first time since her arrival. Her face smoothes like a sheet, then sets like wall compound.

"She looks happy enough. Better to let sleeping dogs lie—maybe later, if she wakes up. Here," and she leans down again, fishing through her purse, "I've got something else for you."

The Rite of Baptism flops onto the table. Christ! She should have known—Faith a religious refugee ever since Mount Cashel opened the floodgates of priestly abuse, and Billy a full-blown agnostic—Joy has tolerated their defection, although she never misses an opportunity to insert the word 'Mass' into a conversation, especially on Sundays, but her grandchild will be a different matter entirely.

"I spoke with Father Simon after our last Parish Council meeting. He said he'd make himself available for a christening the weekend of the twenty-eighth."

February 28th. Three weeks. Dread spreads through Faith's chest, hot at the edges, cold at the center. Her fingertips reach out and push the booklet away.

"I'm not ready. I can't be ready by then."

Joy slides the booklet back.

"When do you think you might be ready?"

Faith's hands slip beneath the table to knead her thighs like a kitten. How about never?

"I'll have to talk it over with Billy. There's no rush, she doesn't even have a name for God's sake."

Joy's face freezes.

"Don't wait too long. Heaven forbid anything should happen to the sweet lamb and her not be baptized." She produces a grim smile. "Pearl had a torturous time after her grandson was taken out in Halifax, two years ago. Remember me telling you how the child was thrown from the baby carriage on impact? And the only comfort she could take in those dark days afterward was the knowledge that the child's soul was safe in the arms of Jesus. Pearl still lights a candle for him every Sunday."

Faith sees it like a waking nightmare—wheels screeching in the frigid air, an innocent life snuffed out—to be replaced by a candle, lit in a gloomy church alcove by a grandmother who'd never even held her grandson. Cold comfort.

"Billy's not sure that he wants her baptized." Coward. Billy doesn't care either way. Whatever you want, he'd said, while their daughter was still theory.

"Oh I don't believe that for a second," Joy says.

"It's true."

"Well then he needs his head read! You were both baptized and raised Catholic and it certainly hasn't hurt you. You were married in that church. How would it look, in a small community like this, if she were not to be baptized? Why, you'd have to be crazy … " She stops, mouth open, teeth poised, hesitating as if that word might tip Faith and spill her all over the table.

Faith takes advantage of her mother's moment of weakness to slide *The Rite of Baptism* back to her. "It's not your decision, Mom."

"Well, you'd better think long and hard miss, before you follow that path." Her finger stabs at the cross on the cover of the pamphlet, nailing it in place. "And that is all I have to say."

It is very quiet, now. They have steered themselves into the silent center of a hurricane. How to escape without loss of life? Faith wills a baby intervention knowing the sight of a bare breast will drive Joy from the house, mumbling about Faith's need for privacy, head down, eyes averted, all the while thinking how her babies were bottle-fed, so much more sanitary, and on a cup by nine months to boot. Come on, kiddo, open your eyes. Demand my nipple.

The baby does not oblige. She sleeps on, a tiny spit bubble forming in the 'o' between her lips, swelling to the size of a pea then popping like bubblegum. Something tugs inside Faith. She reaches out, captures a sleeper-shod foot and rubs her thumb along her daughter's instep.

"Isn't she sweet?" The words drag from her attached to an anchor of guilt. Is this love?

"They all are at this age," her mother says. Pushing off from the table, Joy reaches for her bag. "You wait, your fun is just beginning." She stands and yanks at the zipper of her plum-coloured parka, pulling until it engulfs her chin.

"I'll be off now, I've got errands to run," stepping into her boots. "It's Tuesday, my day to do the shopping for Mrs. Tuttle. Remember her, Faith?"

How could Faith forget, she's heard this story at least twenty times.

"She was the crossing guard when you attended St. Maria Goretti's—always a big woman. You wouldn't recognize her now—shrunk up like a raisin and half-blind to boot. Riddled with cancer. Once a week I do her shopping and stop in for a little chat and she's always so grateful, the poor old soul. Her kids aren't here. One's a Mountie in the Northwest Territories, if you can imagine, and the others are all over the map. People just don't stay put the way they used to." She slings her bag over one shoulder. *The Rite of Baptism* remains on the table.

They hug, after a fashion—chest touching chest, arm across shoulder, eyes averted.

"Alright then," Joy says, easing herself out the door. "You let me know your decision," throwing the comment over her shoulder like a pinch of salt as she makes her way down the snow-packed kitchen steps.

"Be careful, Mom," Faith cautions, exaggerating the care in her voice to make up for her shortfalls as a good Catholic daughter. "Billy hasn't kept up with the shoveling like he should have since the baby."

Closing the door, Faith goes to the table and picks up the booklet, laying it atop the refrigerator. Out of sight, out of mind. Returning to the door, she peeks through the window to ensure that Joy has successfully navigated the path from house to sidewalk. She needn't have worried—her mother is at the end of Faith's driveway, engaged in conversation with Mrs. Kravitz, one of Faith's neighbours. Huddled together, the two women turn in Faith's direction, exhaust rising from their mouths like steam from an iron.

They are talking about her.

Quit it, you're being paranoid. But she knows she is not. Faith drops the lace curtain, obscuring her face, and imagines their conversation.

A SINGLE KNOCK, the doorknob clicks and rotates.

"Faith?" Dr. Sharpe's white-haired head pokes around the edge of the door. "All set?"

"Yes."

Entering the exam room, Dr. Sharpe steps to the counter to tease a pair of latex gloves from a slim cardboard box. "I apologize for the delay. There was a playground injury from St. Maria Goretti's. A little boy needed four stitches."

Faith had heard him screaming.

"He won't be throwing snowballs for awhile." Dr. Sharpe turns back toward her, snapping latex over his wrists. "Now, let's get down to business, shall we? The breastfeeding. How's that going?"

"Fine. Good."

"Nipples holding up okay?"

"They were irritated at first, but they're better now."

"Let's have a look."

Paper crinkles beneath her buttocks as she swings her bare feet onto the examining table. Dr. Sharpe drapes a second paper crust over her waist and thighs, making Faith feel as if she is a pie about to be pinched and fluted. Lying back and gathering the green gown to her neck, she looks off into space while his fingers knead her breasts.

"Everything feels normal...not much milk, here. You must have nursed just before you came."

"Yes, I did."

"Who's got the little one, your Mom?"

"No, my friend, Lisa Sheppard."

127

"Ah, Lisa. She hasn't been in for a while. You tell her to come see me." Pulling the gown down and over Faith's breasts, Dr. Sharpe makes brief eye contact. "Let's move on to the plumbing, shall we?" He produces a red-tipped ballpoint from his shirt pocket and reaches for her chart. "Has your bleeding stopped?"

"Yes." He marks a tick on her chart.

"Anything unusual there?"

"I don't think so." Faith is uncertain. "What would you consider odd?"

"Any large clots of blood?"

"No."

"Unusual colour?"

"No."

"Smelly discharge?"

"No!" Faith begins to wish she had not asked.

Tick. Tick. Tick.

"What about your episiotomy? Any sign of infection around the stitches?"

"No."

"Hemorrhoids gone?"

"Yes."

Tick. Tick.

"Ease your bottom to the edge of the table, will you, Faith and place your feet in the stirrups," a mundane command, as if he might be asking her to take the dog for a walk or change the channel on the television. He is the very picture of decorum: clinical, detached and controlled. Why then does she feel as if Dr. Sharpe might just unzip those polyester pants of his and go to it? *Come on, girl, get a hold of yourself! He's closing in on seventy. He's known you since you were a child. You haven't got anything he hasn't seen a thousand times before!* She fits her left foot, then her right foot into the metal cups, allowing her knees to turn on each other.

Dr. Sharpe sits on a small stool at the end of the examining table, causing Faith to feel for a moment as if she is about to be milked, like the cow on the doctor's hobby farm. Margaret. She heard all about Margaret the last time she came in for a physical. How he and his wife drink Margaret's raw milk. He doesn't sell it, though, or give it away. Not that stupid.

"Legs apart, Faith."

His words are a soft slap. Her face flushes.

Her mother had assured Faith that she wouldn't be bothered by this sort of thing after the baby—not with all those nurses and doctors milling about, sticking their noses in, poking, prodding, pulling. She was wrong, as usual.

Faith feels him place a bundle of sheathed fingers inside the opening of her vagina. She imagines eyes instead of fingernails, scanning her vaginal wall, looking for abnormalities, blinking at her cervix. His other hand presses gently on her lower abdomen.

"How's Billy making out with the baby?"

"He's great with her."

"Does he do diapers?"

"Oh yes! Diapers, laundry, lullabies. You name it he does it. He's a wonderful daddy!" She's gushing, but Billy deserves credit, after everything she's put him through. Besides, talking distracts her from what is taking place at the lower end of the table.

"Used to be all a father had to do for the first five years of a child's life was bring home the pay cheque, and if it was a boy, play a little catch. Nowadays, fathers are expected to be there for every little milestone, digital camera in town. It's all much more hands on."

Dr. Sharpe removes his fingers. His head sprouts like a dandelion gone to seed between her knees.

There is more eye contact.

"Everything seems fine at this end, Faith. You're episiotomy has healed nicely, no signs of infection. Your uterus has returned to normal size. I'd like to do a pap smear while I'm here. That way you can avoid me until next February." A small sound escapes his throat—clinical humour.

She fixes her gaze on the ceiling panels and listens as he pulls a metal table with squeaky wheels to his side. The speculum: she'd noticed it earlier cuddling up to a tube of jelly.

"This may feel a little cold," he warns, as he inserts the metal cylinder.

Her legs begin to shake beneath the paper sheet.

They'd warmed it at the emergency department when she was examined after her last miscarriage—a small act of kindness. Why doesn't he? She'd like to ask him, but not now.

"You may feel a slight pinch."

She does. Dr. Sharpe eases the now warm speculum out of her.

"Alright!" he says enthusiastically, as if they have scored a touchdown together. He places an extra long Q-tip inside a plastic tube, and then he assists her in sitting up.

"This should go off to the lab today." Stripping the latex gloves from his hands, he tosses them into the garbage can. "I don't expect anything abnormal to show up." He begins to wash his hands in the tiny bar sink.

"What about sex."

Turning from the sink, he looks at her slyly, as if she might be a very naughty girl.

"What about it?"

"Well," she says, angry at herself for the second flush that she knows is working its way up her neck, "Billy ... *we* wanted to know if it would be okay for us to go ahead."

"Certainly. I'll write out a script for birth control pills while you get yourself together." He dries his hands with paper towel. "Come into my office once you're dressed."

She waits for him to slip into the next room. Socks, under-wear, sweatpants, nursing bra, turtleneck—returning layers of dignity. When she is fully clothed she goes to the mirror above the sink. Her face and neck are a blotchy patchwork of red, pink and white. No dignity there. She pulls a piece of paper towel from the roll, folds it and wets it with cold water, press-ing it hard against her flesh. There. Better. She knocks on the connecting door to Dr. Sharpe's office.

"Come in."

His desk is a topographical triumph with only her chart—a paper version of herself—spread open before him. He motions to a chair in front of his desk while penning something in her file. Faith tries, but fails to read upside down.

Dr. Sharpe dots with a flourish. He nudges a folded piece of white paper toward her—the prescription, and then he closes her cover. Pushing his chair away from the desk, he looks her up and down, as if she might be hiding something, possibly behind her back.

"How are things going for you emotionally, young lady?"

When he didn't bring it up during the exam, she thought she'd gotten away with it—she should have figured feelings would be discussed across a table rather than when she was on top of a table with her legs splayed.

"Fine," she says, hoping that less is more.

"You are aware that Dr. Kline has been sending me prog-ress notes since you started with her?"

"Yes, she told me." Dr. Kline had asked her permission, in fact. Why had Faith given it? Faith had never questioned Dr. Sharpe's abilities when it came to diagnosing her physi-cal ailments—pneumonia when she was six, sprained ankle when she was twelve, hives at fifteen, but emotional pain? Not so much. A week after the baby was born, she'd come to see him—sleep deprived, weepy, guilty of feeling over-whelmed, of not being happy. His solution? Get Billy to give the baby a bottle, go for a walk, take a hot bath in Epsom salts.

"Are you satisfied with her approach to the post-partum depression?" he asks now, poking her in a different way.

Shifting in her seat, Faith wonders if she could ask Dr. Kline to stop sending Dr. Sharpe updates.

"I'm not thrilled about the medication, but I'm already functioning better with it than I was without it."

"If it had been up to me, Faith, I wouldn't have involved Dr. Kline, but since Billy took you to Emergency, it was their call. I'm surprised, quite frankly, that she put you on any medication, believing as she does that the root of all mental illness is the 'bugaboo' of childhood trauma. It may sound old-fashioned, but sometimes depression is simply depression." His hands swoop together, crash-landing on her chart.

It comes to her, then, about his teenage daughter—must be twenty years ago now—an overdose, wasn't it?

He stands. She follows his lead.

"If there is nothing else, we'll see the baby in two weeks for her first needle." He shepherds her past his secretary, who hands him the next file. "Has she got a name, yet?"

"No, not yet, but we're getting close." They aren't close at all, but the fib is like a vitamin supplement—people seem to need it.

They reach the waiting room. Glancing down at the file tab, Dr. Sharpe dismisses Faith with a name. "Irene Chalmers?"

An elderly woman startles in her seat, hoisting herself up with the aid of a cane.

"And how are you today, Irene?" Faith hears him ask, as she boots her feet and coats her body.

"Not dead, yet, Doc, not dead yet." Her voice crackles like fat in a frying pan as matchstick legs carry her across his threshold.

THE EXHUMATION

REWIND: My father is returning home on the rain-slicked 401 from a four-to-twelve shift at the Pen, when a wheel from a transport truck flings itself into our lives. He is forty-three. The OPP officer informs my mother and me that death was likely an 'instantaneous event'. For some reason, people in our town seize on this seed of information and attempt to plant it in our minds as a comfort.

"At least, he never knew what hit him."

Maybe it was over for him in an instant, but he is still dead. He will not be there to dance with me when I graduate from junior high in June. He will no longer be there to watch my back when my mother is being stubborn. He will not kiss me goodnight again, or put a rose at my place setting on the morning of my next birthday. I say these unbelievable things to myself. I don't know when I will believe them.

I cause a scene on the second evening of his wake, a scene which my mother always manages to bring up on special occasions such as birthdays, Christmas, weddings or christenings.

"Remember," she'll muse, as recently as yesterday when she was having dinner with my new boyfriend, Jude, and me, "poor Mrs. Flagg?"

Of course I remember Mrs. Flagg: old as time, a fixture at all Catholic wakes and funerals; husband deceased, children AWOL The grim reaper in a shiny, black, polyester dress and spike-sized silver crucifix, making my father's death a reality for me, because if she is present then this must actually be happening. Here she is, breath reeking of alcohol (gin, I think), grabbing hold of *my* hand with her claw, declaring *my* father's death to be a sin and a shame but at least comfort could be taken in the fact that he did not suffer.

I bite her ancient, bony wrist.

I don't break the skin. There is no blood. It's meant to be a warning: *don't mess with me any more.* I don't understand why she is making such a fuss. Neither do I understand why the Knight from Columbus, who has sat all evening next to my father's closed casket, a puffed exotic bird in his regimental uniform and feathered cap, feels duty-bound to escort *me* from the room.

"He's *my* father," it feels so good to screech, as he drags me into the papered hallway, "why don't you make *her* leave? She's nothing but an old drunk! She didn't even *know* him!"

My mother follows on the Knight's heels, taking control, steering me by the elbow into an empty visitation room where she slaps me across the cheek. When I bring up The Slap during my mother's reminiscences over The Bite, she always argues it was meant to calm me, but I know she did it out of embarrassment. I can still see her, slim in a tailored black suit, a double strand of pearls, pinching the flesh of both my arms beneath their sleeves, leaving bruises: "You will go back in there this instant and *apologize* to Mrs. Flagg. Your father might be gone, young lady, but we still have to live here!"

She calls it 'swallowing my pride' but I have come to view it as stuffing my grief into a backpack of rage. I offer a sullen apology to the old bat, which I don't mean, a fact that I'm sure both my mother and Mrs. Flagg recognize. They simply choose to ignore it because that is what adults do.

The Exhumation

My mother wears her widow's weeds with remarkable ease. People express amazement at how well she is handling everything: her husband's sudden death, the funeral arrangements, the finances, the difficult teenage daughter (that's me). *She is an example to all of us*, I overhear Father Simon's remark at the gathering in the Kinsmen Hall, after the funeral. I want to bite him too—he obviously does not know about the Valium—but of course I do not. I sit quietly while people sample sandwiches and Nanaimo bars. I do not make a sound.

FAST FORWARD: Mrs. Flagg lives. I serve her with regularity in the liquor store. We make and break eye contact almost simultaneously as I take her cash. Sometimes, when no other customers are near, I growl.

PLAY: I pull into my mother's snow-covered drive. God is fielding another sick joke. She is in the open doorway, completely naked, skin like wrinkled tissue paper, sagging breasts, white pubic hair, black patent leather purse slung over a skeletal shoulder.

"Take me to see your father."

REWIND: The obsession blooms in spring on the heels of a withered relationship. My mother tentatively mentions to me a guy she's been seeing, a few months after I move to the city to attend college. I meet Hal over Christmas. He seems nice enough for a man who is not my father. I get a call from my mother's neighbour in April while I am studying for a marketing exam: "Sunny? It's Marjorie Henson. I'm in the emergency department at the Dieu with Florence. She's had a nasty fall."

Someone has beaten her up. I know this as soon as I draw back the curtain. Broken nose, arm in a cast. Eyes not meeting my face.

I fell from the ladder while cleaning out the eavestrough. Can you believe it?

No. Neither does Marjorie. But we are adults, so we play along. Hal disappears from the language.

She starts to visit my father's grave: on Sundays at first, after mass if the weather is decent. It's soothing. Peaceful. She can't think why she's never done it before. *He really has a nice plot, Sunny, on a rise near a lovely old maple.* Describing it to me as if I had not been there to see him planted.

FAST FORWARD: Florence extracts the pictures from her purse, spreading them out on the kitchen table for Jude to better appreciate. I can't watch. He applies his hand to my forearm as I excuse myself from the table, sliding fingers to my wrist, squeezing gently, before giving his full attention to the photographs. This is when I know I will marry him.

REWIND: We meet in my second year at the campus bus stop. *Nice shoes,* he says, before stooping to tie my laces. Jude is studying criminology. He wants to be a policeman. He's always wanted to be a policeman. He takes me to his apartment and shows me his collection of miniature emergency vehicles. I sit on the edge of his perfectly made bed, legs swinging gently, back and forth, and spill my father into his lap. I don't prepare him for my mother until we are lovers. *She's going three or four times a week, now: digging, mulching, fertilizing. She plants bulbs for the spring, annuals for the summer, Mums in the fall. She takes pictures. She'll show them to you if you ask. Don't ask, okay?*

PLAY: "It's freezing outside Mom," I stamp my feet in a dramatic fashion and blow on my own arthritic hands, hoping to trigger her memory, "you'll have to bundle up if you want to go see him."

Yes, her absent self remarks, as if she is trying to recall ingredients to a complicated recipe that she has not prepared for a long time. A glint of understanding. Then, *I'll get my coat.*

REWIND: *There's something wrong with Grandma,* our brilliant, med-student son declares, while home on Christmas break. *I tried to play cribbage with her and she got mad and threw her cards at me. I don't think she remembers how to play.*

Out of the mouth of babes. It takes months to get a definitive diagnosis. By then, it really doesn't matter.

PLAY: She wipes snow from the top of the gravestone with her mitten-covered hand. *He was a good man, a good husband.* She can no longer remember his name. We stand like statues for perhaps another five minutes, neither of us speaking and then, *I'm hungry.*

BLIND

THE FIRST THING SHE SEES is the last thing she expected to see—stubble on Doyle's cleft chin. A hank of charcoal hair drapes over one bloodshot blue eye, concealing the scar. He is palming her hand. She can feel him turning her wedding ring round and round her finger like a steering wheel.

"What do you see, Cissy?" Doyle's voice tired, hopeful.

Cecile closes her eyes, runs her tongue between teeth and gums, unsticking her mouth.

"I see a man in need of a shave."

"Open them again. Open them for me," he croons. He should know she is past all of that.

A cold, wet, softness slides down her cheek, shocking her eyelids open. A single, yolk-yellow tulip falls away from her and comes to rest on the blue surgical gown between her breasts. Same old Doyle.

She tilts her neck, takes back her hand, brushing the sticky, black piston with her fingers.

"It's so yellow."

"Yes, it is!" He sounds like Mrs. Chelwig, Jake's patronizing kindergarten teacher. "It's from the garden."

Her garden, not his. Not anymore.

"So are these," he adds.

A blur of colour explodes in her face: red, purple, pink, green. She winces and closes her eyes.

"What's the matter Cissy? Are you in pain? Do you need a nurse? Here, let me call a nurse." He reaches for the call button attached to the sheet by a safety pin.

"No! Don't bother the nurses, they've got enough to do." The surgeon, the pamphlets, neither had truly prepared her for this coupling of pain and sight. "Just put them in the water jug."

Doyle turns away. His broad shoulders curve beneath his brown, leather jacket as he bunches the tulips. She considers reaching over to give his cheek a pinch just below the ripped back pocket of his designer jeans but knows he would take it as a sign.

"Ta-dah!" Doyle squeaks on two-hundred dollar heels, his arms open wide, his fingers unfold like petals. His wedding ring is back. Cecile follows it to the tulips. Her eyes narrow, expecting pain. The colours flood her visual field. She takes a deep breath.

"I could spend hours looking at these."

"You used to say the same about me." Doyle's bottom lip plumps out, his top lip disappears—the classic Doyle 'pout'.

"Flowers know when to die," she says.

"Ah, but tulips always return in the spring."

How many times have their conversations steered this way, she wonders, back and forth, tit for tat until they hit a rock cut? No winner, just damage.

"Who's got Jake?" Doyle enquires as his voice and body drift toward the window.

"My mother. I can hardly wait to see him. She's bringing him with her this afternoon to pick me up."

"And does Audrey still adore me?" He fingers the curtain, lifting it away from the glass to stare down at the lake. Cecile knows the lake is out there. The RNA's remarked on her 'lovely view' last evening as they led her to the bed. Maybe when Doyle leaves she'll get up and drown her eyes in it.

"She thinks you're perfect, Doyle, you know that. A perfect shit."

His black head tilts back, his mouth opens and he laughs too loudly.

"Well then, that makes two of us, Cissy. God knows I've treated you shabbily." 'Shabbily'. Which nineteenth-century novel is he lecturing on now, she wonders.

He closes in and reaches a tentative hand to her head. Capturing several strands of her hair between two fingers, he extends the lock to its maximum length, regarding it for a moment before relinquishing it. She used to love when he played with her hair.

"Have you thought about what we discussed before the transplant?" His blue eyes hold her new corneas in traction.

"To be honest? No, I haven't, Doyle. The operation and Jake, what I'm going to do with my life now that I have my sight back. Those have pretty much been my priorities."

He looks petulant. Good. She could watch him squirm on his belly for an eternity. The last one was seventeen, for Christ's sake.

"I've got to run," he says. "I'm teaching in twenty minutes. Tell Jake I'll be there on Saturday. Nine AM sharp."

"I'll tell him." Once she sees Doyle's fast, little car idling in the driveway.

"KATHERINE WALLACE."

The name drops like a sandbag onto Cecile's chest.

"You're kidding."

"No, I'm not. Katherine Wallace."

"The one on the news? The one who had her throat slashed in Scarborough? Outside that women's shelter?"

"That's her. I heard everything went: heart, lungs, kidneys, liver. She was an excellent candidate."

Candidate.

As if Katherine were running for office.

"What's wrong, you look like you've seen a ghost."

"I knew her."

"Go on! Really?"

"A long time ago, when I was younger."

"And wiser?"

"Yeah, right."

"Life is full of surprises," she says. "I've written down her parents' address like you asked. I managed to scrounge some notepaper and an envelope. You'd better get those protective goggles back on or you'll have to stay after class!" Her beeper goes off. Even the volunteers, it seems, need beepers these days. "Oops. Gotta go." She drops the paper and envelope next to the water jug. "Nice flowers," she calls back over her shoulder.

"I'M KATHERINE WALLACE," her grip is a tense surprise.

"Cecile."

"Glad you decided to join us, Cecile. We've got paint and brushes here, cardboard too. We did some brainstorming earlier and came up with some words of wisdom for our chauvinistic friends over there," she cocks a light brown afro in the direction of the co-ed dorm while slapping a damp piece of paper against Cecile's palm. "So, grab a brush and express your outrage." She reaches up on sandaled feet, claps Cecile on the shoulder, then returns to a sign already in progress: "*Brains are beautif*".

There were four. Cecile makes five. Five righteous females in a parking lot, answering a call to arms. Cecile had hoped for more. She reads her palm: 'Brains and Breasts', 'Men Are Pigs', 'Every Woman is a 10', 'Breasts are for Babies'.

'Every Woman is a 10'. Cecile streaks red, painted letters six inches high and tries to summon the rage that must be inside her. They'd only awarded one ten so far this year: to a second-year med-student thrusting up her middle finger as she walked past.

Cecile stands and transfers asphalt grit from her hands to her backside. Damn! She's misspelled 'every'. Her knees give way. She flips the cardboard. By the time she is finished a second clean copy Katherine and her followers have threaded string through their signs and are ready to march.

Katherine, bathed in sunlight, puts her arms around the neck of the tall, flat-chested, Nordic-looking girl and kisses her pale, wide mouth.

What is Cecile doing here? She dresses in kilts and penny loafers. She has a school ring. She wears a bra and believes in lip gloss. She likes men. Why did she come out?

Katherine is the reason—the way she took over the common room yesterday afternoon, flicking off "The Young and the Restless" and jumping on top of the round coffee table, calling for the women of Victoria Hall to unite. She'd pressed strips of paper detailing the time and place into each of their hands and left. Someone turned the soap back on. Crumpled balls of paper appeared on the carpet like mutant popcorn. Not Cecile's. She had felt something.

"Here, Cecile," Katherine offers her enough twine for a noose.

"I'll carry mine." Not wanting to bleed red paint all over her blouse.

"Let's move out!" Katherine leads them through the parking lot and down the block, chanting. People stop and stare. Cecile raises her sign to the bridge of her nose. There are eight of them sitting on the steps to the entrance of the coed dorm with two cases of twenty-four. The catcalls begin immediately.

"Hey, titless, ever heard of Silicone Valley?"

"What's the matter dykes, are we cutting in on your territory?"

Their numbers come up: three, point-zero-five, two, eight, one. Cecile looks at the black-haired boy holding up the eight and smiles. He raises a nine. She laughs. He holds up a ten.

A hand clamps her above the elbow and she loses her grip on her sign.

"Just what are you trying to prove?" Katherine seethes from behind.

"I'm sorry, Katherine. He made me laugh, that's all."

"Why don't you just go over there and chug back a beer with him then, eh?"

"You dropped your sign." It's him, coming to her rescue with his black hair and blue eyes.

"Go to hell!" Katherine's sign sails into his forehead, opening a three-inch gash. He puts a hand to his head and crash-lands on his bum. It might appear comical but for the blood.

"Look what you did!" Cecile screams. The men whoop and yell. A beer bottle explodes on the sidewalk beside Katherine spraying beer up her unshaved calf.

"Come on girls, let's split." Katherine calls. "Are you coming Cecile, or what?"

"NO!" She struggles with the straps of her knapsack aware that the other men are gathering around her.

144

"The name's Doyle," he extends his bloodied fingers. "Doyle Gilbert."

Cecile pulls out a sanitary pad and applies it to his forehead.

"Oh man, that's sick," one of the others says.

"You're going to need stitches, Doyle."

HE MET HER for their first date in the common room with a ten inscribed on a file card glued to a Popsicle stick. She remembered feeling warm and flattered.

Over fish and chips, he offered his past with the vinegar. A native of St. John's, he'd said, where his mother worked like a dog, his father drank like a fish when he wasn't out netting them. Doyle had been both smart and lucky, hooking a mainland university scholarship. Otherwise he'd be in the same sinking boat. He would never go back, he said, holding her hand across the table, swallowing her with his blue eyes. Never.

She mentioned her mother and brothers in passing as she traced his lifeline with her finger. What about your father, he'd asked. We never talk about him, she'd answered.

He'd lit a cigarette afterwards saying he'd like to quit. She could help him with that, she'd said, looping his chest hair around her index finger—she was studying to be a nurse.

FIVE-POINT-TWO.

It was a joke, Doyle whispers in her ear. *You're making way too much of this. It must be the hormones.*

We shouldn't have had Jake. Doyle's last desperate line of defense as she lies with her back to him, his Post-it note tucked between her knees. *I don't know how to be a father—it'll never be the same.*

Tears track silently down her cheeks. Jake is three weeks old. Blood and love drain from her body.

DEAR MR. AND MRS. Wallace: I am sorry for your loss…

She'd given Doyle false hope the other night before her surgery.

Dear Mr. and Mrs. Wallace: Thank you for the lovely set of corneas. They will make it so much easier for me to get around…

She'd almost said yes in a panic as he sat beside her bed wetting her hand with his tepid tears. What if the operation failed? Her disability insurance would be gone in two months. The house would have to be sold. Where would she and Jake go? Her mother had made it clear that they could not stay with her; her nerves would never be able to stand it.

Dear Mr. and Mrs. Wallace: Did Katherine ever mention she was a lesbian? I let her down once and now I see through her eyes.

Sight changes everything.

She can go back to nursing. She won't get full-time, not like before. Still, she can pick up enough shifts to get by. Maybe she'll upgrade, become a nurse practitioner.

Dear Mr. and Mrs. Wallace: Your daughter's generosity of spirit has given me the gift of second sight.

That's it.

There will be no more chances. She'll call it quits, for good this time, when Doyle comes by for Jake on Saturday.

SEEKING LIGHT

"THER-A-PEU-TIC TOUCH," he says, stretching syllables.

Tori's knuckles whiten as she pours tea into Russ's *Star Trek* mug, but she lets it go. He pouted for two days after her cross-examination of aromatherapy.

She hopes the tea is strong enough—it's hard to tell with these herbal varieties. Russ is not one to criticize. He never complained while in hospital about the tea, the rubberized toast or the lukewarm, scum-laden vegetable soup. Tori did— out of earshot and away from his monitor and IV drip. Going so far as to present the head nurse with a written list of concerns—lousy food, dirty linen, dust bunnies under the bed. The staff had come to loathe the sight of her. Too bad.

"The practitioner simply passes his hands over the pathological area and *presto!* the symptoms are relieved. Fascinating! There's a weekend introductory course being offered in Toronto after Christmas. I'm thinking of attending."

They sit in the rejuvenated breakfast nook at the harvest table, purchased last fall before the first, mild heart attack. The triple-paned windows, bordered by stenciled ivy, were installed last spring after the second, more punitive attack.

Hunter-green valances hang above the drawn-up blinds. The early morning sun illuminates Russ. Tori can differentiate each, individual strand of hair on his fuzzy, greying head. His white terry cloth robe falls open to the navel, revealing scar tissue and two folds of baby-soft flesh. The rolls don't bother

147

Tori—the scar does. She has run a fingertip along the seam only once since Russ's return home, allowing the V.O.N. free reign when it came to dressing and cleansing the stubborn incision. Crisp and hard by the time she could bring herself to touch it, reminding her of the dead husks of skin left behind by snakes.

"I thought physio three times a week was enough but, if you think this 'touch' business will speed your recovery... "

"What, me? No, no! You don't understand. I want to *offer* therapeutic touch to my patients after I return to work. Who knows, it might even alleviate your pesky hot flushes."

"They are under control, Russ." The words slip cool and clipped from her mouth.

Flavoured teas, meditation, massage therapy—she's half-expecting him to announce a pilgrimage to Vancouver next. Why should therapeutic touch come as a surprise? Russ is no longer his plodding pragmatic self. He has shed that skin.

Tori checks her wristwatch: 7:25AM She needs to be inside Julia's classroom in twenty-five minutes to scan the daybook before the students begin the slow dance to their seats. Julia runs a tight ship. Tori probably won't need Wordsworth ... still, better safe than sorry.

Russ's hand wanders across the table to make contact with hers. His fingers feel warm, but not too warm, not like the first few days in hospital when he spiked a fever and the nurses made casual references to pneumonia in front of her.

"What about dinner?" Russ asks.

Tori removes her hand from his, tucks it between her knees.

"Don't concern yourself. I'll pick something up."

"I could do that... "

"It seems silly for both of us to be out, Russ. Besides, we agreed I would be your co-pilot for the first while when you started to drive again, remember? I'll get a roast chicken from the deli on my way home."

"Well if you're sure … "

"Positive."

"What can I do around here? Laundry? Dusting? What?"

"Nothing, Russ. Just rest." *Rest, damn it!* Tori's eyes stray again toward the six-week-old midriff to collarbone scar, healing nicely now. Suddenly, she feels a childish urge to locate a pudgy, black marker and play connect-the-dots. Instead, she gathers her purse, overcoat and pumps, going to the mirror over the kitchen sink to inspect her bobby pins and foundation.

"Read a book, listen to the CBC, watch television, go sit in the backyard but bundle up, there's a chill in the air. The last thing we need is you catching your death."

"You don't catch your death, Tori, it catches you."

He's being peevish. She ignores him.

"Whatever you do, don't lift an-y-thing." Her turn to enunciate.

"Yes, dear."

He's sloughing her off!

"Russ, you *do* know how lucky you are to even be here, right?" There, it's out. She's been thinking it ever since he woke up in recovery babbling on about tunnels and lights.

"I'm sorry." He comes into view from behind. "Perhaps I just need to play doctor again." He kisses her lightly at the nape, pressing a familiar stiffness into the small of her back.

"This is not the time, Russ." Matching stiffness for stiffness.

"I know." He smiles at her reflection, backs off and returns to his mug.

"Is Sally still here? I could give her a lift." She offers, knowing her daughter would prefer torture at the hands of some distant, militant faction.

Russ shakes his head.

"Gone. Basketball, remember?"

"Right, I forgot. How does she keep track? Basketball this morning, drama club last night, babysitting for the Lakes the night before ... "

Russ shrugs his shoulders.

"She's fifteen. She's busy."

"But I haven't seen her for two days!"

Mustang Sally—named for Russ's favourite song. Tori wasn't fond of it then, still isn't but she'd named William and Jennifer—it was only fair.

"Stop fretting. Be thankful she has all of these interests. It proves she's evolving."

Evolving yes, but into what? With her black storm trooper boots (Jennifer *never* wore those), her pierced navel, and 'in your face' attitude. Tori found birth control pills in her panty drawer last week. She hasn't told Russ.

"What are you teaching today?"

"Grade Ten English. Julia's class."

"You'll see Sally today, then."

"Maybe, maybe not. She always sits behind some pimpled, gangly boy when I'm at the front of the class."

Russ laughs, reaching out to slap her backside as she walks past him and out the kitchen door to the driveway. Laughter, playfulness—all part and parcel of Russ's metamorphosis.

The surgeon had said to expect depression, had cautioned her not to take anything Russ said to heart. Perhaps he'd been fielding a pun. Sure, there had been pain, colossal pain— she'd thanked God every day for morphine. But depression? Not Russ. It was Tori who couldn't eat, Tori who couldn't sleep, Tori who lost weight and wept into her pillow at night because she couldn't count on being home long enough to ensure that her blouses and dress pants were coming out of the dryer wrinkle free.

She parks the van across from the high school—a brick waffle of a building sprawling the entire block. She's been invited to use the teacher's lot behind the school but Julia has had the finish on her car keyed twice there. Better safe than sorry.

A gaggle of leather-jacketed teens mill about at the end of the block near the butt-bin, smoking a last cigarette before the bell. Damp hair, hands in and out of pockets, heads down, shuffling their feet. One of them might be Sally. Tori averts her eyes—birth control pills being enough of a revelation for one week—and crosses the road, entering through the main doors.

Tori stops at the office and obtains a classroom key. Nostalgia intrudes as she walks the hall. She and Russ were students here thirty-four years ago—high-school sweethearts, walking to class side by side, aching just to hold each other's hand. Of course, none of that was allowed back then. But now? Why, it's all up for grabs. Julia told her over a recent luncheon about two students caught doing it right in the computer lab.

"Can you imagine," Julia had said, snorting into her green salad, "locking loins in a room full of hard drives?"

She'd considered saying, *I can't imagine locking loins anywhere with Russ being the way he is*, but censored the thought before it reached her lips. She didn't mind taking Julia's job on occasion, but she could do without her pity.

Tori nods at a young teacher as she inserts her ancient key into a rusting lock. Shirt, tie, earnest, clean-shaven face—he must be the one teaching European history—the one Sally has dubbed "Herr Dweebmeister". However, to a fifty-two year old female in the throes of menopause he appears no older than the students.

None of her teachers are still here. All are dead or entombed in the nursing home with her father. Tori sometimes catches a glimpse of Mrs. Lawrence (geography) shuffling down the hall in bedroom slippers as she sits patting her father's blanched fist, seeing her reflection in the brown irises of his dead-fish eyes. Each week a harried nurse will stop by while she is at her post, turning him to prevent bed sores, assuring her that it will not be long now. Father Simon has administered last rites twice, still he lingers. What could be worse than having one foot wedged so firmly in the grave? Perhaps when Russ is feeling better he can go to the home and whisper what he thinks he's witnessed into her father's ear, give him the nudge he needs to let go.

Julia's daybook lies open to Nov. 1st:

Dylan Thomas
"Do not go gentle into that good night"
Silent reading and class discussion.
Good luck! Julia.

That's it? One poem? Julia has lost her freaking mind! Thank God she brought the Wordsworth.

Tori hasn't got much time. The photocopy room will be jammed. She opts, instead, for the library photocopier two doors away, returning to the classroom with five minutes to spare, cradling a sheaf of handouts. The flutter of anxiety she felt when she first looked at the daybook dissipates as she slides a bit of Wordsworth onto each desk.

"Occupied students make for productive students and productivity is the goal for any competent supply teacher." *That has a professional ring to it*, Tori thinks. Her philosophy has stood the test of time. Julia confided over the same green salad that Tori is considered the number one choice for staffers now. Tori felt both flattered and relieved. With Russ's illness and William and Jennifer at two different universities on opposite coasts, her earnings have become more than just pin money.

Her popularity as a substitute could have translated into a permanent position this fall. Julia had urged her to go for it, but at her age a full-time job would be more of a curse than a blessing. Besides, there is Russ to consider.

The bell rings as she slips the last page onto an empty desk.

"SALLY?"

Tori has just recited the poem out loud after allowing the students to struggle with it for five tortured minutes. The usual snickers at the mere mention of the word 'gay' in the fifth stanza, which she squashed by raising and slowing her voice while making eye contact with those responsible. And now she has invited them to offer their impressions.

Sally is first to droop in her seat. The others follow suit in a wave, treating Tori to the usual chorus of dry coughs, chair leg scrapings and the irritating beat of a pen on a desktop. No eager, little hands grope for the ceiling.

"Sally?" She says it louder. "Start us off will you?"

She gives her daughter her most encouraging supply teacher smile. Sally knows what is expected. Whenever Tori fills in for one of her teachers they must go through an exhaustive post-mortem at the dining room table with Russ as chief coroner.

Why should I be forced to make your job easier, Mom? You get paid very well for what you do.

Money, which puts food in your mouth and clothes on your back, young lady!

Sally, just help her out for God's sake, it's no big deal.

Oh sure, you always take her side …

"Sally?" The smile has vanished.

Sally burrows further into her seat. A blackened boot slides into the aisle. Her blonde head swivels toward the window.

Tori envisions herself striding forward, slipping her fingers beneath her rebel daughter's dog-collar choker and wrenching her to her feet (Jennifer would never have behaved in this fashion!). The familiar, dreaded flush is beginning to work its way up into her cheeks when Sally's black, raspberry lips finally move.

What?

"I'm sorry," Tori cups a hand to her ear, "I didn't catch that."

"I said two things—I said he's sexist and a coward."

"Please explain."

"Which, the sexist part or the coward thing?"

"Let's start with the sexist part."

"Well, he never mentions women, it's all guys—wise men, good men, wild men, grave men…" Sally dismisses the page with the back of her hand.

"Maybe he was a fag, he does use the word gay." The gangly one who sits in front of Sally speaks out of turn. Tori waits for the laughter to subside.

"What about your second point Sally, Thomas' cowardice? Where is that demonstrated?"

"It's right here, three, no four times: "Rage, rage against the dying of the light." Isn't it obvious? He's afraid to die."

"Not afraid, exactly, more like furious. But then, none of us want to die, do we?"

"I bet if we could ask Grandpa he'd say he wanted to."

Tori's heart trips over this personal remark.

"Your grandfather is not the issue here, Sally. The issue is the poem and how we are to interpret it."

"Well excuse me, but isn't making the poem relevant to your own life part of understanding it? Ms. Cox says it is."

A pox on Ms. Cox! Julia will hear about this one over their next luncheon. The temperature in the room is rising. Tori walks between the desks fanning herself with Julia's copy of the poem.

"I disagree with Ms. Cox. A great poem's a work of art. A closed system, if you will. It doesn't need life support from us."

"Well *I* don't happen to think it's such a great poem. He's all wrong about the light, for starters."

Dylan Thomas is failing miserably as a fan. The flush advances—sweat beading on her forehead, her temples, the back of her neck. Dabbing at it with the palm of her hand, Tori walks to the nearest window and cranks. Cold air flows over her.

"Explain, please."

"It's simple. When Thomas talks about the light dying, he doesn't account for near-death experiences. My Dad, *your* husband, died in September and he saw the light. It didn't die, so obviously Thomas is wrong."

What? Tori turns from the window to face her daughter's glitter green eyes. *Oh no you don't, young lady, not here.*

"Sally…dear, your father did *not* die." She employs her most condescending smile, the one that means stop this nonsense before you embarrass yourself.

"Yeah, he did. His heart stopped."

Sally snaps gum.

"For a minute-and-a-half."

She's an overflowing toilet, Tori thinks, *spilling family business all over the classroom floor!*

"Stop it, Sally! He did not die! He's at home listening to the radio!"

Sally does not quit.

"His spirit wafted up to the ceiling and then he floated into the waiting room and saw us holding hands. Remember us holding hands, Mom—you, me, Jenny, Will, the blue-haired ladies from the volunteer prayer group?"

"I said that was enough!"

"And afterwards? He got sucked into a tunnel and saw this incredible light!" Sally's hands go up into the air and slowly squeeze to fists.

Silence stretches over the classroom. Tori's other students watch Sally with a mixture of wonder and skepticism. Sally's eyes come back to earth and focus on her mother.

"He told me. He told you, too."

Her words plow into Tori's forehead. She presses a hand to her temple.

"Get out!"

A pale girl flinches in the front row, but Sally doesn't waver.

"Go on! What are you waiting for? Get out!"

Sally shrugs and picks up her books. Her boots clip-clop down the aisle and after what seems like an eternity she vanishes.

Tori's clammy hands close the classroom door. Her body crosses the room. She eases the window shut, envisioning forty-one sets of eyes boring into her back, but when she turns to face them, no one is looking at her. Instead, they blink down at their desks, look out the windows or make intense scribbles in their notebooks.

There is more shuffling of feet.

Tori coughs, clearing her throat.

"We will now turn to Wordsworth . . . "

SHE PARKS THE VAN, grabs the roast chicken and bolts into the house. It is three-thirty-seven on the longest afternoon of her life. Her head feels like an unbalanced washing machine set on spin. She steps into the front hall and listens. If Sally is home Tori will leave—she's too angry, too tired to hash it all out right now. Humiliation and outrage have pummeled her throughout the day, whenever she felt adolescent eyes trailing after her down the hallway or the unusual silence as her students filed into class.

Sally will pay.

Her weekly allowance is going to the local food bank. Tori will not be footing the bill for Driver's Ed. in January either and Sally needn't expect any help from her when it comes to paying extra auto insurance for the van. Still, it is not enough. This is Russ's fault. Why did he have to go and burden that child with his post-operative hallucinations?

"Russ?" Tori carries the cooked chicken into the kitchen. No Russ. She spots his battalion style parka through the breakfast nook window—ten meters from the house, beneath the large, bare maple tree and atop her carefully raked pile of leaves. His legs protrude from the parka, bending slightly at the knee. The hiking boots she bought for him three years ago, Christmas—the ones that, until now, had never made it out of the box—are touching the ground at the heel.

He's dead.

Three strikes and you're out, Russ had cautioned, after the second heart attack, gripping her hand through the metal bars of the hospital bed.

His arms are crossed, coffin style. She wonders, as she approaches the kitchen door, whether Russ has made life easier for the Solace Funeral Home mortician, expiring with his arms placed just so. How long does rigor mortis last? She and Russ have had this morbid discussion in their other life, while curled on the couch eating popcorn and watching old Perry

Mason reruns, but now, stepping out onto the cedar deck, she is annoyed by her inability to remember.

As she floats down the stairs, two blue jays hurtle past, taking possession of the miniature pagoda bird feeder—Russ's project while on the bypass waiting list. They land and immediately begin to peck at each other, ignoring the seed. Tori looks from the birds to Russ. His eyes stare fixedly at the sky but she can see, even from this distance, that the tip of his nose is clown red.

"Russ?"

She is beside the funeral pyre of dead, brown leaves. How did she get here so quickly? Her knees buckle. Russ's head rotates toward her in slow motion, as it does sometimes when she enters his study to wake him from dreaming. Tori's hand stretches out to graze his stubbled cheek, checking for fever, finding none. He looks too damned peaceful, smiling up at her as if she has sprouted wings. Something breaks and without thinking she hits him, square in the chest, surprising herself and making him wince. He captures her balled hands before she can do it again and covers them with his own.

"What are you doing out here, Russ?"

His face becomes that of a little boy caught whizzing in the sandbox.

"I got bored in the house. I thought I'd come outside and add to your leaf pile, but it turned out to be too much for me, so I sat down for a minute."

"In a pile of rotting leaves?"

"Correct."

"You weren't sitting when I saw you."

"No." He scratches his head, grabs her forearm and lets her pull him upright. "No, I wasn't."

"You scared the shit out of me, Russ." Tori uses her quiet voice. She wants to scream at him, but then the neighbours might hear. Besides, she suspects that yelling at him will unlock a tidal pool of tears and Russ still needs her to be strong. He's not out of the woods yet.

Russ becomes preoccupied, brushing leaves from his backside, buying time, before stretching a guiding arm across her shoulders. He intends escorting her back to the house, but her knees will not cooperate. He's not getting off this easily, no sir! She wants answers. He feels the resistance.

"I'm not dead, Tori," he whispers into her ear. "And I'm not going to die. Not yet."

His words are a warm, rising promise.

"Then what were you doing? And don't plead fatigue because we both know if that were the case you would have gone inside like the lazy man you are and flopped on the couch."

Russ laughs his new and improved laugh—the infectious one that rumbles up from his toes, laying waste to an otherwise smooth, untroubled face. She stamps the ground.

"Stop it! None of this is funny! None of it! Don't you get what you've put me through this past year? What was I supposed to think when I saw you lying there?"

He becomes serious.

"I'm sorry. I wasn't thinking about you finding me, I ... " And he tilts his head to the side, nodding over her shoulder.

"It was the way the sun was filtering through the branches of that maple. It felt familiar, like that other light you don't want me to talk about."

Here we go with the goddamned light again.

"*Your* daughter talked about it in class today, in front of everybody."

"She didn't!"

"She did. Can you imagine how that made me feel?"

"Oh, I've got a pretty good idea." He looks seventeen again for a second—sheepish, yearning, determined. Something gives.

"I think we'd better talk about it now, Russ."

"You do?" His genuine surprise embarrasses her.

"Before Sally takes it to a talk show. But not here!" looking toward the neighbour's yard. "Inside. Come on."

Grasping his autumnal hand in hers, she leads him like a child toward the house.

THE BIG PICTURE

CONNIE STOPS DRUMMING the steering wheel with her fingertips to check her wristwatch—Jerrie's train is now fifteen minutes late—nothing for Connie to do out here but wait.

Slouching down in her seat, she glances into her side-view mirror. Bob Paget Jr.'s cows are across the road, their peaceful heads grazing greenness. The scene could be rendered nicely on canvas with a dark palette of oils—indigo blue, slate grey, muddy brown, raw sienna, a touch of cadmium yellow to brighten things up—an afternoon in the country with easel and brush—no wristwatch, no worries—just her and Nature.

Right. She can't remember the last time she felt the urge. Not since secretarial school, not since she and Clay made it official, and certainly not since the birth of her boys.

She should have brought *Valencia's Vineyard* from her bedside table. A romance novel purchased on impulse, four months ago, after her mother's stroke. Despite repeated attempts, Connie cannot get beyond the second chapter.

She is a failed romantic.

Perhaps the problem lies with her reading in bed. Perhaps she would have more success with *Valencia's Vineyard* if she transplanted it to the glove compartment of her van. Then she could read in the stands during the boys' soccer matches and baseball games. Yes, but how would that look? A mother with her nose in a trashy bestseller, rather than her head in the

161

game? One thing is certain: if *Valencia's Vineyard* was here with her right now, she wouldn't be staring out at the unmanned railway station, committing each shingle of its steeply pitched roof to her memory.

The station was treated to a vinyl facelift eight years ago, before being closed down altogether. As a courtesy, the trains continue to stop outside the abandoned station twice daily, coughing up a stray passenger or two. Rarely do they arrive on schedule.

This train will be no exception. Connie looks at her watch again—twenty minutes eaten up, just like that!

She hears the putt-putt of a small engine. Here comes Bob Paget Sr.—ten yards to her left—rolling up to a couple of rusted cattle cars on his spiffy new John Deere lawn tractor. The lawn tractor was offered to him as an inspired pacifier by his son, Bob Jr., who, acting on the advice of the OPP, 'misplaced' the keys to the real tractor and his father's black Chevrolet truck after the 'incident'. Stroking his grizzled chin, Bob Sr. stares down at the gravel on the far side of the tractor. His upper body bends away from her for a moment. He reappears holding an accordion length of grey plastic tubing.

What is he up to?

He does not seem to be waiting for the train.

The last time Connie came out here to retrieve Jerrie the train was an hour-and-a-half late. She reaped the benefits of her sons' boredom on that trip because they were barred from school due to rampant cases of impetigo: Joey and B.J., jumping up and down in the back seat before climbing out of the van to pee endlessly into the tall blond grass growing unchecked next to the station house. They were whipping stones across the road at Bob Paget's unsuspecting cows when the train finally pulled in. A man had been hit and killed, her sister explained, as Joey and B.J. 'helped' to haul their aunt's matching luggage across the opposite track. An escapee from the Brockville Psychiatric Hospital, it later turned out.

Surely nothing like that will happen this time, Connie is thinking, when she spots the single headlight of a passenger train off in the distance. Isn't it traveling a little too fast? It barrels past at full speed. Damn!

Bob Sr. catches her eye and shrugs his shoulders, his face lifting into a weather-wrinkled what-are-you-gonna-do grin. He points to his watch-less wrist, then to the track, signaling that another train will be along in due course.

Connie smiles an unsure thank you, wondering how long it will be before Bob Jr. is forced to walk into the nursing home and grovel for a bed like her father, Mutt, had to do with Beryl. It is unlikely Connie will run into Bob Sr. if he does end up at the nursing home. Dr. Mills doesn't expect Beryl to survive the weekend—though her mother has managed to fool all of them on more than one occasion, beginning with her stroke—and once Beryl is gone, Connie has promised herself that she will never return there.

A long blast of horn followed by three staccato blasts.

To her right, at a kilometre-and-a-half distance down the track, is her sister's train, already slowing. Hallelujah! Bob Paget Sr. putts away, keeping to the graveled shoulder, his mission apparently accomplished.

The four-car passenger train comes to a pig-squealing halt. The door to the third car opens to reveal a dark haired young man in a Prussian-blue uniform who drops a set of courtesy stairs to the track before lowering Jerrie's luggage to the ground. Jerrie follows closely behind, her mouth going a mile a minute. The steward takes a moment to throw his head back and rock from toe to heel to toe in a full-blown belly laugh.

Retrieving his stairs, he steps back up onto the train. "You be good now!" he calls, as he slides the cabin door shut, the train already beginning to pull away down the track.

Connie walks around to the back of her van. Fridays are half days at Barnum and Beech, so she has come out here to the station after an afternoon of uninterrupted sanitizing and deodorizing in baggy-kneed sweatpants and one of Clay's tattered "I Am Canadian" T-shirts. The house looks great. She looks like hell. Opening the hatch, she watches Jerrie trip delicately across the tracks in a mauve suit and matching high heels—only one bag this time. Still, it is the biggest one she owns—she is incapable of surviving a weekend without six changes of clothes, half a carton of cigarettes, her deluxe makeup case and, of course, expensive gifts for Joey and B.J.

"Hey, you!" Connie says, kissing Jerrie's powdered and perfumed cheek with more enthusiasm than she feels. "How was the trip?"

"Uneventful," Jerrie replies. "Have we got some time before you pick up the kids? 'Cause I could really use a cigarette."

"Sure."

Jerrie pulls Virginia Slims and a gold-plated lighter out of a miniature purse. She encircles the cigarette with her lavender lips and drops her head, cupping slender fingers around the flickering flame. When the cigarette is successfully lighted, she caps the lighter, throws her head back and flips her blue-black comic book hair over her shoulders. Connie tracks the wispy trail of her sister's exhaust as it breaks up over the top of the van. For Jerrie, smoking is an art form. It is pure devotion. She will never quit.

They stand apart and size each other up in the old cautious way. You're looking good, been working out? Yeah, some. Have you lost weight? Yeah, a little. Jerrie takes a few more drags from the cigarette before dropping it to the gravel.

"It's my new system for cutting back," Jerrie explains to Connie's one raised eyebrow as they get into the van. She tosses the cigarette pack onto the dashboard. "You can't let me have another one until five-thirty."

"Whatever you say, you're the boss."

Pulling out onto the county road, Connie accelerates, which causes the entire front end of her aged van to shudder. She informs Jerrie that it needs a new head gasket, but that Clay is holding off—money has been tight since he bought the old Irving place. He got it cheap. He plans to gut it, renovate it and sell it, fast. Still, it amounts to a second mortgage hanging over their heads until the real estate agent can sweet talk some city transplant into signing on the dotted line.

"How are the boys?"

"Oh fine, you know, the usual. Complaining about the summer program I've got them in, but happy to be out of school. Excited about your visit. Joey informs me that you're going to teach him how to play poker?"

Jerrie smiles. "The kid is a natural. Did he tell you that I want him to come to the casino when he turns nineteen? I'll introduce him to my boss. He'll have himself a job dealing cards in no time."

Jerrie has tended bar at the casino de Hull ever since it opened. She regards it as a step up from her old workplace in downtown Ottawa, where most of the clientele were bitchy federal government employees, coming in to displace their inter-office angst with complaints to her about diluted Scotch whiskey, too much smoke, or the cloying drunk sitting to their right.

"How's the casino? Do you still like it there?"

"Hell, yes. You know, last week, I had a guy slip me a hundred dollar tip? A retired sheet metal worker diagnosed with liver cancer. He won fifty-four hundred at the crap tables. 'Here you go, darlin',' he says to me, 'I can't take it where I'm going. Get yourself something 'perdy.''"

"What did you buy?"

"Lottery tickets."

"A hundred dollars worth?"

Jerrie nods.

"Did you win anything?"

"No." Jerrie laughs, shrugs her lavender shoulders. "Ah well, easy come, easy go."

"What did Stu say when you told him?"

"I didn't. We live together, he doesn't own me."

Connie enters the north end of town, passing by Blodgett's car dealership, the Home Hardware, and a newly constructed tenant-challenged strip mall. Jerrie gets around to the subject of Beryl.

"So, how's Mom? Has there been any change since we talked Wednesday?"

"No, no change. Dad spoke to Dr. Mills last night. He's still convinced it'll be soon, today, tomorrow."

"She's only sixty-six."

"I know, but once the kidneys go, it's time to let nature take its course."

"She's not in any pain, is she?"

"No, no pain. They've got her pretty doped up. I can drop you there if you want, before I go to get the kids."

"Yeah, I guess you'd better."

BERYL PUT HER FOOT down in the spring of 1976.

She'd never liked the old place out on the highway, but she'd allowed Mutt to talk her into it because they were just starting out and it was cheaper than buying in town. Over the years she had come to discover that Mutt was not the least bit handy. She tried not to hold a grudge, but it was hard. The plaster walls were always cracking, the kitchen cupboards were plain old ugly, there was only one bathroom with no shower stall and they were forever priming the pump because of the shallow well.

The energy crisis added fuel to her fire—the rooms grew drafty, the ceilings too high, the thirty-year-old oil furnace expensive and inefficient. The house was going to be a bitch to heat come winter, she could practically see the dollar bills flying out the five-foot windows.

Beryl tossed Jeraldine and Connie in as kindling—teenagers now, always needing a ride to a friend's house, the school dances, their part-time jobs. Town life would be easier all around. Mutt could walk to work at the post office. The girls would finally get a chance to wear out a pair of shoes before outgrowing them. Beryl, who worked shifts for Ma Bell up in Kingston, would keep the new Corolla. They'd sell the old Ford, which was, let's face it Mutt, a gas guzzler and ready for the scrapheap.

They would put a bid in on one of those airtight, three bedroom bungalows in the east end of town. She'd had her eye on one for almost a month, but they'd have to move fast. In two years they would save enough money in heating costs alone to be able to afford a week, maybe ten days in Jamaica.

Buy small, live big, is how Beryl put it.

What could Mutt say?

They took possession on September 1st, with Beryl hyping the low maintenance exterior like a tourist attraction while Mutt, craning neck over shoulder, carefully inched the U-Haul down the slanted driveway toward the single car garage door. Beryl drew Connie and Jeraldine's attention to the honey glazed oak cabinets as they lifted scavenged liquor boxes onto the countertops. She ordered the three of them to shed their shoes and socks in the living room to become acquainted with the shag carpeting. One-and-a-half bathrooms made Beryl feel as is she'd died and gone to heaven. She'd never need to lift the lid off of a can of paint in the basement because of the wood paneling. Painting the rest of the house would be a piece of cake. She and Mutt had sex that night for the first time in six months.

Beryl found the hole in the kitchen wall the next morning when she got up early, intent on fixing Mutt a special breakfast.

"Why would anybody leave a calendar hanging up for two years? Oh my God! Mutt! Come quick!"

Detective Beryl stood in the middle of their newly mortgaged kitchen in her crumpled housecoat and fuzzy pink slippers. She stabbed an unlit cigarette toward the pothole in the gyproc.

"He must have driven her head clean through. Look, you can still see a few strands of hair. She didn't even bother to wipe away the lipstick! I heard he could be a real S.O.B. when he drank, but my Heaven's. You just never know, do you Mutt?"

Mutt had to agree.

He made three failed attempts to patch the wall before Beryl gave up on him. They would have to wait until they could afford to hire a goddamned professional. Until then, it would be up to her to figure something out.

Beryl's solution came from the grocery store, where every ten dollars spent brought her one stamp closer to a mass-produced 'old master' cardboard print of her choice, complete with real wood frame, while supplies lasted. She decided on 'Sunflowers' by Vincent. She would never be crazy about

Vincent or his sunflowers—Connie, at fourteen, could draw more realistically—but it did cover the hole and, more importantly, it didn't clash with Beryl's gold appliances or brick floor tiles.

Vincent and the Sunflowers started popping up all over town.

Connie took to announcing each sighting. Her best friend's mother had hung the painting in their bathroom above the toilet. Ms. Witherspoon, the gym teacher, had it dangling in her tiny windowless office. Connie noticed it in Dr. Mills' waiting area as she arrived for one of her bi-weekly allergy shots. She found it positioned above the change table in Jenn Morrison's room when she went there to babysit.

"Oh, and by the way, Mom? Vincent was his first name. His last name was Van Gogh," Connie lectured Beryl one evening as she set the table for dinner. "My art teacher says he signed his paintings that way because he didn't have a lot of self-confidence."

Beryl took another careful look at the picture as she poked the boiling potatoes with a fork to see if they were ready.

"Well, it's no wonder, if that was the best he could do."

Connie sighed and shook her head at her lost cause of a mother.

A few weeks later, Connie breezed into the house with an essay about Vincent Van Gogh featuring an unruly red 'A" in the top right-hand corner. She dropped it onto Beryl's lap as she sat knitting a tiny yellow sweater for the next Morrison baby, due in April.

"Here," she sniffed, "why don't you read this and get educated?"

Beryl neither dropped a stitch nor batted an eyelash.

"Perhaps I will," she replied, letting the report slide from lap to floor, "after I finish this row."

BERYL HAS BEEN gone less than six months when Connie's sixty-eight year old, widowed father announces that he is in love. Her name is Mae. She lives west of town, a stone's throw from Mutt and Beryl's first home. He's moving in with Mae next week.

Mutt listed the bungalow on January 2nd and was handed a solid offer five days later, prompting his envious son-in-law, Clay (who barely broke even on the Irving property), to wax poetic: Your goddamned father, Mutt/ Has horseshoes up his butt!

Despite the suddenness of it all, Connie has a good feeling about Mae. She has stepped nicely into the role of surrogate grandmother—Joey and B.J. are out at her place right now. And Mae and Mutt have a lot in common. They are the same age, born within days of each other, a fact which Connie finds extremely romantic. Both prefer country life, enjoying long walks along the highway, hand in hand, wearing their butter yellow slickers. Mae likes to bowl and play golf, two of Mutt's favourite pastimes. She was a letter carrier, too, working in town for a while in the mid-seventies before accepting a transfer to Kingston. She moved back to this area a couple of years ago upon retirement.

They make such a cute couple.

Jerrie does not agree.

She is convinced that Mae is a gold-digger who is after Mutt for his equity and their parents' hard-earned RRSP's. Jerrie informed Mutt of her suspicions over the telephone when he called on New Year's Eve to wish her and Stu a Happy New Year.

Mutt hit the roof, Connie has never seen him so agitated, and now he and Jerrie are not speaking, which has put Connie in the middle just like in the old days. Only then, it was Connie defending Mutt's muted point of view to Beryl as she pitched his soiled golf shoes out the front door or slammed the toilet seat down hard enough to crack it or threatened to call in a team of electricians because Mutt couldn't be counted on to change a bloody light bulb, much less a fuse.

Connie hates being in the middle. No matter how hard she strives to clarify the issues, everyone becomes angry with her. Take the sale of her parents' house and her father's decision to move in with Mae. Jerrie says their father is moving too fast. Connie told Jerrie that Mutt might not be making such a hasty decision if a certain someone had been able to keep her opinions to herself until she'd at least met the woman.

Now, every time Connie calls Jerrie and Stu's apartment, she is greeted by the bored, affected voice of Stu's pubescent daughter, Tiffany: Hi. Stu and Jerrie aren't here right now, but if you care enough to leave your name and number they'll try to reach you later.

She has left several messages.

—Hi, it's Connie, give me a dingle later on tonight. We need to clear the air.

—Hey, it's Connie, again. I want to speak to you, Jerrie, so if you hear this message please return my call as soon as possible.

—Jerrie? Are you there? Pick up … This is silly, you're acting just like Mom. Call me, okay?

—It's Connie. I'll be at Dad's all weekend clearing out the rest of his and Mom's stuff. If there is anything that you want you'd better let me know because Goodwill comes on Monday.

171

Better yet, why don't you stop this nonsense, get your ass down here and make up with Dad? That's all I have to say. Bye.

Jerrie has not returned a single phone call, but she did e-mail an itemized list: *my 11 x 14 framed baby portrait, the Collected Works of Sir Arthur Conan Doyle, Mom's wooden tennis racquet, my baptismal certificate, my half of the good china which includes six place settings and the gravy boat. (We flipped a coin, remember? You get the cream and sugar.)*

Connie has put it all aside, except for the baptismal certificate, which up until today she has been unable to locate. It was Mutt who suggested she check beneath the false bottom of the cedar chest that sits under her parent's bedroom window.

She meets with success—both baptismal certificates, hers and Jerrie's, rolled and ribboned, lying next to a rectangular, translucent, plastic container filled with bite-size pieces of coloured pastels, several small sketch pads, drawing pencils, paint-stained brushes and ten or twelve partially squeezed, curling tubes of oil paint. And beneath the container? She can hardly believe it—her high-school essay about Van Gogh, and Vincent's Sunflowers, warped slightly, but still in its original real wood frame. Connie smiles. Putting the essay aside, she lifts Sunflowers out. She touches her nose to its surface, closes her eyes and breathes in her adolescent self.

THE HOLE IN HER parents' kitchen wall stayed hidden behind Sunflowers until September of 1980. Connie remembers the date because it coincided with her enrollment in the Fine Arts Program at Queen's. After the wall was professionally treated, Beryl spent her spare time wallpapering and painting the kitchen, accepting minimal input from a colour-blind Mutt. Vincent's Sunflowers disappeared, replaced by a clock in the shape of a bloated oak leaf. Connie noticed its absence when she came home at Christmas to confess she wasn't cut out to be an artist. Now what she wanted, more than anything, was to become a legal secretary. Connie had not asked about Sunflowers. Beryl never offered.

Connie flips the print over front to back, curious to see if the four-line biography has survived. And there it is:

Vincent Van Gogh, 1853-1890: An artist of the Impressionist school. Although plagued by mental illness, he was still able to produce an impressive body of work in his brief ten-year career. Best known for cutting off his own ear, he committed suicide at the age of thirty-seven.

Below it, Beryl's careful upper-case printing: FOR CONNIE, THE ARTIST OF THE FAMILY.

Connie has a little cry, realizing in the process that despite its tackiness she has no choice but to display the print some-where. It is from her mother. Connie slips her sister's baptismal certificate into one of the cardboard boxes marked 'Jerrie'. She picks her own certificate up along with the art supplies, the essay, and Van Gogh's Sunflowers, and then takes one last look around her mother's bedroom before locking up the house and driving home.

Connie has no difficulty finding the stud-sensor, a hammer and a nail in Clay's immaculate basement workshop. The ques-tion is—where should she hang it? Walking through the rooms of her house, she glances down at the flowers, up at the walls.

The sunroom addition, built in fits and starts by Clay during low points in the construction business, is the obvious choice, given Van Gogh's fascination with light. It is also the location Clay will be most likely to criticize—I worked hard on that room and now you want to hang this piece of crap?

Well, it's her house, too. She'll lay it on thick—tell him it was a gift from the grave. She locates the stud in the sunroom wall and positions the print at eye-level. Then, like she's watched Clay do so many times before, she marks the spot with a flick of her pencil, and she hammers the nail home.

Dappled sunlight dances across Vincent's flowers. For a second, they appear to turn their droopy heads.

This would make a great little studio, they slyly point out.

Connie cannot help but agree.

BUZZ BOMB

DESCRIPTIVE PARAGRAPH by Dylan Lansing/English 9A/November 11th, 1995:

Grandma Hattie is a very important person in my life because she survived the bombing of London during World War II, and if she hadn't, I would never have been born! Over the years, she has shared many exciting stories about the war with me, but my favourite ones concern the buzz bombs, invented by German scientists. Buzz bombs were warheads carried by unmanned airplanes across the English Channel during daylight hours. The airplanes made a distinctive ticking sound while in flight, but when the ticking stopped, Londoners knew to run for cover because the sudden silence meant the bomb was about to drop and blow someone or something to smithereens. During the war, a person never knew when their number might be up, but Grandma Hattie has always maintained it never stopped her from living her life. Grandma Hattie is almost seventy years old now, and she still rides her bike 25 kilometres three times a week! I think that is fairly good for her age.

HATTIE LANSING, clad only in her peacock-blue overcoat, plastic rain-hat, and white walking shoes, reaches the end of her street as the first drops of rain begin to quench the pavement. Glancing upwards, she takes a moment to admonish the dark grey clouds for releasing their load earlier than forecast before proceeding to scramble over the knoll that curves in front of her eight-storey apartment building. The bag from the drugstore that she carries in her left hand contains two purchases —a small bottle of *Dettol* and a vial of artificial tears. In her mind she returns to the drugstore to reassess the advice of the cashier at the checkout counter, an underfed, inked young woman pierced at eyebrow, nostril and lip, jet-black hair framing a ghost-white forehead.

"Do you really need a bag, Ma'am? Why not tuck them into one of your coat pockets. That way the plastic won't end up in a landfill."

What are the landfills for if not to take our refuse, Hattie volleys back, garnering a dismissive sigh and a whispered 'Whatever!' from the little trollop.

Hattie is thinking about how much she loves the sound of the word 'trollop'—it reminds her of England, of home before Canada became home, and of how her grandson's generation seem to prefer 'ho', as if a woman of questionable morals could be confused with a gardening implement, minus the 'e', of course—when her right foot slips from beneath her, the grass already slick from the weatherman's promised deluge. Regret immediately floods her mind—she should have continued around by the sidewalk instead of taking the shortcut over the knoll, she's too old to be climbing like a mountain goat— but regret, as usual, washes ashore too late. Down she goes onto her right knee, reconstructed by that wonderful man, Doctor Skelton, in 1997. Thankfully, her other foot does not lose traction, and with her right hand—the one without the plastic bag—clutching at a clump of lawn, she ends her downward slide. No harm done, but for the rapid beating of her heart and a dull throb located somewhere in the vicinity of her four-year old porcelain hip joint (also Doctor Skelton's

handy work). She'd best get up fast, or one of those cars zipping towards King Street on its way to the university campus
will stop to disgorge an over-educated Samaritan who will
insist on escorting her to the Emergency department, especially if they happen to detect that she is naked beneath her
coat. At eighty-three, having reared three unhappy, ungrateful
children, having spent thirty-five years under the thumb of
her now deceased ex-husband (yes, she outlived him and only
right that she should, the bugger), she feels that she has earned
the privilege to act in whatever way she damned well pleases.
Clothes, no clothes, breakfast for supper, television at four in
the morning. It's no one's business but hers.

But also at her age, she is keenly aware of what will happen
should the health care system express a renewed fondness for her.
Bye-bye apartment, hello nursing home. She's seen it happen
far too often with friends and acquaintances, the latest casualty,
Alice Martin of her bridge club—poor foolish Alice, signing
over all of her assets to that son of hers after Clarence's sudden passing. "I've never handled the finances, Clarence always
took care of that. Why, I'd never even been inside the bank until
Eddie took me to the TD and we got everything straightened
out. I get an allowance now, don't have to worry about a thing,
and Eddie's very generous, bless his heart." A slip in the tub,
two cracked ribs and a broken elbow, and darling Eddie had his
mother in a nursing facility before she could towel herself dry.
And Alice glad to go! Refusing to be a burden to little Eddie and
his double-D-cup bimbo of a wife—his second, the first one
having had enough sense to dump him after he invested thou-
sands in the slot machines at the charity casino located twenty
miles down the highway, outside the town that Hattie used to
call home. How could Alice be so gullible, so weak? Did everyone's backbone crumble as they aged, literally and figuratively?

Not Hattie's. Case in point—her son and daughter-in-law's recent plea that Hattie relinquish her flat when the lease comes due next month and take over that dingy apartment in the basement of their house. Tired of renting to strangers, they say, but still requiring the income, what with Terry's recent lay-off at the plant and Patricia's never-ending 'nerve troubles'. Hattie would be helping them out, big time, Terry says, and isn't that what family is for? Well, when did Hattie ever get any help from her family? *You made your bed, missy, now lie in it.* Her father's grim summation when she rang her parents, long distance, to say that her Canadian soldier turned small-town fire chief wasn't the man she imagined him to be. Thirty-five years she lay in that sodden, abusive man's bed, no one to help her, and then the bastard locks her out of her own house and moves his little trollop in, with the whole town lining up to take his side! It's a good thing Hattie had the sense to retain a lawyer or there's no telling where she would be now.

"Ma'am? Ma'am, are you alright?"

A voice hails her from the far side of the road, which is when Hattie realizes that, though standing upright with hands on her hips, prepared to argue all over again with Terry about why she will not consider moving back to that oppressive little berg, she hasn't budged an inch from where she first slipped. How long has she been standing here, back to the street, staring up at her building? Oh well, no matter.

"Ma'am, are you okay?"

Hattie turns to face her inquisitor—a bespectacled, blond test tube of a man, at the wheel of something low, dark and European.

"Never better," she says, throwing him a mock salute meant to put him at ease.

"Are you sure?"

"Absolutely. Now move along, young man," she says, waving her arm in the general direction of King Street, "before your misplaced concern results in a traffic accident. I assure you that I am as right as this rain falling down upon me." She feels a song bubbling up—*I'm singing in the rain, just singing in the rain*... Gene Kelly. Now there was a handsome man, and could he ever dance!

Oh, for God's sake, her Samaritan appears to have switched off his engine. He's opening the driver's side door, climbing out of his car.

"Are you lost?" he calls, striding across the pavement, narrow shoulders scrunched due to the rain, thumb and index finger pulling at a pink earlobe. "I'd be more than happy to offer a lift, if you can tell me where you live."

She's no fool—this is a test—he's attempting to determine if she is confused. Where do you live, what day is it, what year, can you name our illustrious prime minister? Oh, she'd like to box the ear that he is so tenderly pulling, and the other one too, for good measure. Who does this young man think he is? She can see hospital credentials dangling from what appears to be a shoelace strung round his razor-scraped neck—he's an intern, then, possibly a resident.

"I *am* home," she says, her voice too loud, since he is now only an arm's length away. She jerks a thumb over her shoulder "that's my apartment building right there. I live on the fifth floor, apartment 506. I have a sublime view of the lake, and a cat named 'Pebbles'."

How many more details about her life will she be required to divulge before this young man judges Hattie sane enough to be left alone? Perhaps he'll ask to see her papers, next—oh wait, that was wartime, except being old is like being in a war, isn't it, since there always seems to be someone eager to detain you, question you, tell you what to wear, where to live, how to dispose of your trash. To make matters worse, the young man's eyes have now traveled south of her chin, then caught the space shuttle straight back up to her face. A red flush is now advancing up the contours of his neck. Hattie glances down. Oh dear. The belt of her overcoat, cinched at the waist before she left on this little expedition, seems to have loosened during her tumble—it's not gaping wide, but obviously he's seen more of her girls than he was expecting. Her heart almost goes out to him. Poor pet must only be an intern if a bit of geriatric flesh can incite such an embarrassed reaction.

Hattie pulls the edges of her overcoat together and tightens her belt.

"Laundry day. I haven't a thing to wear," she says. It's a lie, of course. Her clothes closet is bursting with the fabric artifacts of her life—the burgundy suit she was married in, sweater sets brought over from England (which no longer fit), housedresses from the sixties (which do still fit, but are housedresses from the sixties ...), a pantsuit or two, a handful of dreadful sweatsuits that her daughter-in-law, Patricia, has purchased for her as Christmas gifts over the years, several pairs of navy, grey and brown elastic-waist polyester pants and shapeless cotton blouses that seem to be her lot in life, now that her waistline has joined forces with her hips—she just hadn't felt like putting any one of them on this morning. Truth be told, she found herself unable to choose between gray and brown pants, flowered or striped blouse. She had only needed to pop out to the drugstore to purchase the *Dettol*, which she required to mask the smell of urine that had recently begun to waft up from her favourite reading chair, and the artificial tears prescribed yesterday by her family doctor to keep her eyes from turning to stone. Twenty minutes walking the streets in her birthday suit. Who would be the wiser?

This young man, apparently—she peers at his credentials—Dwight … something, can't make out his last name. Dwight Blight. That makes her giggle. Of course, Dwight Blight has no idea why she is giggling, which causes her to snort and guffaw, which results in alarming the poor chap even more.

Dwight's lips purse together, having made their decision—he reaches out, splayed fingers firm beneath her elbow.

"Look Ma'am, it's pouring out here, and I'm running late. I'll walk you to the door of your building," he says, each word upbeat and glittering, as if Hattie were a child, or an invalid, or a feeble old woman. She tries once more to shake him off by appealing to his sense of self-preservation.

"But your car, your very pretty car … "

"Is fine. See, my four ways are flashing. We'll only be a minute. I saw your fall. I just want to make sure that you get inside safely."

A knight in shining armor—who would have thought they still existed?

"Well, if you insist … "

"I do."

He's right of course—it does only take a minute for them to reach the foyer of her building, and before she knows what is happening, Dwight has seated her in one of the foyer's overstuffed chairs that face the electric fireplace, and what's this—he's attempting to unknot the ties of her plastic rain hat. Such a decent young man—she's a bit sorry, now, that she made fun of poor Dwight's name, if only in her mind. She should offer him a tip—not the loonies from her change purse, which she is sure he would refuse, no, a life lesson tip, based on her years of … well, *acquired wisdom*—don't marry the first man who happens by just because he looks dashing in his Canadian uniform. Though, in Dwight's case, that bit of advice wouldn't translate, unless he's a tad light in the loafers. *Not that there's anything wrong with that*... God, she loves *Seinfeld*. Jerry and Elaine and Kramer and George—it's been in reruns for years, but their shenanigans never get old. What would she do without her television?

Dwight's lips are moving.

Pardon me? Well, that didn't make any sense at all. The urge to box Mr. Blight's ears is once again upon Hattie. Her left hand is game, but for some reason her right hand has welded itself to the armrest of the foyer's overstuffed chair and is refusing to let go. Her right leg appears to be similarly afflicted.

And now Dwight is speaking in tongues once again—his eyebrows are floating free on his forehead, which suggests that he is asking Hattie a question, but for the life of her she cannot understand a word. The Samaritan pats her right hand, then fishes a cell phone from the inside of his jacket. Hattie watches him punch 9-1-1, click, click, click.

Suddenly she is fed up with playing the part of a nice old lady who has accepted aid from a kind, young stranger. All she wants is to return to her apartment, so she can call out for Pebbles and have him curl his warmth around her calves as she secures the deadbolt behind her, and at Hattie's age, is that really so much to ask?

CATCH AND RELEASE

THE PHONE CALLS BEGAN in April—sporadic at first, then each night for two weeks in May. They petered out completely at the end of June, after Clarke's terse 3AM suggestion to Lou that she try phoning at a decent hour. Lou was in therapy, kicking a drug habit, and reaching out to her cousin, Gail, for affirmation and understanding.

Gail didn't mind.

Lou's calls made Gail feel needed, though not in the same way the children needed her, and not in the way that Clarke needed her. She felt visible when she spoke to Lou over the telephone, despite the fact that she could not see her own hand in front of her face—visible and valued. That's all.

Gail even went so far as to purchase a self-help book, the glossy cover of which guaranteed sound advice. She made it to the end of Chapter Three. By then, Zoe and Garrett were out of school. She hadn't heard from Lou in weeks. Soccer practice, baseball games, drama camp, science camp, the Art's and Crafts Club, power skating, music lessons. Who had time to read?

Lou's letter arrived with the fall round of stomach flu. Zoe and Garrett, hanging their helpless heads in cold-sweat misery over recycled ice-cream containers. Gail, pressing cool, damp cloths to the backs of their feverish necks, disinfecting tooth brushes, cups and spoons, scrubbing her hands like a surgeon, watching with perverse satisfaction as the skin on her knuckles cracked. Then Clarke, who had slept soundly through each germ-infested night, who had escaped to the relative safety of his orthodontic practice each fever-racked morning, fell ill.

Gail heard the clank of the mailbox lid as she prepared Clarke's diluted tea and salted soda crackers. She slit the envelope open in the ensuite, as Clarke groaned, sipped and nibbled in the bedroom—a note and a pamphlet. The note, scribbled in red ink on the back of a grocery tape: *Gail, why don't you leave those kids with their papa and come away with me for a weekend? I'll call. Lou.*

Pinecrest Lodge: On the front panel, a photograph of a couple riding an outcrop of black rock—lovers peering off through an intimate mist with nary a barf bucket in sight. A number of package deals offered inside, including a women's only weekend, which Lou had circled several times in red ink. Not cheap, not expensive, not long from now.

Funny how life is: if the telephone had not rung at that precise moment she might have shown it all to Clarke. They could have shared a quiet laugh together before tossing it into the white, wicker wastebasket. Imagine Gail leaving her family to go off to a cabin somewhere, for an entire weekend, with a cousin that she barely knew.

"Ms. Flannery? Dr. Premont's secretary calling with the results of your urinalysis." A ruffle of paper. "Congratulations!"

Looking at the couple on the rock as the words leeched into the walls of her stomach, Gail conceived a bloated belly, labour pains, hemorrhoids, breastfeeding, diapers, sleep deprivation—all over again.

She said nothing for two days, waiting to hear from Lou, waiting for a pasty-pale Clarke to rise, walk out the door and return to his dental impressions, spacers and braces, and to his perky new assistant, Daphne.

Gail announced her intentions over dinner as she cut Garrett's spaghetti.

"I'm going away for a weekend at the end of the month with my cousin, Lou."

Clarke pierced a turkey meatball with his fork. "And the kids?"

"You'll be here."

"Me?"

"Sure. Why not? You're quite capable."

He'd lifted the meatball to his mouth, chewing it over, staring at her while she stared back.

"Yes," clearing his throat, "I suppose I am."

LOU LIGHTS UP, inhaling through drawstring lips. Gail rolls her passenger-side window down another notch. It is Lou's fifth cigarette since they left Clarke standing in the circular driveway, with Zoe wrapped around his waist, and Garrett, clinging to his left thigh.

An hour and a half on the road—so far, it hasn't been too weird, despite Clarke's passive-aggressive attempt at sabotage as Lou's red, rusted, pickup truck rolled up to the house and she crossed the paved driveway on dime-store running shoes.

Perhaps we should have insisted on a urine sample.

She'd forgotten how much of a snob the father of her two children could be. Sure, Lou was down on her luck, but so what? It didn't mean that she couldn't be trusted. There was no time for Gail to challenge him—the kids were desperate for last second kisses and hugs, Lou was eager to hit the road and, truth be told, so was Gail. She let it slide.

And now, here she is, driving the road less traveled— Highway #2—with a cousin she has not set eyes on in over twenty years.

"Do you remember when we last saw each other, Lou?"

"Can't say that I do."

"I was eleven." Pixie-cut hair, breast-less nipples, training bra. "My parents and I came to Kingston for the day. It was just after Uncle Fred kicked your brother out of the house."

"I remember when Dad gave Sean the boot."

"You were wearing one of those red and white striped tube tops and hip-hugger cut-offs. Your hair was down to the middle of your back."

They had all been sitting around the kitchen table—Gail, her parents, Uncle Fred, Aunt Winnie. The men were drinking beer, the women sipped gin and Wink. Aunt Winnie, the solitaire junkie, had just passed a deck of well-worn cards to Gail: *Here honey, build me a house*, when Lou came in. Swinging a beaded, buckskin purse, chewing a wad of bubblegum, she jiggled past all of them on her way out of the house. No hellos, no goodbyes. Uncle Fred's massive belly propped the screen door open as he pretended that he was still the one in charge: *Be home by twelve, miss, or don't bother coming home at all!*

"You didn't spend a lot of time with us," Gail says, now. "I think you had a date, or something."

Lou snorts.

"Or something," she says.

"You were so beautiful—exotic, really. I remember wanting to be just like you."

Lou chuckles. She takes another drag—smoke in, smoke out. "How the mighty have fallen, eh?"

Fifty-pound weight gain, grey streaks tracking through her black hair. Lou's metamorphosis has taken some getting used to.

"You know, Lou, it wouldn't take much—a decent diet, an exercise regimen, some hair product. You'd be back to your old self in no time."

"My old self was kind of a bitch, if I remember correctly."

"Aren't all teenage girls?"

"True enough." Glancing into her rear-view mirror, Lou runs a hand through her hair. "That visit with your parents, it must have been just before my mom punched out."

Aunt Winnie's spirit enters the truck, her wrists oozing iron-rich blood: *Here honey, build me a house.*

"Yes, I guess so."

Gail looks to the window—bloated pumpkins, ravaged cornstalks, maple, oak and birch trees licked by fire. Her parents had attended Aunt Winnie's funeral. Gail was left behind with a neighbour. They never visited Kingston as a family again. Only last March, did Gail learn the truth. She, Clarke and the kids were visiting her parents over the school break at their Florida condo. They'd gone out for breakfast on her parent's dime—a grease fest at Denny's. Clarke wanted to know how old Gail was when she got her braces. Gail thought she was twelve, but her mother argued that she was eleven, employing her aunt's suicide as a touchstone.

—Remember, Gail? It was a couple of months after Winnie did that to herself.

—Did what, Mom?

—You know, dear.

—Mom, what are you talking about?

Suddenly, Gail feels light-headed. Fresher air is required. Rolling the window down all the way, she sticks her face through the opening. Autumn air rushes past at ninety kilometres an hour, causing the skin around her eyes and cheekbones to pull facelift tight. Can't see, can't breathe. Why do dogs enjoy this? She pulls her head back inside.

Lou glances over. She seems put out.

"You said you didn't mind about the smokes."

"I don't," pausing to swallow a splash of bile, "but I think the baby might."

"Baby?" Lou butts out, and then tosses her pack of cigarettes through the open window. "Jesus, Gail, why didn't you say something? I never would have lit up if you'd told me."

"I just found out, myself, yesterday," she lies. "Anyways, a little second hand smoke at this stage won't hurt a thing."

Lou doesn't look convinced.

"How far along are you?"

"It's early—seven or eight weeks—nothing to worry about, Lou. I've been through this twice before, I ought to know."

"Don't you mean you ought to know *better*?"

A long-lost, ex-addict cousin lecturing Gail on prenatal care? A change of subject is required.

"How's Uncle Fred? Mom said he moved to Arizona."

Lou takes the hint—there ain't no flies on her.

"Yeah, he got his pension from the Pen and split, must be half a dozen years ago, now. He's shacked up in a trailer park with some woman young enough to be my sister. Sean was down to see him last winter. Says he hasn't changed much— still sucking back a two-four every three, four days, still pissed about Sean's 'alternate lifestyle'."

Right. Sean's gay. The other piece of news gleaned from Mother over breakfast at Denny's: *That's why Uncle Fred asked him to leave the house, dear. You mean, I never told you?*

"Dad is never going to accept it," Lou says, now. "I don't know why Sean even bothers."

Gail knows. Right now, at age six, Garrett would do anything to win Clarke's approval, and that little boy is always going to be there, lurking inside the grown-up man.

The pickup abruptly slows to a crawl. Gail's hands rein in her purse. Lou points toward a cluster of wooden arrows nailed to a greying post: Pinecrest Lodge, painted in the same truncated black lettering as Ernie's Fishing Lodge, Stoney Lake Cabins, Water's Edge Trailer Park and Farley's Bait and Tackle.

"We are here, we are here, we are heeeeere!" she announces.

Manoevering around a yawning pothole, Lou turns down a similarly afflicted lane. Bumpity-bump. Gail needs to pee. She crosses her legs. Her eyes strain for a view of something, anything other than the canopy of red, orange and golden leaves, but the road continues to bob and weave. Creatures dart out in front of them—a black squirrel, a variegated chipmunk, something fast and brown—each squatting briefly before scurrying away. At last, a clearing. They pull up to an old frame house marked 'office'. Gail jams her hand between her legs like a child.

"I've really got to pee."

"There must be a john inside," Lou says, shooing her cousin out of the truck. "Go on, I'll get us registered."

Gail doesn't stop to appreciate the hard blue lake, the sagging docks or the tiny silver cabins that ring the neck of shoreline like beads on a child's necklace. She sprints through the office door.

THE OTHER WOMEN wear black rubber boots, pliant, faded blue jeans, and heavy woolen sweaters that stretch across their baby-boomer abdomens. Huddling together for warmth at the lake's edge, they murmur like a flock of congenial pigeons. Each one grips a fishing pole.

Gail and Lou have arrived late because Lou misplaced the key and Gail refused to leave until they could lock the door behind them.

One woman breaks away from the others and steps forward to greet them. She reminds Gail of the secretary at her old high school—the one who used to write out the late slips with a determined hand. Gail resists the urge to apologize.

"You must be the Flannery sisters," she says, offering each of them a pole.

"We're cousins," they both say.

"Well now, I didn't think you looked much like sisters!" She laughs, her eyes flitting from Lou to Gail, back to Lou.

"I'm Faye, by-the-by," and she sticks her hand up like a mime wiping non-existent glass. "Um, have either of you had experience running an outboard?"

"Plenty," Lou affirms. "My last man was a fishing guide near Picton. He took a swing at me with a walleye. That's when I split."

Faye's mouth blinks in an uncertain smile, revealing impossibly large teeth.

"Okay, then! I'm sure that you two cousins won't mind pairing up." Turning her back on them, she increases the volume on her voice. "We'll have two to a boat, as planned. Your bait and tackle are part of the package and are already aboard. You'll have three hours out on the lake, ladies, and please, remember to watch for shoals. You *will* be held responsible for any damage done to your boat." Faye casts a meaningful look over her shoulder at Lou, then turns back. "Now, let me see, did I forget anything? Oh, yes! There's a prize for the biggest fish. The lucky winner will receive a Pinecrest Lodge sweatshirt! That's a forty-eight dollar value, ladies. Let the games begin!"

GAIL THROWS UP over the side before they make it fifty feet from shore.

Lou passes her a stiffened rag from the bottom of the boat. "Do you want me to turn back?"

Gail catches a whiff of gas fumes from the cloth as she wipes her mouth and she retches once again.

"No," she says. "Give me a couple of minutes. I'll be fine."

She reaches inside the pocket of her jacket for a roll of mints. Offering one to Lou, she takes one for herself, and then closes her eyes, stick-handling the mint with her tongue, glazing the entire inside of her mouth.

Lou throttles down, shuts off the motor. They glide silently toward a miniature island overwhelmed by a three storey, glass-fronted cottage. Refracted sunlight hits Lou's face as she glances up.

"Somebody's got money, eh?"

She drops a pitted wheel of cement, attached to a fraying rope, over the side.

"I won't go any farther in case you need to pee or do the other," her hand swoops over the edge of the boat by way of explanation.

She passes a rod to Gail, and then removes the plastic lid from a Styrofoam container filled to the brim with convulsing black earth. "You want me to bait your hook?"

"Don't be silly," Gail answers, "I have been fishing before." With her father when she was seven, in order to qualify for her outdoor Brownie badge.

Lou's thumb and forefinger slide a third of the way down the worm's glistening body and pinch. She hands Gail the smaller, decapitated section. It wriggles and writhes in the palm of Gail's hand, but she shows no mercy, threading her hook through the center cavity.

"What would happen to fishing," she muses, "if worms were ever to evolve to a point where they could scream when pulled apart and impaled on a hook?"

Lou pulls her rod back, snaps it forward. Her line arcs upward, her worm takes flight, spinning through air for a few moments before dropping into the water thirty feet from the boat.

"It wouldn't matter. We'd fish just the same, only then we could feel like pricks about it."

Gail's attempt to emulate Lou's technique fails—her line drops five feet in front of her. She hates the word 'prick'.

"You don't seem to have a lot of faith in human nature, Lou," Gail says. "Is that what therapy has done for you?"

"You should try it sometime. Everybody needs to take stock once in a while."

"I'm doing just fine, thank-you-very-much."

"You don't seem too happy about having another kid."

Gail doesn't bite.

Lou reels her now blue and rubberized worm in, only to fling it out again. "I got caught, once. I was young, gullible. Don't remember much about the guy, but I sure remember the 'procedure'." She looks out over the quiet water.

A protective hand goes to Gail's abdomen.

"I could never do that."

"You mean you wouldn't consider it? Not for one, itty-bitty second?"

"No, of course not!"

"How is Super-dick feeling about it all?"

"Clarke doesn't know."

Silence.

"Well, it's not like you can't afford another one. Everywhere I look I see kids with their mouths chock full of metal. You two play your cards right, you'll be inviting me up to a cottage like that one in a few years."

"It's not money. It's time. Zoe and Garrett are both in school all day now. I was just starting to get out by myself again. I'd even thought about going back to work for Clarke."

"So? Get a sitter, what's the big deal? Lots of people do it. Hang on, I've got something."

Lou's rod bends. She pulls back, her reel clicking.

"Geez Gail, it feels like a friggin pike. Get the net!"

Gail yanks the net away from the side of the boat and stands, placing one hand on the aluminum edge. A wavy, watery self confronts her.

"It's coming, get ready Gail … Oh man, look at that," Lou's voice drips with disappointment as a striped back comes close to the surface, zigzagging back and forth. Gail watches her watery image give birth to an eight-inch perch.

"And I thought I had myself a keeper." Lou brings her catch to eye level. "You wouldn't satisfy my sadistic cat."

The perch's tail flaps back and forth, its mouth opening and closing over the ingested line.

"You swallowed the hook didn'tcha?"

Gail can't look.

"Pull it out, Lou."

"I'll try." Holding the line with one hand, Lou brings her other hand up from beneath the perch, her fingers splaying like a fin. "Let's see what kind of a mess you're in, little fella."

She tugs lightly on the line, and then pokes her index finger inside the fish's mouth.

"It's no use. I can't even feel the damned thing." She lowers the fish into the lake where its fins mark time with the current.

"Now what?"

"I'll have to cut the line, there's nothing else I can do." Reaching across Gail for the tackle box, Lou locates a set of embroidery scissors. "These should do the trick."

Bending out over the side, she sets up a rocking motion that brings Gail's head to her lap. "All done," Lou announces.

The perch descends like a striped submarine, out of sight. Lou rinses her hands in the lake. "Who knows, he might live to tell the tale."

She looks over at her cousin's bowed head.

"You feeling sick again? Want to go back?"

Gail nods, keeping her head low as Lou pulls up anchor and starts the engine.

"Geez Gail," she yells over the sound of the outboard as they putter back toward shore. "Are you always this much fun?"

The winner is a seven-inch sunfish.

"YOU WANT ANOTHER blanket from inside, Gail?"

"No, I'm cozy, thanks." She is touched by Lou's concern—a mug of instant cocoa, warm blanket across her shoulders, fire-wood from the cottage to elevate her feet. She can't remember the last time anyone took such good care of her.

"You've built a great campfire, Lou."

"Yeah, well, we all have our talents I guess." She skewers marshmallows onto two long-handled forks.

The hot fire rises to meet the cold, crisp night air. A net of stars twinkles above. The moon reflects on the lake's surface, shattering like fine crystal.

"How far could this fire be seen, Lou?"

"On a night like this? Pretty far." She plunges the fork past dancing flames to pulsing embers, turning it slowly. "Why, what's the matter Gail, you need to send an SOS?"

"No, I'm having a great time." She is ambushed by her own sincerity.

A burst of communal laughter lures her attention from their site down toward the beach, where black-silhouetted women sit like paper cut-outs in Adirondack chairs around a larger campfire.

"They sound as if they're having a grand old time," Lou says, offering her a blackened and smouldering marshmallow. Gail discards the carbon crust and licks the oozing center.

"Go down, if you like. I won't be offended."

Lou glances toward the beach and shakes her head.

"Naw, I'd feel like a gatecrasher now." She pulls off the outer skin of her marshmallow, popping it into her mouth. "Besides, I didn't see you all afternoon."

Three workshops had been offered as part of the package: Fine Stitching by Faye, Let's Do Pottery or Life-Writing. Gail opted out, preferring to steal a nap. Lou bummed a pen and returned three hours later clutching a fanned sheet of paper like the hand of a child.

A poem about her abortion. After insisting that Lou read it aloud to her, Gail had burst into tears.

"Jesus, Gail, it wasn't your fault," Lou had said.

Lou jabs at the fire now, with one of the forks. Sparks fly, wood crackles.

"For a woman who says she's fine, you seem awfully damned low, Gail. The way you reacted this afternoon . . . I know the hormones can get a little out of control when you're pregnant, okay, but geez, it was just a lousy poem! If you want to go back to work, go for it."

"Clarke doesn't need another dental assistant right now. He's made that very clear."

"So? There are plenty of other orthodontists in the sea, right? I bet that'd freak Clarke out, eh, you working for the competition?"

"I think he's doing something with her."

Lou stops poking the fire.

"Who?"

"Daphne. His new assistant."

"Something other than adjusting braces, you mean?"

Gail nods.

"Let me see if I've got this right—you think Clarke is putting it to his receptionist?"

"Orthodontic assistant."

"Whatever, and you let yourself get pregnant?"

"It wasn't well thought out."

"You got pregnant because you didn't have the guts to ask him a simple question? Gail, that's pretty messed up!"

Gail is crying again, absorbing tears with the sleeve of her jacket.

"It's more complicated than you think, Lou. I've spent the last eight years of my life changing diapers, learning the alphabet, going to play group, zapping aliens. I don't feel like me anymore. I didn't know how to ask him."

Lou pulls two more marshmallows from the bag. She hands one to Gail along with one of the forks.

"Well, honey, you'd better find a way."

THEY LEAVE IN THE morning after Gail throws up her scrambled eggs and sausage.

"Thanks for not smoking."

"Not a problem. I'd been thinking about quitting for a while. Should we stop for a pee?"

"No, I can make it."

"That sure was fun."

"Yes, very."

They take stabs at safe subjects: gay marriage, global warming, the Iraq war. Gail is ready to jump out her side of the truck by the time they reach the driveway, but Lou insists on releasing her where she was picked up.

Garrett and Zoe explode through the front door and squeal "Mommy, Mommy!" Clarke appears with a dishtowel slung over one shoulder. He smiles his approval as Gail is peppered with hugs and kisses.

"You're early. We just finished brunch."

"Daddy squeezed real juice from real oranges," Garrett announces. "*And* he made blueberry pancakes!"

"He needed help, though," Zoe sniffs. "He almost used a tablespoon when he was supposed to use a teaspoon."

"We weren't going to tell that part, remember Zoe?" His eyes twinkle over Zoe's head at Gail. "There are leftovers if anyone is interested," he adds, including Lou in his gaze.

"Thanks, but I've got to shove off. It was nice meeting you kids," she says to Zoe and Garrett, causing them to crowd in closer to their mother. "And you, Clarke." She reaches over and pumps his hand. "You've got a great gal, here. Keep it in mind the next time you and whats'ername ... Daphne, have to work late."

Ignoring Clarke's look of confusion, Gail peels Zoe and Garrett from her forearms. She follows Lou back to the truck.

"Why'd you say that?"

"Don't get your arse in an uproar, Gail. You said you didn't know how to ask him, remember?" Lou climbs into her truck. "I mean, what if you're wrong?" She begins to back down the driveway, then stops, sticking her head out the window. "I'll give you a call in a couple of weeks to see how everything works out."

GAIL SHOULDN'T HAVE EATEN the pancakes, but Zoe and Clarke were looking so proud of themselves when she walked into the house. How could she say no?

There is a knock at the bathroom door.

"Gail? Can I come in?"

Clarke. She retches again—a dry heave this time—which her husband accepts as an invitation to enter. Water runs in the sink, then stops. Clarke drops to the floor behind Gail, his weekend jean-clad legs encircle her. A cold wet facecloth adheres to her neck.

"Where are the kids?" she asks.

"Family room," Clarke says. "Watching a DVD."

His chin comes to rest on her shoulder.

"Is it the flu?" he asks.

She takes a long shuddery breath.

"No."

"I didn't think so."

Gail begins to cry. A waterfall of words escapes her mouth. Clarke's arms reach round her. Shushing her, he rocks them both side to side, which, though she hopes it is intended to calm and reassure her, only succeeds in making her feel nauseous again the way she felt in the motorboat with Lou—she really has had enough of puking for one day. Breaking loose, she un-spools a bit of toilet tissue to blow her nose, and then she waits for him to sink their boat.

"Look, Gail … she's really pretty, okay, but I'm not … I would *never* … When are you due?"

"May 1st, give or take."

His chin finds her shoulder again, but this time he keeps his hands to himself.

She sips some air, still waiting.

"So," he says, "when do we tell the kids?"

Gail closes her eyes for a moment. Resting her cheek against the cool lip of the toilet bowl, she listens as the tank refills with water until the sound of the water rising stops with a satisfying *thunk*.

BINGO

I WAS FOURTEEN when Grandma died—my first personal loss.

Liver cancer.

Quick and relatively painless, compared to the slow decay that we witness here, in our line of work.

One-by-one, she called up her daughters on the telephone—"I've got the cancer," the inveterate bingo player announced, "they tell me my number will be up in six weeks." Vintage Grandma—no histrionics, no melodrama—this is how it is, now please, let's just get on with it.

My mom, Alfreda, and her five sisters, determined that their mother remain in her own home until the end, took turns keeping Grandma company—Alfreda less often than the others on account of her full-time job and being a single mom and living two hours away.

I went with Mom the one time, before Grandma got really bad—she was yellow, all right, the whites of her eyes yolky, but she was still game for a round of cribbage with me. Not eating much, losing weight, but able to laugh and gossip, to be critical of her daughters, their husbands or lack thereof, while doting on her grandchild. Same old Grandma, I remember thinking, right up until Mom and I were about to leave. That's when Grandma crooked her index finger at me and led me over to her china cabinet—chockablock with knick-knacks and fancy tea cups that she had collected over the years—dust catchers, my mother always called them. Opening one of the cabinet doors, Grandma reached in and withdrew a ceramic figurine—someone's idealized version of a grandmother, I'd expect—white hair wound in a bun, black spectacles perched on the end of a tiny nose, a floor-length white and red polka-dot dress, a red apron, hands grasping a large, hollow, black cauldron.

"This is for you," she said, her voice, in hindsight, a little gruffer than usual. "A keepsake from your ol' grandma."

That was the last time I saw her alive.

I still have that figurine. Funny how a bit of dime-store porcelain can mean so much to a person, isn't it? I keep her on the dresser in my bedroom. I look at her often, and deposit this and that inside her black cauldron—mismatched buttons and single earrings, a cat's eye marble, a small tube of vanishing cream, a spent ticket from a Barbra Streisand concert, a nickel from 1929—that sort of thing.

Grandma's final days were difficult—I recall a number of one-sided telephone conversations between my mother and her sisters—morphine dosages, hemorrhaging, messing in the bed. When she died, we trekked back to Trenton for the wakes and the funeral. Stayed with my Aunt Marta and Uncle Rod because they had no kids and a spare bedroom equipped with a double bed, which meant my mother and I wouldn't have to sleep on an air mattress or worse. Three of my five aunts were doped up—glistening eyes drawn to half-mast, voices slurring. I got called 'dear' a lot. The creepiest thing was Mom's insistence that I accompany her to the casket, not only to view Grandma's corpse, but to touch it, as well.

"You need to touch her," Alfreda said, "so you will accept that she is really gone." Whereupon she placed her own warm hand on Grandma's rouged and unresponsive cheek, a gesture of affection that Grandma would never have permitted in life, and one my mother would not have dared to extend. "See, Barbie," she said, reaching for my hand, turning toward me with a crazed smile, "it's easy. She won't bite."

"Not anymore," I said. Yanking my fingers away, I disappeared into the washroom to bawl my eyes out in private, because that body in that casket was not my grandma.

Later, I found my way back to the casket, while Mom was outside the main visitation room comforting Aunt Marta— one of the two sisters who wasn't high on Grandma's leftover pain meds—and what I discovered was that I wasn't nearly as freaked out to look at her *by myself* as I had been with Alfreda hanging over my shoulder. She wasn't my grandmother anymore, that's true, decked out in an unfamiliar blue dress and creamy white blazer, but she *was* what *remained* of her and I would miss her very much. One of my aunts had tucked a handful of bingo cards into the V where the edges of the blazer crossed over Grandma's sternum. And for some reason, likely because Grandma loved her bingo so much, I decided that I needed to have a card to remember her by. So, when no one was looking, I reached out and pilfered one, planning to fold it up and hide it away inside the figurine that Grandma had given me when we'd last seen each other.

I still couldn't bring myself to touch her, though.

"I'M NOT NEARLY so squeamish now," I tell Chloe, before biting into a ham and cream cheese sandwich. We are seated in the staff room. It's well past midnight and we are ten minutes into our supper break. Somewhere down the hall, a resident's bell goes off—*ping, ping.* Chloe begins her Pavlovian response. Stopping her with a raised palm and a mock scowl, I finish chewing and swallowing.

"Don't," I say. "Let Marie get it. We're on break." Marie of the heavily penciled-in eyebrows, her hair teased and puffed, her face only puffy—the remaining staff member in our section on this skeleton crew. Two personal support workers and a practical nurse versus forty long-term care residents—thirty-nine, now—hardly a fair fight, even at night, but one that we have become accustomed to waging.

Ping, ping.

Chloe looks toward the door.

"Seriously," I say, "if you cave now, Marie and the others will exploit it. You'll never get a proper break." I point at her square plastic container and juice box, raise my voice an octave. "What did mommy make you tonight, honey?"

Chloe smirks at my dig about her living arrangements. She may be young, but at twenty-two, with no responsibilities and a full-time job, she's old enough, at the very least, to be making her own sandwich.

"Egg salad. But I'm not feeling very hungry."

"Is it Audrey?" I ask, referring to the recently deceased resident in room 204. Discovered, still warm, but no longer breathing by Chloe during evening bed check, less than an hour ago. We are waiting for Audrey's family doctor to drive in from his acreage on Golf Club Road to pronounce her dead before we contact the funeral home.

Chloe nods.

Her first death on the job—she hasn't been with us long—two weeks. I thought the story about Grandma would help, apparently not. These young ones—so full of life themselves, have a hard time embracing death—even in here, where so many of the residents long for an end to their misery. *Kill me, kill me now*—how many times have I heard that or something similar in the twenty years I've worked here? But I don't express my view. Instead, I try a softer approach.

"She was ninety-two," I say. "Blind, bed-ridden. Skin beginning to break down all over the place."

Chloe blinks rapidly.

"No family nearby to visit her."

The knuckle of one hand reaches up to block the progress of a tear.

"Yeah, I know, but she was just so sweet."

"She lived a long life, Chloe, she died in her sleep. What more could a person ask?" I take another bite of my sandwich, then reach over and pop the lid off her plastic container, the smell of egg, onion and dill wafting into the air. "Now eat," I say.

MY MOM WASN'T so lucky when her time came—too early, by anyone's standards—lung cancer at forty-nine. It took my breath away (it honestly did—I remember feeling as if I'd been kicked in the mid-section), along with any faith I might have harboured about a loving and merciful God. Never smoked a day in her life, though exposed to the second-hand variety for twenty-five years at the restaurant where she was a waitress— this was long before the government stepped in to ban smoking from public places. Who could imagine a world without the no-nonsense, always-on-her-feet-and-moving Alfreda, before she even had a chance to celebrate her fiftieth birthday?

I was twenty-nine when Mom was handed her death sentence—my daughter in grade five. I'd finally finished up my degree at night school and made the shift from part-time personal support worker to full-time practical nurse, which meant a steady pay-cheque and benefits, not to mention the promise of our own apartment, free and clear of Alfreda, at last.

"Don't get me wrong," I say to Chloe, "I loved my mother, but I didn't want to live with her for the rest of my life. She could be quite overbearing. Her way or the highway."

Multiple tumours the size of tennis balls in both of Alfreda's lungs, lymph nodes gone haywire in her armpits and neck, a couple of hotspots located in her cervical spine. The oncologist offered radiation to slow the progress, but he stressed it would only delay the inevitable, not influence the outcome. Mom would have none of it. She came home to die.

I stopped looking for an apartment.

IT IS NOW THREE AM—the doctor and funeral home representatives have come and gone. We are stripping Audrey's bed of its sheets, pillows and bedspread. In the morning, housekeeping staff will, for a fee, box up Audrey's personal belongings and put them in storage until a family member can claim them—her elastic-waist pants and flowered tops, her stretched out bras and ankle socks, the crocheted blanket flung across the shoulders of her red-velveteen sliding rocker, the framed black and white wedding photo positioned on a lace doily atop her dresser, the pig slippers—a gift from a granddaughter—which she never wore, but could not bring herself to throw out, a little clay bowl of smooth, coloured stones on her nightstand.

Once housekeeping has packed away these remnants of Audrey's life, the maintenance man will arrive. By five PM, the room will have received a fresh coat of paint. A new resident will be moved in the next morning.

I take the sheets, pillowcases and pillows, Chloe gathers up the comforter and we leave Audrey's room, closing the door behind us. In the morning, the news of her death will filter through the dining room before the hot cereal and toast have been served. Some of the residents will break down and cry, requiring a pat on the shoulder, a hug, if we have the time. Cassie Cross—eighty-five, confined to a wheelchair due to Parkinson's but still sharp as a tack, will carry on to anyone who will listen about the Angel of Death being amongst us. The Catholics will seek comfort in their crucifixes and rosaries. A few, lost inside their own minds, will have no reaction at all. After breakfast, a small parade of wheelchairs and walkers will pass by room 204, like motorists slowing down on the highway to gawk at an accident. Move along, the closed door will silently proclaim, nothing to see here.

"I remember when I came home from the nursing program that first time," I say, as Chloe and I head down the hallway to the laundry bay. "It was Christmas, I was eighteen years old and scared out of my mind to tell Mom I was pregnant. Well, she slapped me pretty hard, straight across the face. *It was supposed to be different for you, you were supposed to be smarter than that!* I thought I was."

I continue the story of my mother's passing as Chloe and I walk back toward the nursing station. How I cancelled our plans to move out and took a leave of absence from work. How I managed, with the help of the V.O.N. and Doctor Mills, to keep Alfreda at home in her own bed until her last rattling breath, the way she insisted it should be. How, in the end, the brilliant granddaughter whose embryonic existence Mom had cursed when she found out that I was carrying her, provided my mother with the only comforting proof that her life had not been a waste after all.

"Justine's in her second year of university now," I tell Chloe. "Full scholarship. Fingers crossed."

Ping, ping.

I glance down the corridor and locate the pulsing red light above Arthur Crown's door.

"Oh, oh, Arthur's got himself out of bed again. Have you met Arthur yet?"

"No," Chloe says, "although I've read about him in report."

"Well then, follow me," I say, before filling in Chloe on our most stubborn patient.

Arthur Crown—retired butcher, and long-distance runner, who, in his youth, nearly made it to the Olympic trials. Arthur did everything right—exercised, ate properly, drank moderately, never smoked—and yet here he finds himself at sixty-five with a neurological disease, as yet to be diagnosed, that has robbed him of his mobility—could be Parkinsons, ministrokes, Lou Gehrig's, or something I have not heard of. Never compliant about staying in his wheelchair, or ringing his bell when he needs assistance, he falls in his room on a daily basis.

Sure enough, Arthur is on the floor of his bathroom, pajamas pooled around his ankles, dry diaper at mid-thigh, a lump forming on the left side of an already bruised forehead.

"Arthur, Arthur," I say, going down on bended knee. "What did you do?"

"I needed to take a piss," he says.

"Go get Arthur an icepack, would you please, Chloe?"

After she has left, I touch the bulge on Arthur's forehead. He doesn't even wince.

"This is no way to live," he says. Encircling my upper arm with a large boned hand, his hold tightens like a blood pressure cuff. "I'd put a dog down long before now. Know what I mean?"

"Sure, Arthur. I understand."

I pat him on the shoulder, and peel his hand from my arm. Chloe returns with the icepack. Between us, we get tall, skinny, shaky Arthur back up on his feet and shepherd him to his bed. I point to Arthur's trophies and medals on a table beside his television, displayed there by his daughter from Vancouver on her most recent visit. "Why don't you tell Chloe about those," I say, before directing Chloe to stay with him for a few minutes, icepack to his forehead, until the lump recedes, or another bell goes off.

As I make my way back toward the nursing station to file an incident report on Arthur's latest fall, I finger an antique button in the pocket of my uniform—I found it on Audrey's nightstand in the small dish of shiny smooth stones, this was after Chloe came running to tell me something was wrong, after I pulled the sheet up and over Audrey's peaceful face, after I told Chloe to go back to the nurse's station and put a call in to Dr. Mills, long after I slipped the needle into Audrey's vein.

I've had enough. Please, let me go.

My mother all over again.

Black onyx, silver filigree all around—the button is very pretty—perhaps one of several that once graced a fine old blouse, but now singular. I will tuck it away in Grandma's little black cauldron with all of my other treasures.

No one will miss it.

No one will ever know.

CHILDREN @ PLAY

HALLOWE'EN AND IT'S Saturday night—that only happens once every seven years ... or is it every six years? Maybe it's six years. Maybe leap year messes everything up.

Chrissie asked Griff this very question last evening, as he was packing his lunch bag for the final midnight shift of the month before switching back to days. Lil' Griff had gone down for the night, finally, and Chrissie was about to settle in on the couch to watch a DVD—*Scream*, the original. *Is it every six or seven years, Griff?* The look he gave her. And what he spat out on the heels of that look: *Only you would give a shit about something like that.*

Mr. Grumpy-McGrump!

Now that the midnight shifts are over, at least for a couple of weeks, and Griff has had eight hours of uninterrupted sleep—Chrissie and Lil' Griff became nomads for the day, walking to the library, the town park, and after that, to her parents' place—the man of the house is in much better humour, looking forward to a couple of days off and to the Hallowe'en party tonight at Lisa and Taylor's. In fact, he was in such a good mood when he woke up that he offered to change the baby's diaper and dress Lil' Griff in his Koala bear costume while Chrissie rushed around, preparing her own costume and gathering items for the diaper bag, all of which has put Chrissie in a pretty wonderful mood herself.

Last stop before the party, the LCBO, and what a grim place it turns out to be—a reaper draped in black, Jesus Christ in sackcloth and prickled crown, Zombie Michael Jackson, a werewolf and Heath Ledger's Joker, all of them haunting the aisles and looking for booze. The older female employee, the one who generally mans the cash register, is re-stocking the Chilean wine section with an axe lodged in the crown of her head, grey matter trailing down the back of her blue shirt.

Clearly, Chrissie and Griff are out of sync with all of the dead, undead, and tortured souls in here. Griff, studying the whiskey section, is sporting the same tired costume he's worn since forever: blue face paint, Maple Leaf jersey and hockey helmet. Chrissie is clowned out in white face, a red nose, polka-dot bow tie, suspenders and baggy pants ... not up to her usual standards, but it hides the pounds she hasn't managed to shed since Lil' Griff was born, which is all that matters. Griff beats her to the checkout—*he's* not lugging a sleeping five-month-old koala bear—and sets down a forty of Canadian Club, which is definitely not the twenty-sixer they had agreed upon.

Behind the counter—the Phantom of the Opera, also known as Roy Thompson.

"Hey, Griff, how's it going?" Scanning the forty.

"Good."

"Your team's playing tonight."

"Don't I know it."

"Against my team—*les Habitants*."

"I feel sorry for you, then."

Standing in line behind Griff, cradling their son in one arm, a bottle of white *Fuzion* in the other, Chrissie cannot help feeling deflated. She has come to expect this guy version of small talk from Griff, but is that the best Roy can manage while dressed as the Phantom?

She saw him perform in the town park during the festival years ago now, must have been the summer before grade twelve.

She and Griff were broken up at the time, had been since before the prom, and she was with Cooper. Poor, sweet Cooper. Roy had performed *The Music of the Night* a cappella, his voice a pleasant surprise. Who knew a middle-aged manager of the LCBO could possess a hidden talent? He'd gone on to appear in a couple of community theatre shows in Kingston after that, which caused Chrissie's father, deeply suspicious of talent, to begin referring to him as 'the thespian'. *I'm playing eighteen with the thespian*, he'd say, injecting an extra 'th' into the middle of the word, until Roy got fed up with him and asked him to stop.

Would it kill Roy to sing a few bars now, or even hum something?

"Anything else, Griff?"

Nudging Griff farther along the length of counter, Chrissie places the bottle of wine in front of the Phantom.

"This," she says.

Scan. Roy adjusts his white silken tie, clears his throat. Staring down his half-masked nose at her, he shifts into Phantom mode.

"Air Miles, my lady?" Well, it's something.

"Sorry, no." She has a card—it's with her money, inside her purse, which is stowed in the trunk next to the diaper bag and the Pack and Play. A calculated move on her part—they'll run out of diapers by tomorrow and Griff never seems to have cash on hand when it comes to the baby. Video games, hockey sticks, the latest cell phone sure, but diapers, clothing, toys— uh-uh, that's her department, he says.

The least he can do is pay for the booze.

"$44.80, please." The Phantom selects two paper bags, one twice the size of the other. Whipping the larger bag open with an operatic flourish, he nestles the forty into place, surprising

Chrissie with a conspiratorial wink, before setting to work on the wine.

She glances at Griff—see that? There was a time, twenty pounds and one kid ago, when Griff might have taken offence to such a wink, even if Roy is a friend of her dad's and is way too old to mean anything by it. Griff's eyes are on her but not because of anything the Phantom might have done. He's looking for her purse. He wants her to pay. Sorry, honey, her shoulders mime. It's in the car.

"I guess the clown isn't paying," Griff says.

"Clowns never do," the Phantom solemnly allows.

Griff drops two twenties and a ten into the Phantom's expectant palm. Not waiting for the change, he lifts the bag trophy high and roars: "Let's party!" to no one in particular before charging for the exit as if heading for open ice. What a tool. If Chrissie's face weren't painted white it would be flaming red.

The Phantom gathers change from the register, tut-tutting under his breath.

"Boys will be boys," he says, tumbling coins into Chrissie's upturned hand.

"I remember when you sang in the town park, a few summers ago," she finds herself saying. "You were good."

"Well, thanks," he says, smiling down at Lil' Griff, who is still asleep in the crook of her arm. "Seems like a long time ago now, doesn't it?"

"Sure does."

Zombie Michael Jackson appears at her side—Peach Schnapps.

"You tell your dad I said 'hi'."

"I will."

*

212

In the two months since they've been together, Chrissie has accepted, for the most part, Cooper's habit of glomming onto her hand at every opportunity—walking along the main street of their small town, lining up at the movie theatre in Kingston, drifting through the Cataraqui mall, he's forever reaching for her fingers, claiming them for his own. It's sweet. It really is, but sometimes it makes her feel a little bit like a Chihuahua on a diamond-studded leash. Cooper reins in her hand now, as they settle onto the grass in front of the town-hall stage.

There is a bigger, professional stage down at the waterfront, with state-of-the-art lighting and sound equipment, a giant blue and white striped canvas bonnet stretching high overhead, but it's reserved for the real festival entertainers that show up every summer—Blue Rodeo or Great Big Sea, Randy Bachmann, or a totally hot Sam Roberts. Grumbling over the additional cover charge despite the purchase of a festival button, the crowds open up their lawn chairs and camp chairs and their umbrellas if the sky threatens rain, plop themselves down with their arms folded, and dare the musicians to entertain them.

This stage, erected on the lawn in front of the town hall, is not quite so grand as the waterfront one. Chrissie's father, a local fireman, has expressed concern about the solidity of its construction. Knocked together over a period of three or four days by a volunteer crew of sketchy unemployed labourers, he says it has the look of a gallows, minus the noose which, he allows, may be fitting when he considers the calibre of talent that is likely to be showcased.

A whiteboard easel has been placed at the bottom of the stage steps, red and white helium balloons are attached to either side of the easel by lengths of ribbon and the balloons float and bob in the breeze. On the whiteboard, printed in a dry erase rainbow of colours—the names of those who have come out to strut their stuff—six acts in all. The first act is the three death metal guys from school—Garth, Phil and Kev, who are calling themselves "What the Fuck"; shortened today, by order of the Festival Council to WTF. Chrissie saw them play last summer at Phil's parents' cottage, when she was still with Griff. She got really wasted that day, even smoked a joint or two with Phil's mom, who is way cooler than her own mom, so she doesn't remember much about the band's sound, but she does remember them arriving with a lot of equipment—guitar, base, drum kit, microphone stands, extension cords, speakers. Shouldn't they be setting up by now if they are the first act? After them it's a couple of old farts with fiddles, followed by "The Amazing Caroline"—a ten-year-old juggler in a silver-sequined jumpsuit and matching bowler hat. Then it's Roy Thompson, her dad's buddy—looks like he's wearing a Tuxedo—pretty fancy for a talent show, she wonders what he will do, followed by a clogging group. And then, Cooper. He hasn't told Chrissie what he's going to perform, despite her repeated attempts to tease it out of him. There is a guitar in a black gig-bag slung across his back, though, which should tell her something.

Despite the beautiful weather and the non-existent entrance fee, the audience is sparse. A few old people, who always enjoy getting something for nothing, have commandeered the three park benches that ring the stage. As well, there are a number of mothers with young children—some in strollers, others running round the stage and the nearby bandstand, up the steps, down the steps, up, down, oblivious to the dagger looks that the old folks are shooting them. Beside Chrissie and Cooper is a toddler—tight blond curls, massive blue eyes, sitting ramrod straight in his stroller, pointing out the red and white balloons to his mother. Me, mine, he says, sweetly. Me, mine? No, honey, no. Waaaaaaah! Me, mine! Me! Mine!

Cooper squeezes Chrissie's hand, inclines his head toward the stroller.

"Poor little guy," he says.

Yeah, right. Spoiled rotten, more like it. Chrissie is *never* having kids.

*

Griff's silhouette is hunkered down in the passenger seat, his head thrown back, chug-a-lug, by the time Chrissie and the baby reach the car. Chrissie is pissed. First, he embarrasses her in the liquor store, and then he starts pre-drinking?

Opening the back door, she nestles Lil' Griff into his infant car seat, don't wake up, little man, don't wake up. Straps over his shoulders, buckled in tight, tip the door shut—*aaaand* he's still asleep. Score, Mom!

Chrissie scoots round to the driver's side of the car, settling into the seat as Griff is screwing the lid back onto the top of the bottle. Her steady gaze is not returned, but she doesn't let that stop her.

"What about the talk we had?"

"Relax," Griff says. Bending forward, he slips the rye bottle back into the paper bag. "No shots when I get there. Just rye and ginger ale, like we said."

THE PARTY AT LISA and Taylor's is in full swing when Chrissie pulls up to the curb. Every window in their rented townhouse is aglow, and music pulses out onto the street. Chrissie will have to insist they turn the volume down. Baby eardrums, people. Baby eardrums.

"Oh man, looks like we're the last ones to get here," Griff says. Taking full responsibility for the liquor bag, he exits the car, slamming the door shut, which wakes Lil' Griff, who begins to cry. Griff is up the walk and inside the house before Chrissie can unbuckle the baby from his car seat.

Lil' Griff is really wailing—a little help would have been nice, frig! She'll have to send Griff out later to retrieve the diaper bag from the trunk.

"Come here, baby. You are the cutest koala bear ever! Look at you in your little costume. What a good boy, what a good boy!"

Three jack-o-lanterns glow outside the house—one for each of the concrete steps leading up to the door. She points them out to her son, one at a time. Look, Lil' Griff, look—*spooky*, but by the time she reaches the last one he has turned his attention towards the door and the music—a party animal just like his daddy.

Chaos inside, the usual suspects and a few she doesn't recognize. Music—Black Eyed Peas, now—loud, distorted and thumping. First things first—yelling in Taylor's ear—turn it down, can you please turn it *down*? Moving into the kitchen where emptied shot glasses form a drunken line along the counter, but also beer bottles, wine bottles, liquor bottles, and bags of junk food. Her two best friends, Lisa and Brittany, and Courtney Smith, whom Chrissie has never trusted because she is always giving Griff the eye, are dressed as three curvaceous little pigs—stubby piggy noses, velvety piggy ears, sparkling, feathery pink bustiers. They are making margaritas, blender swirling, but they take a time-out in order to create a minor big deal over Lil' Griff, passing him around while Chrissie locates her bottle on the counter and pours herself a big glass of wine. Lisa, her cheeks aglow, practically inhales a margarita as she is filling Chrissie in on the gross-out moment of her day, little Kiefer's naptime 'poo-splosion' in the crib—*I've never seen anything like it—shit everywhere! Crib, sheets, stuffed animals, up his back, in his hair, his ears. I almost lost it. Swear to God. Thank goodness my mom was able to take him for tonight.*

Leaving the kitchen, wine glass in one hand, baby on her hip, intending to head upstairs to scout out a quieter place to nurse, Chrissie wonders why Lisa or Brittany didn't ask her to be a little piggy, too.

STRAIGHT, GLOSSY BROWN hair, smooth, bared shoulders, bangles sliding down toned, coppery arms. Kohl eyes. A golden snake crown perched on her head.

"Oh my God, isn't he cute? Coop? Where's Coop? He *has* to see this baby."

Not only is this girl blocking Chrissie's access to the second floor, but now it turns out she is here with Cooper? Cooper is at this party with this girl and Chrissie is dressed like a clown?

Fuck my life.

Her name is Andrea—pronounced 'An-dray-a'—she hates it when people say her name wrong. She's a size two—does Chrissie know how hard it is for a tall slim girl to find clothes that fit? It's so much easier for the plus sizes these days, what with the obesity epidemic and everything—Andrea is a personal trainer, she knows what she's talking about. That's how she and Coop met—at the gym.

"I'm Cleopatra, in case you couldn't tell," she says.

"Of course you are." Chrissie smiles a fake smile, takes a healthy sip from her glass and swallows. "And Cooper?"

"Mark Anthony, do you even need to ask?"

"You know that didn't end well, right?"

"What? Oh, there he is. Coop! Get over here. You've got to see this baby! Oh my God, he's so cute."

Breastplate, helmet, sword and shield—Cooper always did have a flair for the theatrical—looking more buff through the chest and arms, but with the same skinny, hairy legs.

"Hi, Chrissie."

"Hi."

"He's a cute little guy," chucking Lil' Griff under the chin, making him smile. "Lisa said you'd probably bring him. What's his name?"

"Griff. We call him Lil' Griff, though, to differentiate him from his dad."

"Hi Lil' Griff," Cooper says, his voice cracking over an octave. "You gonna be a rap star when you grow up? Eh, little man?"

Lil' Griff becomes shy, turning his head away from Cooper, grinding it into the safety of his mother's shoulder and then back to him again.

"Awe," Cleopatra and Cooper both say.

"Have you seen his dad?" Chrissie asks Cooper. "'Cause I really need him to bring in some stuff from the car."

"Out back with the other guys, I think. Kev brought a little…"

"Right."

Chrissie becomes aware of the three pigs, then—huddled together at the outer edge of her vision—whispering, giggling, plotting some kind of drama, Chrissie is sure of it. Suddenly, Andrea is swarmed by the little oinkers and nudged toward the kitchen with promises of the best margaritas she will ever taste, leaving Chrissie and Cooper alone. Awesome. What do you say to an ex-boyfriend you haven't seen in three years, especially after the way you broke up with him? Cooper, ever the gentleman, helps her out.

"So," he says, "I hear this party has become a tradition," which allows Chrissie to brief him on the history of the

Hallowe'en bash, held every year since their last year of high school.

Well, for sure he must remember the first party, says Chrissie, the one at her parent's house, where he and Griff got into it over her and some of her mom's china dolls got smashed, not to mention, like, his rib.

So, the year after that it was up at Kev's apartment in Kingston, but things got out of hand there, too, and the police showed up, cleared the whole place out. Last year, she and Griff hosted it at her grandma's cottage, where more stuff got wrecked and Griff acted like a total asshole. Her mom is still pissed about that one—all *Thank God your grandmother wasn't alive to see the mess—yadda, yadda.* This year, it's Lisa and Taylor's turn, which Chrissie thought was going to be pretty cool because they have a kid a few months older than Lil' Griff so maybe the big boys would smarten up this time and act more mature. But apparently Lisa managed to guilt her mom into taking Kiefer for the night, so now Lil' Griff is the only kid here, which means that Chrissie is the only one who can't cut loose.

But it's okay.

"It's not like I can drink a ton anyways, what with the breastfeeding and all."

Cooper's eyes drift toward her chest and then away.

Chrissie was expecting the usual gang. So imagine her surprise when she saw Cooper, who hasn't changed a bit in three years, skinny legs and all.

"Yeah, well, it fell on a Saturday, so I figured why not come home from school, give Mom and Dad some extra face time, see what everyone's been up to, show Andrea my home town. I feel ridiculous in this get-up, but Andrea said we had to match, and I wasn't about to argue."

Chrissie *really* doesn't want to talk about Andrea.

"So, still in engineering?" She asks.

"Yep, third year of a five-year Bio-Chem degree at Mac. I may apply to med school afterwards, still not sure."

Chrissie almost chokes on a sip of her wine.

"Seriously? You'll be in school forever. One term at Ottawa U was enough for me—too much partying, flunked two courses, barely scraped by in the others, and my parents unwilling to piss away any more of their hard earned cash."

"And Griff? I heard he went to college."

"Pfffft. Yeah, right. Some of us aren't cut out for higher learning."

"Not you," Coop says. "You had great marks in high school. I thought you wanted to be a teacher? What happened there?"

"Well sure, yeah, I did, but that was before I realized how totally different university was from high school, more work, crowded lecture halls, not knowing any of my teachers. Plus, I missed Griff like crazy what with me in Ottawa and him at college in Kingston—slut capital of the planet, by the way. It's okay, now, though. We both have jobs—Griff's dad was in tight with the head of security at the casino, so Griff snagged full-time there, and I got my old job back at the grocery store. Except now I'm on maternity leave, so money's been a little scarce, but it's okay, we're getting by."

And she loves being a mom—she hastens to assure him, since the look he's giving her now is making her feel kind of pathetic. It's almost like being a teacher, except she only has one student and the pay sucks, and she never gets a break. It sure would have been nice if Mom and Dad had volunteered to take Lil' Griff for tonight, even for a couple of hours. It's not like she didn't drop plenty of hints when she saw them today, but apparently *they* had plans, so whatever.

"He's been pretty good so far, though, haven't you sweetie? Yes you have! You sure have!"

Except she really needs to nurse him now, and he's going to need a diaper change after that, but as usual Griff is nowhere to be found! If she gives Cooper the keys, would he mind running out to the car and grabbing the diaper bag from the trunk for her?

"Thanks, Cooper. You're the best."

*

It's really hot out here in front of the town hall, and Chrissie would like to retrieve her hand from Cooper's sweaty-palmed embrace, but she doesn't want to risk hurting his feelings, especially now when he's getting set to perform. What The Fuck didn't show up—in their place, Phil's twelve-year-old brother, with a note for the emcee—*It appears that the uh, the band, that WTF has decided not to perform, citing, uh, artistic and creative differences with the Festival Board. Oh well. Not much of a loss, really, now is it, folks? Ha, ha.*

The fiddlers were actually pretty good, and the Amazing Caroline? She only dropped one of her three juggling balls, while her dance-of-the-seven-Hula-Hoops came off perfectly. And Roy? Oh my God, Roy. Chrissie's father won't believe her when she tells him. The Phantom of the Opera thrilled and surprised everyone in the audience, his voice so powerful and the swirl of his cape so dramatic that he received a standing ovation. But the cloggers, in their 1950's costumes, showing a little too much middle-aged, blue-cheese leg? Chrissie could definitely have done without them.

And now it's Cooper's turn. When the emcee calls his name, Cooper looks over at her with those puppy-dog eyes, lets go of her hand, and scrambles to his feet. Chrissie can't believe how nervous she feels for a guy who, six weeks ago, she considered more acquaintance than friend, until he stepped up and offered to take her to the prom, no strings attached, after he heard about Griff dumping her for some Regis chick. And now? Well, she'd have to say he's more than a friend, but still less than what Griff ever was. She and Griff dated on and off for almost three years, and during that time she did to him and let him do to her almost everything he wanted. But Cooper? She hasn't let him make it past her breasts—she's no slut, after all, she doesn't need that kind of thing getting around. Besides, it's not like Cooper is complaining. She's his first girlfriend. He says he's happy to take it slow, to not pressure her. He knows she's still hurting. Such a nice guy, she thinks, as she watches him mount the stage, un-sling his gig-bag and pull out his guitar—Chrissie really wishes she felt more attracted to him.

It doesn't help that Griff has been getting in touch again. Emails on her computer, text messages on her phone: *I made a fucking mistake, okay? I just wanna talk to u can I come by ur house? it isn't over we're not through chrissie? u there?*

"I'd like to dedicate this song to a very special girl in the audience," Cooper says, and then he starts to strum.

Wonder Wall by Oasis. Oh man. That's hardcore. How sweet. How very sweet. People are looking at her—feeling gooey and happy for her, even the little kid in the stroller is smiling, as if he was in on the whole thing. And the worst part of it is that there is nowhere for her to hide.

*

Kiefer's nursery decor is all about Super Mario. Heavily moustached Marios frolic across the wallpaper, shooting fireballs, avoiding Mario-eating plants. Red crib-sheets, blue baby blankets, a mushroom lamp, a red rocking chair in the corner. Look, Lil' Griff—Super Mario—encircling his wrist with her fingers, Chrissie stretches out his arm, allowing his fingers to graze the raised graphics on the wallpaper. Oooo, he says, as if he is in the presence of something holy. It cracks Chrissie up.

The sounds of the party downstairs are muffled for the most part up here, but a certain sweet, acrid smell has floated its way into the nursery from the back yard—Lisa must have left the bedroom window open a crack in the wake of Kiefer's 'pooh-splosion'. As if the smell weren't bad enough, accompanying it is a single drunken, loud voice, which she soon recognizes as Griff's, going on about that fucking loser, Cooper, being here, and that hot bitch he brought to the party, and how if Griff wasn't with Chrissie and they didn't have a fucking kid, he'd show Cleopatra what it was like to be with a real man.

What???

She's at the window in a second.

"Oh really, Griff," she shouts down to him. "Is that so?" A chorus of drunken and wasted voices, then—*Oh man. You're in trouble now. In the doghouse now, buddy.* Fucking losers. Chrissie slams the window shut.

Her sudden shout, the slamming of the window have scared Lil' Griff. He begins to cry. *It's okay, sweetie, it's all right. Mommy got a little mad, that's all. Let mommy calm down.* Chugging the rest of her wine, she places the empty glass on the bureau. Big breath. *Sorry, baby, sorry.* Taking a seat in the rocking chair, Chrissie yanks up her blouse and unclips her nursing bra. *Here, honey, here you go.* Contact. Normally, there would be nothing better than having Lil' Griff at her breast. Not only is it best

223

for him, it's way cheaper than formula. And truth be told, and she's never admitted this to a soul, not even to Lisa, because she's pretty sure people would think she was totally sick, but all that sucking has on more than one occasion caused her to, well, she can't even admit it to herself. Maybe *that* wouldn't happen if Griff would stop making wisecracks about her weight and pay attention to more than just himself in the bedroom. Never mind showing Cleopatra what it's like to fuck a real man, how about showing the mother of your child, asshole?

Big breath.

In.

Out.

Calm down, Chrissie, calm the fuck down.

In. Out.

There.

Okay, little man, time to change sides.

Of course, the downside of breastfeeding is that Griff never has to take responsibility for feeding his own son and apparently, by extension, for changing his diaper, or doing anything else with him. And since Lil' Griff won't take a bottle Chrissie can't leave him with anybody for more than a few hours at a time. This too shall pass, her mother has assured her, whenever Chrissie has complained about having no time to herself. And the older women who stop her on the street when she takes Lil' Griff out for a walk in the stroller back her mother up— *Isn't he sweet, isn't he adorable, look at those eyes. Enjoy it while it lasts, they grow up so fast.* It drives Chrissie crazy. Seriously, have they forgotten what it's like?

Why didn't anyone tell her before she got pregnant? Where was the chorus of well-meaning women then, huh? *Just so you know, dearie, you'll never have two minutes alone to yourself again for as long as you live.* And now here she is, still a kid herself, twenty-one years old, nursing a baby, *her* baby. She loves Lil' Griff, doesn't know what she would do without him, but there are times, like right now, where she aches for the days when she could sleep in on weekends and be the centre of the universe, when life was all about Chrissie and what she wanted out of it, even if she didn't know exactly what that was. And just like that, her earlier excitement about Hallowe'en and the party and spending time with her friends evaporates.

Griff will be good and hammered by the time she goes back downstairs; even if he doesn't try to hit on Cleopatra, he'll be of no use to Chrissie as a father. Chrissie will end up watching the baby all night, hating herself for eating too many chips and pretzels and Cheezies, and not drinking nearly enough alcohol to compensate. And worst of all, there Cooper will be with his hot little girlfriend and his big plans for medical school, watching it all go down with those sweet brown eyes—him feeling sorry for Chrissie, instead of the other way around. There is a timid knock at the nursery door.

"Chrissie?" Speak of the devil—it's Cooper. Took him long enough—must have got waylaid by her highness. "Chrissie, you in there? I've got the diaper bag."

"Great," Chrissie says. "So, like, can you bring it in?"

"Yeah, sure."

He pushes the door open, causing light from the hallway to sweep across the room. At the same moment, Lil' Griff, no longer hungry and now more interested in the light and the voice at the door than his food source, unlatches from Chrissie's nipple, giving Cooper an unobstructed view of Chrissie's breast.

"Oh, shit," averting his eyes. "I mean, *geez*," hand flying to his temple to form a blind, "I'm so sorry, Chrissie, I didn't mean to, you know, *look*."

"Cooper, it's okay," she says, laughing, a little, to herself because of his embarrassment, while at the same time not rushing to cover up her breast. "Relax. Breastfeeding is totally natural. Besides, it's nothing you haven't seen before, right?"

And later on while providing a tearful and heartfelt statement to the town cops, after the ambulance has driven away with a sobbing Cleopatra and her unconscious Anthony, after Griff, Kev, Phil and Garth have been removed from the scene in handcuffs, after her parents have been called to come and collect Lil' Griff, Chrissie will recall this moment—when she slowly tucked her breast back into her bra, pulled down her shirt, and decided to mess with Cooper and Griff's heads, just a little bit, for ruining her night.

THE STONE LION

"SUN-DOWNING," DOCTOR MILLS CALLS IT, when Sylvia describes what has been happening. Jack isn't with her—she's left him back at the house with Iris, the home-care woman—the one who plays twenty-one with him.

"The time of day," the doctor is explaining, although she doesn't need him to, she's heard the expression before, "when Alzheimer patients, like Jack, can become agitated, a bit out of sorts. Anxious. If you can get him out in the fresh air—take him for a good long walk in the morning or early afternoon—your evenings might go easier."

Take him for a good long walk. As if he were a dog on a leash—a Doberman, maybe, or a German shepherd, something muscular and unpredictable.

Doctor Mills scribbles an indecipherable word onto a piece of paper and hands it to Sylvia. It's true, she thinks, what they say about doctors and their handwriting.

"Melatonin," he translates. "You should be able to get some over the counter at the drug store. Follow the directions on the label. It might help to regulate his sleep cycle. And I know this last suggestion will be tough, but *attempt* to get him to cut back on his coffee."

She looks at him as if he's the one who is off his rocker, not her husband.

"He drinks eight, ten cups a day, doc. He'd rather die than give up his coffee."

"Try him on decaf, then, only don't tell him. My wife did that to me—mixed regular with decaf, then gradually increased the decaf. I didn't know until she confessed. I promise, he won't notice the difference."

But you aren't the one who'll catch hell if he does, are you? Last week, Jack accused her of poisoning his food, threw his plate at the wall, missing her head by inches. A chicken stir-fry—green onions and bean sprouts, mushrooms, chicken and stir fry sauce—all of it sliding down the wall.

Sylvia walks from the clinic to the drugstore, picks up the melatonin. She still has about an hour. She decides to stop off at the bakery for a coffee and one of those chocolate croissants. Iris, the card shark, is supposed to be on duty for a full three hours, but often, if Sylvia doesn't leave the house, Iris will beg off fifteen or twenty minutes early. She says it's because she needs to get to another client's house by such and such a time and the scheduler didn't factor in her driving distance. That's what she says, but the other women always stay the full time, so Sylvia has learned to run her errands on Iris days, returning home just as the bell on the town's clock tower is striking the hour.

"Where's Jack," Sue, the baker's assistant asks, when Sylvia places her order at the counter. Everybody knows Jack—when he was walking the beat so many townspeople used to wave at him from their cars, from across the street, that he joked he should walk around town with his hand up.

"He's back at the house with the homecare woman."

"Good for you," Sue says. "Sometimes you need to take time for yourself."

Sue's father suffered from Alzheimer's, she confided to Sylvia on a previous visit, while Jack was in the washroom and she was cutting Sylvia twin slices of lemon meringue pie. It was hell for her mother, she said, but before she could elaborate Jack returned to the counter. Just as well. Sylvia wasn't interested in hearing the details. One Alzheimer patient was enough. Still, it was comforting to know that this younger woman, whom Sylvia didn't know from Adam, understood, in a shorthand kind of way, how much a walk to the bakery by herself might mean to Sylvia.

Sylvia orders her croissant and coffee, sees a table near the back with an abandoned newspaper and makes for it. The local rag—better than nothing, she supposes. Sitting down, she takes a sip of coffee and a bite of her treat. Out of habit, she turns to the police-beat section of the paper. Often, when Jack was still with the force, the only way she would find out what he'd been up to on the job was to read about it in the police beat—domestic disputes, drug busts, fender-benders, break and enters, driving under the influence, the odd sexual assault, even a murder/suicide, once—all there in the paper. No names with any of the charges—a male, 58, a female, 32, a young offender—but it was a small town, the details got around. Sometimes accurate, sometimes not.

Jack didn't like to talk to Sylvia about the job—said it was for her own good. She'd understand if she'd grown up here, he said, folks in town could be awful nosy. He didn't like putting her in that position. She couldn't tell what she didn't know. And he was right. It surprised Sylvia how often, in the early days of their marriage, a person would accost her on the street, sometimes a person she couldn't even put a name to yet, and ask what she knew about so and so and the drug bust on Arthur Street, or that fellow and his wife over on Kent Drive. Nothing, she'd say. Jack doesn't bring his work home. It made her feel proud of her husband, that he could hold all that inside and not tell a soul.

Of course, it came out in other ways, ways she didn't understand until the kids left home and went off to university and then came back and tried to talk to their father about PTSD, about why he got so angry with them when they were little, and so controlling when they got older, about why he drank so much. Mouthing off, Jack called it, before he told them to mind their own business, but she thought she could see what they were getting at. It might even explain that woman, the one who almost wrecked their marriage—the one he sometimes confuses her with now when the light begins to waver and fade at the end of the day.

"Sylvia!"

She looks up. Beth-Anne McGuire—sixty-six, same age as Sylvia—bulging out of a younger, slimmer woman's skirt and blouse, and fresh from the manicurist, her long, fake nails elegantly painted. Someone ought to take her aside and tell her to dress her age.

"Hi Beth-Anne."

"Where's that man of yours hiding?"

Always the flirt.

"He's back at the house, with the home-care woman."

Beth-Anne pulls out a chair, plunks herself down, crowding Sylvia's coffee and treat to the round table's edge with her enormous gold-clasped purse.

"And how's our Jack doing?"

Our Jack. Wouldn't the old Jack roll his eyes at that one?

"Oh, you know, about the same."

It's the response Sylvia reserves for a busybody like Beth-Anne who only wants to know Sylvia's business so she can run off and tell it to somebody else. If Beth-Anne really cared one iota for Jack or Sylvia she'd offer to come over to the house and spend some time with them, like one or two of his retired buddies from work do, or she'd speak directly to Jack when she met them on the street together, instead of talking only to Sylvia.

"Well, Sylvia, at least he's company. You're not all alone."

Like me is what Beth-Anne doesn't add. Five years since her husband died of bowel cancer, she loves to go on about how hard it is to live in that gigantic house all by her lonesome, how difficult it is to find a like-minded travelling companion for her trips to the Caribbean and abroad.

Poor dear.

Sylvia could play the pity game and win, give Beth-Anne a real earful—tell her about how she will often wake in the middle of the night, Jack next to her, pulling on his thing as if he were a six-year-old—the same man who, ten years ago, refused to raise the subject of not being able to get it up with his doctor because it was a goddamned embarrassment. Or the times when he can't remember who *he* is, let alone her, their neighbours and friends, one of the children. Or the way he speaks to people on the television as if they've suddenly come to life and are standing right there in the living room. Or how suspicious he can get about the food she puts in front of him, mistaking a hardened edge of pasta for a shard of bone, thinking she is feeding him bits of babies. *Babies*. She could win the pity game all right, but what would she lose?

Doesn't matter. Beth-Anne has moved on to other topics—she's been nattering away at Sylvia for a couple of minutes now, and Sylvia has no idea what she's been saying.

"So what do you think?"

"About?"

Beth-Anne administers a light pat to her hand.

"Poor Sylvia," she says. "Mind off somewhere else is it? That's okay. I completely understand."

No, Beth-Anne, you don't.

THEIR BOYS, closing in on middle age themselves now, make a joke of it—call it "The Big A". She'll be talking to one of

231

them on the telephone, having given them an update on their father's illness, and they'll forget the name of something—a book, a movie, a household item—or they'll be apologizing for forgetting her birthday or their dad's, and with a chuckle they'll announce that they must be getting 'it'.

She doesn't find it funny.

She knows *why* they do it—Jack's mother died of the same thing—wasted to nothing, curled up in a fetal position on her single bed in the nursing home. At least she was eighty-three. Jack is only sixty-eight, so not old at all. The boys are terrified that their father's illness is hereditary and with good reason. It very likely is. If they are not cracking wise about it, they are filling her in on the latest research—how they read on the Internet that drinking red wine provides a benefit, how keeping active will stave it off, how doing crossword puzzles improves the memory, how researchers think a miracle drug is just around the corner—all of it too late for Jack.

Their daughter, who lives down east and is the farthest from home, doesn't find any of it funny, either. A head nurse on a surgical floor at a hospital, she copes with her feelings by reading all the Alzheimer's literature that she can lay her hands on, talking to her friends and co-workers who may have parents going through a similar thing, and by bossing her mother around, long-distance.

Sylvia was on the telephone with her this morning. She's been quite concerned for Sylvia's safety ever since Sylvia told her about the plate of food flying past her head and crashing into the wall. She wants to know if Jack's done anything else.

"Has he hit you, Mom, shoved you?"

"No, no, nothing like that."

"Because he used to be pretty free with the palm of his hand when we were little, remember?"

That again.

"Yes, I suppose he was."

Sylvia decides not to mention the other morning, when she woke up to discover Jack sitting next to her on the edge of the bed. Staring at her, glaring at her.

What did you do with it?

What?

My... my... And he made a pistol out of his hand.

His service revolver.

You don't have that anymore, Jack. You had to give it up when you retired. Remember?

Their daughter wants assurances from Sylvia that she would call 9-1-1 for assistance if she ever felt that she wasn't safe. She's heard from a co-worker how that can sometimes become necessary.

Yes, of course she would. Although, she likely wouldn't—Jack would never hurt her.

"We're going for a walk as soon as I get off the phone with you, dear."

"Yes, I'll make sure he wears a hat."

"Yes, I've already sprayed on the sunscreen."

"I'm quite aware of the heatwave. We'll stop at the bakery for lemonade, before we go on to the park."

"No, he's never done that. Not once. He's not a wanderer."

SINCE THE DOCTOR'S APPOINTMENT, she and Jack have developed a nice morning routine. Let's go for a walk, she'll say, after Jack has communed with the morning news anchor on the television, and her husband will get up from his living-room chair and head to the closet to find his shoes. He can't tie the laces on his running shoes anymore, but she refuses to buy him the ones with Velcro closures. He's sick, he's not a three-year-old. Once Jack's got his baseball cap and sunglasses in place, she checks to make sure that all his shirt buttons line up, that his fly is zipped. Then, directing him to sit on the deacon's bench in the hallway, she gets down on her creaky knees and ties his laces—perfect little bunny ears. He always says thank you. He's become so polite, thanking her for every little thing that she does as if she were a stranger, which these days, she supposes, is the truth more often than not.

Leaving the house and walking down their street, they'll stop to say hello to one or other of the neighbours, if they happen to be outside watering the lawn or tending to their plants. No one has moved from this street in decades, unless they've left on a gurney, a sheet covering their motionless body. The neighbours know what Sylvia's been up against, the last three years since Jack's diagnosis—even better than the children. If you ever need a shoulder to cry on, more than one has said to her, man and woman alike, but that would never be her way. Except for that dark period in the early nineties, Jack is it—her best friend. Even now, with the way he can be—his eyes staring vacantly off into space, or worse, the anxious, muddled look he adopts when he doesn't know what is happening, where he is—she can't imagine another shoulder being of any use to her.

Once they leave their street, she will ask for his hand. He's always been a fast walker, the disease has not slowed him down much, yet—taking hold of his hand is the only way for her to keep pace with him. She wouldn't want him becoming disoriented and stepping into traffic because she fell a few steps behind him.

"Slow down, partner," she'll say, or "Whoa, Nellie, give me that hand," and he'll smile, almost like he used to and oblige her.

And off they will go—down to the berm to look out at the water and watch the boats putting in and out of the marina, then across the swing bridge, and up to the main street, where they will stop at the bakery for a treat and a beverage before heading off to the town park.

Today's weather is no different from any other day this week. Still sunny, still humid, still hot, but the town park has some lovely old shade trees—maples, mostly, and a few strategically placed wrought-iron benches with the town's name punched out in the centre of the backrest—*Kanawasaguay.* Sometimes, not often, all the benches are occupied, but today they can pick and choose. Sylvia steers them toward the bench next to the stone lion.

"Look, Jack," Sylvia says, like she says every other day when they come to the park, "it's your lion." She resists the ever present impulse to add 'remember?', because if Jack doesn't recall, he can become quite agitated.

"Is this a test?" he'll say. "Is this a goddamned test, Sylvia?"

The stone lion is not really his, and it's not really carved out of stone—it's a concrete cast of a reclining male lion, set onto a concrete plinth—God only knows when or why or how it ended up in the park—there is no memorial or historical plaque explaining its origins, but there it sits, like it has since before she moved to town. The children, when they were small, used to take turns straddling its back when she would bring them out for a walk. Many years later, when Jack retired, Sylvia bought him a digital camera as a gift—he'd often mentioned that he'd like a nice camera. A hobby would do him good, she thought. Keep him from getting underfoot. And for a few months, that fall, he did disappear for hours at a time, coming home to download hundreds of shots onto the computer—birds, flowers, squirrels and raccoons, cloud formations, trash cans, sunrises, sunsets, store fronts, boats, and one that Sylvia really liked—a black and white close-up of the lion's grey and crumbling face—it's stone pupil-less eyes fixed and staring at nothing.

Downloading the picture onto a memory stick, she took it uptown to the photography shop to have the photograph printed and professionally framed, and then she gave it to Jack for Christmas. By then, of course, he hadn't touched the camera in months, but she still hoped he would be surprised and pleased. In hindsight, she supposes that may have been about the time that he began showing the first signs of his illness.

Was he surprised by the framed photo? Yes. Pleased? Not really. He looked from it to Sylvia, then back to the photograph again. He scratched his head, wouldn't meet her eye.

"Well?"

"Well, what?"

"Do you like it?"

"Sure, it's fine, I guess," he said. "But I'm no photographer, Syl. I'm no 'artiste'."

She tried to involve him in the decision as to where she should hang it in the house—she'd paid good money for the matting and framing, she was determined to display it somewhere—but he refused to offer an opinion.

"Do whatever you like with it, Syl," he said. "It's your picture now."

Fine.

She hung it in the hallway above the deacon's bench.

Last year, the town hired a summer student to paint all of the fire hydrants on the main street, transforming them into two-foot tin soldiers—an attempt to add charm to the downtown, she supposed, to keep the tourists interested, although if council had been serious they might have hired someone with a bit of talent. For some reason they must have given the kid the go-ahead to paint the lion, too—a brassy gold, his eyeballs painted white, a black dot for each pupil and black whiskers to match. It is not an improvement. In fact, it looks so awful that Sylvia has seriously considered writing a letter to the editor about it. The toddlers still come with mom or dad and straddle its back, but who would ever want to take a picture of it, now?

Jack stares at the lion, grimly shakes his head.

"They sure made a mess of it, didn't they?" he says.

And Sylvia smiles, so happy that he's remembered. He must be having one of his good days, she decides.

"Yes, Jack, they certainly did."

They haven't sat down on the bench, yet.

Jack's hand goes to the front pocket of his trousers. He often has a collection of coins in that pocket—loonies or toonies—a couple times a day he will fish them out and cup them between both hands, shake them next to his ear. The sound of cold hard cash, he said the first time, when she asked him what he was doing. It's odd that he would do that here, in the park. New. But his behaviour changes every day, so she doesn't become too concerned until Jack takes his hand from out of his pocket and instead of a handful of coins he is holding a small paring knife from the kitchen.

Oh, oh.

"Jack, what are you doing with that?"

"I'm going to fix the…I'm going to fix him," he says, pointing the knife in the lion's general direction, and before she can think of how to disarm her six-foot tall, dementing husband, he is down on his knees, scraping at the whites of the stone lion's eyes, his tiny black pupils.

"Jack, I really don't think you should," but it's as if he hasn't heard her.

The paint flakes away quite easily. Jack's almost got one eyeball scraped clean before his actions begin to attract an audience. A little girl, no more than three, walking hand in hand with her mother has come to the park, as Sylvia and Jack's children did when they were young, to climb onto the lion's back. Sylvia doesn't know the mother or the child. The little girl takes one look at Jack stabbing the lion in the eye and her bottom lip begins to quiver.

"Mommy, is he hurting the lion?"

Mommy takes in the scene. She looks to Sylvia, who throws up her hands in a 'what should I do' kind of way.

The mother lifts her daughter up.

"No, sweetie, no," she says. "The man is just giving the lion a haircut!"

"But he's not cutting his hair, Mommy."

"Why don't we come back later to see the lion, when the nice man is finished? Okay, honey?" Transferring her daughter to one hip, she walks off down the street. Sylvia watches wearily, as the young mother pulls a cell phone from a pocket and places it to her ear.

In her position, she would have done the same.

ACKNOWLEDGEMENTS

I raise my glass and propose a toast to:

My ideal readers—Cathy Sheppard, Danielle Maitland, Rick Gagnon and Sue Danic.

The Trio of Awesome and Writers on the Rocks.

Susan Pye—for her Latin expertise.

Kim Jernigan—editor at *TNQ*, who published several stories, and who cares so much about promoting and nuturing new writers.

Antanas Sileika (Humber School for Writers)—for his excellent mentorship in 2003, and for his cheers from the sidelines ever since. You were right: it was a marathon, not a sprint.

Isabel Huggan (Humber), Charlotte Gill (UBC), Dianne Warren (Banff) and Diane Schoemperlen—for their thoughtful edits, generosity and good will.

The emerging writers I have met in workshops and classes.

My extended family—the Gagnon brood and the Maitland clan.

Al Maitland—for first readings, technical know-how and emotional support—I love you, honey.

Our kids—Josh, Sam, Danielle and Jaime—who called me a writer long before I would do so, myself.

Kris King—Photographer extraordinaire.

John Metcalf—for providing just the right amount of push and praise, for the books, and for all the splendid telephone conversations.

The fearless duo: Tara Murphy and Dan Wells of Biblioasis.

Cheers, all.

ABOUT THE AUTHOR

KRIS KING

Colette Maitland has published widely in such literary magazines as *The Antigonish Review*, *Pottersfield Portfolio*, *Descant*, *Room of One's Own*, *The Nashwaak Review*, *Wascana Review*, *The Prairie Journal*, *Freefall*, *The Puritan*, *The Fiddlehead*, *Event* and frequently in *The New Quarterly*. She lives in Gananoque, Ontario with her husband, Al.